APPETITE

FOR

INNOCENCE

LUCINDA BERRY

APPETITE FOR INNOCENCE

First Edition. First printed in the United States of America

ISBN-13:978-1544763828
ISBN-10:1544763824

10 9 8 7 6 5 4 3 2 1

DEDICATION

To my biggest fan, Gus. You inspire me every day with your creativity.

SARAH

(THEN)

SHOVE MY EARPLUGS in as far as they'll go to drown out the sounds of her cries. I hate the crying, and they always cry. In the beginning, I used to try to get them to be quiet. Calm them down, but nothing ever worked. They were as terrified of me as they were of him. They'd claw at me like wild animals, raking their nails across my arms and scraping my face if I tried to hold them. A few hit me. One even spit at me when I offered her a glass of water. I gave up trying to soothe them a long time ago. Now, I just let them cry.

The worst part is not knowing how long the wailing is going to last. I used to try to figure out a way to predict how long they'd carry on before being moved to Phase Two, but I was always wrong. The weak ones give up within a matter of hours because they succumb to shock or simply resign to their fate, but the fighters can go on for days. It's hard to tell the difference between the two, but I don't care as long as they stop crying. I want to yell at them to stop screaming—nobody can hear you. Sometimes I do, but it only makes them cry harder.

I hate the fighters. They make my days so much more difficult and throw me out of my routine. Things work best for me when I stick to my routine. They take away my sunshine and I need my sun.

I'm pretty sure this one is a fighter. He had to sedate her for the car ride which is never a good sign. The weak ones are paralyzed by their fear and keep quiet in the car. Not the strong ones. And this one is strong even though she's small.

Before I went to bed, Paige and I watched her on her cot, asleep out of protest with her arms and feet bound with zip ties, her mouth covered in duct tape. Not the gray kind. He never uses gray. This time, he used red with white stripes. Even in her drug-induced sleep, she didn't look peaceful. Her forehead was still lined with a fight.

Paige shook next to me even though she tried to hide it. Her eyes were filled with questions I couldn't answer.

"It's not fair," she'd whispered as I left her laying on her cot next to the new girl and retreated to the privacy of my own space.

A few years ago, I hung a sheet from the ceiling. I wish it was a real wall, but at least it separates me from them. I didn't bother to turn around as I walked away from her.

"There's nothing fair about life," I said.

The drugs wore off shortly after I laid down and she woke up. She started screaming—the tortured screams they make when their mouths are taped shut. It's been over an hour now and she still hasn't stopped. I put my headphones on over my earplugs and press play on the CD player he gave me last Christmas. I didn't complain it was old-fashioned or that nobody listens to CDs anymore. I was just grateful to have music. Out of all the things from my old life, music is what I miss the most.

ELLA
(THEN)

TERROR JOLTS ME awake. My eyes snap open. There's water between my legs. A scream stuck in my throat. I want to rip off the gag but I can't because my hands are still tied, the skin torn from my movements. My legs are tucked underneath me, bound at the ankles. Every part of me aches. My throat is raw.

In an instant, it all comes flooding back to me. The man. His baseball cap. Perfect, white smile. The way his eyes lit up when I told him my name. I never should've told him my name. The way his hand felt on my arm as he gripped it. The awful pain in my head. It still throbs in the same place.

My eyes can't adjust to the darkness and burn like a thousand pieces of sand are stuck on them. I want to rub them, but can't because my hands are too awkward in the way they're tied. I edge myself up slowly, my bones screaming in protest as I pull myself into sitting position, resting against a spongy wall behind me. I bring my legs up to my chest, wrapping my arms around them as best I can.

I furtively scan my surroundings. I can see every inch of the room from my bed. There's thick foam covering every surface. The walls, the ceiling, even the stairs. It's bumpy like if you threw yourself against it, you'd bounce off. Thick, gray shag carpet covers the floor. So thick you could comb it. There's no windows. Nothing that speaks of light. Some kind of wall to my left. A narrow staircase. An outline of a toilet in the far right corner. No sink. It smells musty like dirty socks.

"Hey, you're awake," a voice comes out of the darkness and startles me. Panic shoots through me.

My head snaps to the side—the outline of a body lying on a cot next to me.

"I can call Sarah to take the tape off your mouth, but you can't scream. She'll put it back on if you scream." Her voice sounds kind.

Who is she? Who's Sarah? What does she want with me? Why am I here? Do I know her? I squint into the darkness, but it's too dark to make out her face. I'm frozen. Can't move. Can't speak. I just stare. My heart pounds. I'm dripping in sweat.

"Do you want me to call her?"

I shake my head. I don't want her to call anyone. I want my mom. Hot tears move down my face. They run over my tape. I'm thirsty. I've never been so thirsty. How long have I been here? Where am I?

And then I hear it. Gut-wrenching sobs. But they're not coming from me. My tears are silent. They're coming from the girl on the cot next to me. Why is she crying?

Terror rises in my throat.

ELLA

(NOW)

"TELL ME ABOUT the basement." He works his jaw as he talks. He has a closed face, the kind that reveals nothing. His white Oxford shirts stretches over his well-toned chest and is tucked into his navy blue pleated pants. A phone is clipped on his black belt.

He's already asked me about the basement. Three times. They both keep asking me about the basement. I hate the basement. I don't want to talk about it. I just want to go home. The medicine the doctors gave me makes it hard to think. I can't remember how to breathe. My body is on fire. Everything hurts.

"When is my mom going to be here?" My voice cracks.

The other man speaks, the one with the crew cut. "Her flight should be in the air by now. We're having one of our agents meet her at the gate and they'll escort her here." He checks his watch. A thick plastic one. "As long as traffic is okay, she should be here in about three hours."

The nurse pipes up from the corner of the room. "Can I get you anything?"

I shake my head. I want everyone to leave me alone. I just want to sleep. I'm so tired.

"Are you in pain?"

She walks over to the bed to get a closer look at me. Her green eyes are kind, but I look away. She's staring at me in a way nobody's looked at me before. Is this how everyone is going to look at me now? I bow my head, refusing to meet her eyes and stare at my arm. It looks funny wrapped in a purple cast. I've never broken a bone before.

"What's your favorite color?" the doctor asked after they'd set the bones back in place.

I said purple. Purple has always been my favorite color. I don't know if it is anymore. I don't know if my world still has room for color.

"Is the victim's advocate here yet?" The serious man speaks again. His name is Brian or Blake. Something with a B. I can't remember. He speaks around me like I'm not here. I wish I wasn't. I want to disappear.

Their lips move, but the sound is turned off. I want to interrupt them and ask the question burning my lips, but I can't. I'm too afraid of the answer. Maybe it's better not to know.

SARAH

(THEN)

THE ALARM DOESN'T summon me awake. It's always strange to wake up without it. I hate Phase One. It has no order and I need order. He knows that but he doesn't care. I've been begging him for years to just let me stay upstairs until they're ready, but he refuses. Says he needs me. I'm the only one that can do it right. I wish he'd do it himself. But I do what he tells me to do. No argument. I know better than that.

I stretch lazily. Today will be a day without coffee. I don't make coffee in the basement. Coffee is for upstairs. It helps to keep the two separate even if it makes it harder on me. My head will be throbbing by noon.

Both the girls are already awake. Paige is curled up on her side crying and the new girl has flattened herself against the wall trying to make herself as small as possible like she might be able to make herself invisible. Paige pays me no attention but the new girl is glued to my every move. The whites in her eyes are visible even in the dark. I make my way over to the corner and use the toilet. I walk through the room, flicking the lamps on after I'm done and flood the room with dim light.

The new girl flinches and frantically looks around, checking everything out now that she can see. She surveys the padded walls, every inch of space covered in foam including the ceiling. She searches for a way out and her gaze rests on the stairs. It's what all the girls do. They think the stairs hold the key to their freedom but it doesn't take them long to figure out they're safer in the basement. She keeps scanning, back and forth and back and forth, as if she might be missing something or find a clue hidden in the walls somewhere.

I can see her heart beating through her blue t-shirt. Her face is lined with terror and sweat drips from it. She's small but muscular like she plays sports. She's still in her running shoes. Her shorts are black and short—the tight Nike ones I've seen on TV. Maybe that's what he liked about her.

I crouch down in front of her making sure not to get too close. Even though her legs are tied, she could still try to kick me if she wanted to.

"Hi, my name is Sarah. I know you're totally freaking out, but I'm not going to hurt you. I promise." I keep my voice even, as neutral as possible.

The vein pulses in her forehead. She's working her jaw underneath the tape.

"I can take the tape off you, but you can't scream." I point around me. To the walls. The ceiling. The thick carpet underneath us. "Nobody can hear you if you scream. This place is completely soundproof. Do you understand?"

Her eyes are wide, unblinking. She just stares at me as if she hasn't registered what I've said. Maybe she's still in shock. It takes some of them awhile to snap out of it. Some of them never do. I pull off her tape in one swift movement. It's easier that way, just like a Band-Aid.

"Get away from me!" she screams. "Help! Somebody help me! Please help me!"

I roll my eyes. I've been through this routine too many times. "Nobody can hear you. I already told you that. You can scream for days and nobody's going to come."

My words have no effect on her. She continues to scream. Her voice growing more and more frantic, filled with panic as her screams are absorbed by the foam.

Paige slowly moves over to her cot and sits next to her. The new girl jerks away, rolling off the cot and landing on the floor.

"Leave me alone!"

"We're not going to hurt you." Paige's voice is kinder than mine. She's always so sweet. She used to have younger siblings so she had lots of practice calming people down. "I get it. I was terrified too, but she's right. Nobody can hear you."

The new girl scuttles to the corner. Her body is shaking. Her eyes dart back and forth between us.

"Who are you?" Her voice quivers.

"I'm Paige." Then, she points to me. "That's Sarah. What's your name?"

She looks back and forth between the two of us before deciding to answer.

"Ella."

ELLA

(NOW)

"**IS PAIGE OKAY?**" I ask.

I can't take it anymore. I have to know.

The man and woman in my room exchange looks. She's wearing a dark blue uniform so there's no mistaking she's a police officer, but he's in plain clothes so I can't tell who he is. The woman nods toward him. He takes whatever cue she's just given him.

"There are officers on the premises now and we should know more soon." He glances down at his phone. He's been anxiously checking it since we got into the room. He may have been in the room during my examination. I'm not sure, though. I disappeared into the blank space in my mind once they spread my legs and inserted the metal inside of me.

My mind and body are separate now. I used to just be me. One person. But now I'm split. I have a body and a mind. I can go back and forth between the two but they rarely ever meet. I can't help but wonder if I'll ever go back to just being one.

At least police officers are at the house. I want to pray to God that she's okay, but I quit praying after God stopped answering my prayers. I don't believe in God anymore. I wonder what Mom will think about that when she finds out.

"And Sarah? What about Sarah?" I ask. I'll never forget the look in her eyes when she figured out what I was planning.

"Don't do it," she'd begged. "You'll get us all killed."

I'd never seen her so desperate or afraid. She didn't like for us to see her afraid. What if she was right? What if I saved myself but got them killed? I start to sob.

The female officer moves toward me. She looks like she's going to hug me.

"Don't touch me!" I cry.

She steps back.

"Okay, okay." She retreats to the corner of the room. "I understand how hard this must be for you. You've been through something terrible and the FBI is going to send a victim's advocate to work with you. She'll help you get through all of this."

The FBI? I'm going to have to talk to the FBI? Am I going to be in trouble? But I didn't do anything wrong. I was just trying to get away. I don't know how to talk to the FBI. I don't know how to talk to any of these people. What if they're coming to talk to me because I'm a murderer?

My sobs come in hiccupping gasps. It feels like someone is shoving my head underwater. The female officer reaches over and presses a button on my hospital bed. A nurse appears in my doorway.

"I think she's hyperventilating," the officer says.

The nurse hurries to my side. She puts her hand on my back. I flinch. It only makes me gasp harder. Struggle more.

"Sweetie, you just need to try to relax. You're safe now. You're okay. Take some deep breathes. Just follow me. One." She takes a deep breath. "Two." She lets it out. "Three. Follow me if you can, sweetie."

I focus on her words. Her counting. Her breathing. I try to match mine to hers. I hiccup less and less until finally they've stilled. I can breathe again.

"There you go. Good job, sweetie. Now, I'm just going to have a few words with the officers, but I'm not going anywhere, okay?"

I nod, too exhausted to speak.

She motions to both of them and they huddle in the corner of the room by the door. Her movements are stiff and robotic as she motions back and forth between them and me.

"I understand you have a job to do, but this girl has been through hell. You need to ease off on the questioning. You know that," she hisses, trying to do it quietly, but I can still hear her.

"She was the one asking questions. We didn't do anything to get her riled up," the man says.

I cover my ears. His voice is too perfect. Too calm. Just like John's. I don't want to think about John.

SARAH

(NOW)

I RIP OUT THE CORDS they're trying to attach to my body and pull the mask off my face.

"Where is he? Have you found him? Please tell me you've found him?"

The EMT tries to push me back onto the bed. "Just relax. You're safe now. He can't get you here. You're safe now."

I frantically shake my head back and forth. "No! No! No!"

They don't understand. They don't know him.

"Please, you've got to let me go. You've got to let me out of here." I struggle against his arms. "Please, let me go!"

They don't have any idea what they've done. I told Ella not to do it. Told her not to try. She didn't listen. She should've listened to me.

I'm screaming now. I can't help myself, but I don't recognize the sound of my voice. It's someone else. Someone who doesn't belong to me. There's too much movement. This space is too close.

"John!" I scream just as I feel a sharp sting on my arm. I fall back onto the bed. My head is swimming. Swirling. I can't catch my thoughts. My lids are so heavy. I can't fall asleep. But the darkness is so powerful. I have no choice, I give in.

When I open my eyes, I'm in a hospital room. There's a police officer sitting in a chair next to my bed. A needle taped into my arm attached to an IV bag. This is all wrong. It's not supposed to be happening.

"Where's John?" I search the room as if he might be hiding somewhere out of my sight, waiting for the perfect moment to grab me.

They have to know he'll find me. He's not going to just let me go. Not like this. He won't stand for it.

"I'm Officer Malone." The police officer stands and walks to my bed. He has to be at least forty. Maybe older. His dark hair threaded with slivers of gray is cropped close to his head. "And you must be Sarah?" He sticks out his hand.

I cling to it. "Please, you don't understand. You have to let me go. I can't be here."

His brown eyes fill with tears. "Look, I have two daughters of my own. Right about your age too. And if either of them had been stolen by that monster, they'd be terrified too. I want you to know that I'll protect you like you're one of my own. He's not getting into this room."

"So, you haven't found him? You don't know where he is? He's still out there?" My voice raises a pitch with each word.

He shakes his head. "Unfortunately, he did a pretty great job destroying the crime scene, but we're going to find him. He couldn't have gotten far." He grabs my other hand. He leans in close, holding tightly to both of my hands. He has a broad nose. Full lips. "I can promise you one thing. We will find him and make sure he's punished for what he did to you girls."

He knows there's others? Ella made it? I can't believe she made it. How did she get over the gate? The sound of the alarms still rings in my ears. I'm not sure it will ever stop. I've never been as afraid as I was when she pushed through the door and the alarm went off, not even the first night I stayed with him and I didn't think I could ever be more scared than I was that night.

"The others?" I ask.

"Yes, your friend Ella is two doors down."

I wouldn't call her my friend, but I want to see her. I have to talk to her.

"Can I go to her room? Can I stay with her?"

"For now, we're keeping each of you in your own rooms. I'm not exactly sure why the hospital set it up that way, but I can definitely talk to my boss about getting both of you in the same room. Would that make you feel better?"

I nod.

"Are you sure you'll find him?" I ask.

"Honey, I'm not going to quit until I find the man that did this to you."

I wish I believed him, but he doesn't know John. Nobody knows John. Not like I do.

ELLA

(THEN)

I EXHAUST MYSELF SCREAMING. I think the girl, Sarah, is right. Nobody can hear me down here. When I woke up, the other girl, Paige, was sitting on her bed reading a book. She's reading a book in this dungeon like it's perfectly normal. Why aren't the other girls tied up? How come I'm the only one?

I try to sleep, but it's impossible to sleep when your limbs are melded together. There's no comfortable spot. Every time I move, another part of my body cries out in pain.

I am so thirsty. My throat is on fire. I'm afraid to ask them for something to drink, though. What if they put something in it? But I don't know how much longer I can hold out. My mouth is so dry my lips are sticking to my teeth. My tongue is taking over my entire mouth. Eventually, I'm going to have to drink. The body can't survive without water. That much I know. I don't know how long I've been down here. It's hard to tell when there's no light. I've never lived without light.

And it's so quiet. Painfully still. I strain my ears for sounds. A voice. A car. Train whistle. The sounds of traffic. Any clue as to where I am. There's nothing. I listen so hard it makes my head hurt.

Am I still in the city? The same country? Did he put me on a plane?

My brain is foggy.

I remember everything right up until the car. The car is where it gets fuzzy. The images blur together. The fabric over my head. Heavy and rough. It made me itch. I couldn't breathe. I puked. I might have peed myself too. I'm not sure.

My smells permeate the air around me. It makes me want to gag.

I moan through the thick tape covering my mouth. Sarah put it on again after I wouldn't stop screaming. Paige begged her not to, but she wouldn't listen.

"She's giving me a headache," she said. "Help me hold her down."

"I'm sorry," Paige said as she sat on top of my legs while I bucked.

Sarah planted herself on my stomach, pinning my arms above my head. She peered down at me. "It doesn't have to be this hard," she said through gritted teeth, her face lined with exertion. "We're not trying to hurt you, but you have to listen."

"Then, get off me! Let me go! Please! What are you doing?" I thrashed back and forth, but they held tight.

"Just calm down."

I heaved my legs up, throwing Paige off me. She tumbled onto the floor next to my bed. Sarah wrestled on top of me. Paige scrambled back up.

"Stop, please!" Paige yelled. "She'll call him and he'll come down here. You don't want him to come down here. He'll chain you up." Her eyes filled with the same terror that surged through my body.

I let myself go limp. Sarah quickly slapped another piece of thick tape across my mouth.

"There," she huffed. "Be quiet or we're all going to end up in trouble."

I sat on my cot out of breath like I'd just one run of my cross country races.

Sarah is still behind the curtain. I think she works for him, but I can't tell. Who are these girls?

I study Paige as she reads. She looks younger than me, but it might just be because she's so tiny. She's wearing a pair of black sweat pants and a plain white t-shirt. Her hair is cut short, a cute pixie bob framing her petite face. She has a cute button nose, pointing up at the end. Her fingernails are painted pink. She looks innocent, but a few hours ago, she was pinning me down so she can't be all that innocent.

I need water. I think I'm going to die if I don't get something to drink and I can't die. I have to stay alive long enough to figure out a way out of here or someone to find me. Mom has to be frantically searching for me by now. She probably put together one of those crews they do when a child goes missing. I can't imagine how worried she is. I always come home on time. I don't break rules. It will destroy her if I don't make it out of this. All I have to do is hold on until she finds me.

I make an exaggerated coughing sound to get Paige's attention. She turns to look at me. Her eyes are green and covered by dark lashes. Her skin is soft and clear. She looks like a doll.

I try to communicate with my eyes that I want her to take my gag off. I promise to be quiet, but my words come out muffled.

"Sarah?" Paige calls.

Sarah sticks her head out from behind her curtain. Unlike Paige, her hair is long, tucked up into a messy bun on the top of her head. Her face is square and angular with perfect cheekbones like the ones you see on models in magazines.

"What?" she asks, clearly annoyed.

"I think we should try again," Paige says.

Sarah walks over to me. She's taller than I thought. She's long and lean with a confident and poised strut. She's wearing the same black sweatpants and white t-shirt as Paige. She towers over my cot where I lay curled up.

"Are you ready to be quiet now?" she asks.

I nod my head and try to look compliant.

She tears off my tape. I don't even flinch this time. She doesn't move from her spot. Her hands are on her hips.

"We aren't the enemy," she says.

I'm not sure I believe her.

"Can I have some water?" It hurts to talk.

She walks back behind her curtain. This space is tiny. It's smaller than my bedroom at home. When she returns, she's holding a water bottle.

"Can you untie me?" I ask.

She shakes her head. "Not yet. We have to be sure you're not going to hurt us."

They're smart. I've already tried to figure out how to overtake them.

She brings the bottle to my lips and pours. I gulp it up hungrily. Some of it spills out of my mouth and onto my shirt, but I don't care. I'm just so thirsty.

"Can I feed her?" Paige asks.

"I don't care," Sarah says.

She hands her the water bottle. She goes behind her curtain and comes back carrying a box of crackers. They're the Saltine kind Mom feeds me whenever I have the stomach flu. She tosses them to Paige and then leaves us alone except it's not as if we're really alone because her sheet is so close to Paige's cot she could reach out and touch it if she wanted to.

"Do you want a cracker?" Paige holds one up tentatively.

I shake my head. My stomach is too twisted to eat. It's coiled in on itself.

She munches on a few herself, taking a few dainty bites. She brushes off the crumbs that fall on her bed.

"I've been where you are," she says. "I know how it feels."

She has? Really? Or is she trying to trick me? But the fear in her eyes was real when she mentioned his name. Whoever he is. I'd never seen him before last night. Can she help me? Maybe we can help each other.

"How old are you?" I ask.

"Fifteen."

I would've guessed thirteen but she's only a year younger than me.

"How did you get here?" I ask.

"Same way you did."

She was running too? Did he ask her about his lost dog?

"Did he ask you if you'd seen his dog?"

She shakes her head.

Of course he doesn't have a dog. None of his story was real.

"He asked me if I knew his daughter." She stares at the wall as if she's seeing something I can't. Her gaze is faraway. "I was walking home from the library when he took me."

Relief washes over me. I'm sorry she's been kidnapped too, but there's something comforting about not being alone in this.

"Where do you live?" I ask.

"I lived in Phoenix," she says.

How did we get here together? I'm from Aurora, Colorado. Phoenix isn't even close.

"But I'm from Colorado..."

She shrugs her shoulders. "I don't know how that part works. I don't even know where we are. We could be anywhere."

Panic washes over me.

"Do you–we just stay down here?"

Her eyes fill with despair so real I could touch it. "No."

Hope rises in my chest. If we get to go outside, maybe I can escape. "When do we get let out?"

She shakes her head. "We don't ever get let out, but he does take us upstairs."

"What's upstairs?"

She picks her book back up. "You don't want to know what's upstairs. It's better down here."

SARAH

(THEN)

LISTEN AS PAIGE TAKES care of business for me. She's doing a good job explaining things to her. There's always a million questions. Who are we? How long have we been here? Is there any way to get out? Who is he? What does he want? Can we escape?

Paige has one thing wrong, though. Upstairs is way better than here. I hate the basement. It's not even a real basement. It's an old wine cellar that he gutted to create this prison. There's so much stale air and the walls feel like they're closing in on me. I hate the smell. It always stinks no matter how many times I clean or how careful I am with the toilet. When the upstairs door opens, it's the first time I can breathe without feeling like I'll choke on the air.

Being down here with a new girl always reminds me of what it was like when I was new. At least these girls have someone to talk to and help them figure things out. I didn't have anyone.

It was just me. Me and the darkness for days. I thought I'd die from the loneliness and never-ending silence.

Not to mention the boredom. You start to go crazy after a while when there's nobody to talk to and nothing to do, especially when you're used to living in the outside world. It takes a while to forget the old world. I started to talk to people that weren't there. I made up all sorts of people to have conversations with and created things to do to keep myself busy. I tore off chunks of foam from the wall and meticulously picked out pieces of it until I made a family. It took me lots of tries, but I did it. Once I'd built my family, I started working on other characters, seeing if I could create different things—horses, dogs, trees. But then he noticed the holes in the walls and was furious because he thought I was trying to escape.

He ripped into the holes, clawing at the foam until he exposed the brick underneath. "See this?" He pulled my head and smashed it up against the wall. "This is brick. There's no tunneling out of here. This isn't *Shawshank Redemption*."

I hadn't even considered trying to dig through the foam and into the wall. All I wanted was something to do with my hands and to occupy my mind. He didn't know what it was like. He wasn't the one who had to live alone in a dark basement.

"I wasn't trying to escape." The tears flooded my face. I hadn't learned how to swallow them yet. That takes a lot of practice. "I just wanted something to do. It's so awful down here with nothing to do." My voice sounded small. Like it did when I was a little girl.

After that, he started bringing me coloring books and crayons. They were the first gifts he gave me. I'd always hated coloring before, but I devoured them. I colored every page. Sometimes twice, going over pages I'd colored with different colors. I felt like a toddler, but didn't care. There wasn't anyone to see me doing it anyway and it kept me from going stir-crazy.

These girls don't know how good they have it. It's nothing compared to what I went through. I fear the day he decides to take everything away and goes back to doing things how he used to do them. That's why I work so hard at keeping them in their place. They don't understand it. They just think I'm mean, but they don't know what it used to be like or how much worse it can get.

I wonder how long this one will take. He didn't say anything to me last night when he carried her down. He used to but he doesn't anymore. I've learned the routine and I don't ask questions. He hates questions. I know my place. I've worked hard for this place.

I've already missed *The Today Show* and *Dr. Phil* is on now. I really wanted to see the gambling addict he was going to have on today. I should've thought to record it, but I didn't know he was going to go on a run. Usually, I do and then I make sure to record my programs for the next few days so I don't miss anything. It gives me something to look forward to while I wait down here. But he didn't tell me he was leaving and didn't give me any of his usual clues. No bags packed. No itinerary taped on the refrigerator. He was barely on his computer and he usually spends hours on it before he grabs another girl. He was just gone. I was as surprised as Paige when we heard the door open long after he'd locked us in for the night.

ELLA

(NOW)

SHE RACES THROUGH THE doorway, pushing the officers out of the way.

"Mom!" I cry.

She throws herself on my bed, wrapping herself around me. "My baby! My baby!"

We sob together, forming a giant wave. She squeezes me so tight, I can barely breathe, but I want her to squeeze me tighter. I want to disappear inside her body. She is solid and strong. She smells of comfort the way she always has.

She pulls me back and cups my face in her hands. "It's you! It's really you!" Her eyes are a mixture of pleasure and pain. "I was so scared I'd get here and find out it'd been a huge mistake. I was so scared to hope. I didn't want to be devastated all over again. But it's you. It's you. You're really here. My Ella Bear."

I sob like I will never stop. She plants kisses all over my face, drinking in my tears. I cling to her shirt. I'll never let her go again. She pulls me close again and I inhale her chest, taking in the sweet smell of her. She rocks me back and forth just like she did when I was small.

"Mommy..."

I haven't called her mommy in years.

"I'm here, Ella Bear. I'm here."

I can finally rest. I'm so exhausted. I haven't been able to sleep without being woken by paralyzing terror in months, but I fall asleep in her arms—a place I never thought I'd be again.

When I wake she's still in the bed next to me and for a moment, it all feels like a bad dream. But then I look at the new lines in her face, the haunted look that's never been in her eyes before, and it all comes flooding back. It wasn't a dream.

The FBI officers are standing at attention in their respective spots in the room. The female officer, Melanie, is sitting in a chair by the door, flipping through a *People* magazine. There's another police officer outside my door.

Mom strokes my hair. "How are you, baby?"

I don't know how to tell her how I am because I don't know who I am anymore or what's become of the me I used to be. I'm afraid to tell her the things I've done. What's been done to me. Afraid of what she'll say if she knows. She might not love me anymore.

"I'm okay," I say even though I'm not sure I'll ever be okay again.

"You were so brave to escape the way you did." Her chest puffs with pride.

I force a smile, but I know the truth. I wasn't brave. I was terrified.

SARAH

(NOW)

I DON'T LIKE THE MEDICINE they keep pumping into me. It makes my thinking cloudy and hard for me to stay awake. I need to stay awake. I can't keep falling asleep. It's too dangerous. I wish they'd stop giving it to me.

Officer Malone hasn't left my side. Every time I open my eyes, he's still here. He jumps up from his chair at my slightest movement, asking if I need anything. He has linebacker shoulders and looks like a man who once had a lot of muscles, but the years have taken their toll on his body and they sag in places they used to bulge. He doesn't smile very often with his lips, but his eyes do all the time and the eyes never lie.

I'm sure he's a great father. His daughters are lucky. He helped the nurse prop me up in the bed and told me there are officers from the FBI coming to talk to me about what happened, but even with his forewarning, I'm not prepared when they stride into my room.

They aren't dressed like any police officers I've ever seen. They look like they belong in an office with their collared shirts and dress pants. FBI badges hang from the lanyards around their necks. They have the same matching short haircut as if they're in the army. Both of them are built like they spend hours in the gym.

"Sarah, I'm Agent Blake Erickson. This is my partner Phil. We're with the FBI kidnapping unit and we're here to ask you some questions. Are you up to answering some of our questions?" I can hear the military in his voice.

I nod, too intimidated to speak. Their presence takes over the room.

Blake reeks of authority and he motions for Phil to take a seat in the chair in the corner while he remains standing. Phil sits on the edge of the seat, his long legs sprawling out in front of him. Blake sets his briefcase on my bed and opens it. He pulls out a small notebook and a pen.

"Mind if I take some notes?" he asks in a tone that indicates I don't really have a choice in the matter.

I nod again.

He fires his questions quickly.

"Can you tell us your full name?"

"Sarah Smith."

"Middle name?"

"I don't have one."

He raises his eyebrows. "No middle name? Are you sure?"

Of course I'm sure. It's my name.

"Yes. Just Sarah Smith."

"Can you tell us the date he took you?"

This is a hard one.

I shrug my shoulders. "It's kind of hard to remember."

"Try. Do you remember the day? The month?"

"I remember the year."

It was 2012. I'd just turned twelve.

He nods. "That's something. A good place to start. What was the year you were taken?"

"2012."

Four years ago. It feels like four centuries.

"Do you remember the month?"

"It was fall, I think."

Or was it winter? There were so many dead leaves in the park that day. It could've been either.

"We're going to take it slow with the questions. If you start to get overwhelmed, just let us know and we'll stop."

I nod. So far, Phil hasn't spoken. He just keeps staring at me like I'm a puzzle he's trying to solve.

"Where were you when he took you?"

"In the park."

"Which park?"

"I can't remember what it was called. The one by my house."

"Do you remember your address?"

I shake my head. I willed myself to forget everything from before. Deleted the memories. It was easier that way.

"Where are you from?" His gaze pierces me.

"California."

"Sarah, if you could be as specific as possible that would be really helpful. Try to give us as much detail as you can about things."

"You're doing great, kiddo. I know this is hard," Officer Malone pipes up.

I'm glad Officer Malone is still here. I don't like these men.

"I used to live in Redlands. Before... before..."

I don't know how to finish the sentence. For so long, I've told myself there wasn't a before. Don't think about your past—it's what I tell the girls. I drill it into their heads right away.

"What are your parents' names?"

I freeze. I can't talk about my parents. These are the questions I can't answer. The world tilts and then stills. My heartbeat explodes in my ears. It doesn't take long for the silence to grow uncomfortable.

His forehead wrinkles. "Sarah, what are your parents' names?"

"My mom's name was Destiny." My voice sounds strange to me. I haven't spoken her name in years. The word doesn't feel right in my mouth.

"Was?" Blake cocks his head to the side.

"Yes. She's dead."

Blake and Phil exchange a look. Phil has leaned back in the chair and spread his arms out behind him trying to be casual, but there's nothing casual about this conversation.

"When did she die?"

"Two days after I was born."

Officer Malone reaches out and takes hold of my hand again. I can feel his pity surrounding me, but it's not that big of a deal. You can't miss someone you never knew. I don't know what she looked like. I've never even seen a picture.

"How did she die?" It's the first question from Phil.

"She overdosed on heroin."

"And your dad?" Blake asks.

"I don't want to talk about my dad."

They exchange another look.

"What does all of this have to do with finding John? I want to know where he is."

Phil leans forward in his chair. "You're safe here. He can't get to you. We have officers surrounding the hospital and outside your door at all times. Any information you give us is going to help find him. Is there anything you can think of that might help us?"

They don't need to worry about finding him because he'll find me if they wait long enough and I can't stay in this hospital forever. Eventually, they have to let me go and there's no way he's going to let me get away from him. He'd never let that happen. Not in a million years.

"Like what?" I ask.

I know every detail about him because I've studied him for years. I know how he moves when he's upset and when he's calm. I can read what kind of a day he's had by the way he holds his silverware. I know how he takes his coffee and the foods he doesn't like to eat. I can tell the difference between his fake laugh and the one that's real. I know the shows he likes to watch on TV and how he likes his laundry folded.

"Did you see him today?" Blake's back to asking the questions.

I nod.

"Did he leave the house?"

"Yes, he leaves for work at 7:30 every morning unless he's traveling on a business trip."

"What was he wearing?"

"He was wearing a suit and tie. He wears a black suit, a white shirt, and a black tie every day. He wears Gucci leather loafers with silk knee-high socks."

And red silk boxers with white spotted print.

"Do you know what kind of job he has?"

I shrug my shoulders. "I'm not sure. He never told me. But he's got to do something important and make a lot of money. Did you see how big his house is?"

And then I remember, of course they haven't seen his house. The house is gone.

ELLA

(THEN)

EVERYTHING IN THE basement moves in slow motion. Time stands still. My body radiates with pain. The parts that aren't on fire are tingling. My skin rubbed raw. I keep telling myself I'm having a nightmare and any minute, I'm going to open my eyes and wake up tucked under my pink comforter in my own bed at home. But it's not a nightmare. This is real. It's really happening. To me. My tears are hot against my skin.

Nothing bad has ever happened to me. Not really. My dad left when I was a baby and I've never met him but lots of people are raised by single parents and I have the best mom anyone could ask for. She's always been a morning person, up at five even on Saturdays when she didn't need to. She was so happy and cheerful when she'd flick on my lights and pull up the blinds, flooding my room with light and making me squint in revulsion.

"Rise and shine, sweetie," she'd say.

I'd groan and pull my pillow over my head. Now, I'd give anything just to hear her voice.

She's my best friend. Teenagers aren't supposed to admit that, but it's true. I trust her more than I trust anyone else. Maybe it's because we've always been so close. When I was small, she couldn't afford daycare while she worked, so she carried me in a Mobi wrap tucked close to her chest while she cleaned hotel rooms. As I got older, she switched to carrying me in a hiking backpack while she worked. I was rarely away from her. No matter how hard she worked she never complained. Ever. She went without just so I could have things and if there was ever a choice between her happiness or mine, she put me first.

I loved her laughter. She had one of those contagious laughs and could brighten up a room with it. Everyone commented on it.

"Your mom has the best laugh," my teachers would always say.

She always found the good in situations no matter how bad they looked, like the days when they scheduled her to work on Christmas or holidays and she refused to be sad about it. She just made Christmas a different day. When I was younger, I didn't know the difference and it didn't matter to me as long as I got to spend the day celebrating with her.

It hurts to think about her in the past tense. Why am I already thinking of her in the past tense? She's not dead and I'm not going to die. But what if I am? What if he's going to come down here and kill me? But what about the other girls? He took Paige too and he hasn't killed her. I don't know if he kidnapped Sarah, but she's still alive too. I take a deep breath, willing myself to calm down.

My bladder is full. I've been holding it so long it hurts. I'm either going to wet myself or have to use the toilet. I can't get to the toilet with my legs bound together at the ankles.

"I have to go to the bathroom," I announce.

Paige jumps up from her bed, looking happy to have something to do.

She pulls me up to a standing position. "I think you're just going to have to hop over there."

She puts her arm around me like we're about to do a three-legged race and I start hopping. I'm grateful for her body to lean against because my legs are so weak I feel like they won't hold me. We hobble-hop over to the toilet. Paige giggles.

I stare at her. "What are you laughing at?"

"We just look so goofy." She smiles.

How can she laugh and smile about any of this? I'm mortified because I have to pee in front of her and I'm an incredibly shy person. I don't like to be the center of attention for anything, especially not when I'm going to the bathroom, but I don't have a choice because it'd be even more humiliating to pee on myself. I can't get my shorts down by myself. Paige notices at the same moment I do and pulls them down in one swift movement.

I take a seat on the toilet wanting to die of embarrassment but I have to go so bad I can't hold it. The pee makes a weird sound as it fills the toilet. I quickly look down between my legs. There's not water in the toilet. My pee is flowing into a large bucket. I look up at Paige. She reads the confusion in my eyes.

"It's not a real toilet. I mean, it's a toilet, but it doesn't have a pipe or whatever," she says. "It's an old person's bedpan."

"What do we do with it?"

She quickly rattles off the list of rules for the use of the toilet. First, we try to limit the amount of times we go to the bathroom each day. Second, only two sheets of toilet paper are used to wipe because the toilet paper fills up the bowl faster. Three, the lid on the toilet must be closed except when we are using it to try to keep the smell down. Fourth, since I am the new girl, cleaning the toilet is now my job.

"But what am I supposed to do with it?" I ask.

"Sarah empties it. She takes it upstairs to the real bathroom, but when she brings it back down, you're the lucky one who gets to clean it each night." A wide smile spreads across her face. "Sorry, I'm just so excited not to have to be the one to do it anymore."

As mortifying as it is to pee in front of someone else, I can't believe I'm going to have to poop in front of them too. I don't even poop outside of my own house unless it's an emergency situation and there's no way I can hold it.

"Why can't we just have a regular toilet?"

She shrugs. "Who knows. I stopped trying to figure things out here a long time ago."

I don't like how resigned she is to her fate. That is not going to happen to me. I won't get used to this no matter how long I'm here.

The day drags. I lay on my bed staring up at the padded ceiling. I imagine my mom out searching for me, walking the streets of Aurora and begging other people to help her. I'm sure she's called the police by now. I can almost feel her desperation. I try to send her telepathic messages that I'm okay—I'm alive, I'm going to get through this. Thinking about my mom makes me cry on and off all day.

Paige keeps trying to get me to eat. I don't want food. I may never eat again.

Sarah stays behind her sheet and I can't help but wonder what she's doing behind it. Why does she get a sheet? What makes her so different from us?

Sometime during the day or maybe it's the evening—I'm not sure, it's impossible to tell when I can't see outside—a loud buzzer goes off. The room becomes alive immediately. Paige sits straight up at a ninety-degree angle on her bed. For the first time since this morning, Sarah appears from behind her veil. She stands at attention at the end of the stairway.

"Sarah, you may come upstairs now," a loud booming male voice calls out from what sounds like an intercom. It's like the intercoms they use at my school every morning when they make announcements.

Sarah doesn't turn around. She rushes up the stairs. I hear three short beeps and then a long beep, followed by the sound of a door opening. Then, the beeps again. Same pattern. I turn toward Paige.

"What's happening?"

"This is how it works," she says as if that's supposed to explain anything.

"How what works? I don't understand. What's happening? Is he going to come down here? What happens if he comes down here?" I can't keep the hysteria out of my voice.

"He doesn't come down here unless it's an emergency." She quickly adds, "Or to bring a new girl."

"How long have you been here?" I ask.

"Five months, I think? It might be a little longer. I'm not sure. I used to try to keep track of the days but I lost count after a while. All the days are the same so it doesn't really matter."

There's no way it will take Mom five months to find me.

"How about Sarah?"

"She's been here for years. Forever maybe." She leans in closer. "She's his daughter."

SARAH

(NOW)

EVERYTHING CHANGED WHEN I told the
officers I was John's daughter. They fingerprinted me
and swabbed my cheek for DNA with a Q-tip like I've
seen them do on TV. Officer Malone left the room for a few
minutes. He was more shocked than all of them. It must be hard
for him to imagine. He's back now, but he just keeps staring at
me like there's clues hidden in my face somewhere.

The FBI agents are gone. They promised to be back shortly
and told me someone called a victim's advocate is going to be
here soon to talk to me. I don't know what a victim's advocate
is, but I don't need one. All I need to know is where John is.

I did just like he taught me. We'd gone over the plans so
many times I had each step memorized by heart, but this is the
part we hadn't planned on and now I don't know what to do.
I waited and waited for him, but he never showed and he was
supposed to come for me. That was the plan. Instead, the police

showed up. First, it was just one squad car, but as soon as they noticed the fire, things moved really fast, so quickly I had a hard time keeping up. But I kept my eyes peeled the entire time, always searching for him amid all of the emergency vehicles, trying to catch a glimpse of him. I waited for him to step out from the chaos and grab me when they weren't looking.

What is he going to do when he finds out I'm here? He isn't going to be happy. That much I know. I hope he's madder at Ella. She's the one who did it. Not me. I told her it was a stupid idea. I warned her what would happen if any of us ran. She didn't listen to me, but then again, she never listens to me.

She was so stubborn from the minute he brought her home. She questioned everything we did. She was constantly drilling Paige with questions. Always asking about things. Any answers we gave her just led to more questions. It was exhausting.

And she wouldn't eat. She refused food for six days. I didn't have the patience for it. Paige tried everything. Not that she had many options, but she tried every item we keep in the basement. She wouldn't even open her mouth. She didn't even try to make things easier for herself.

He said I could uncuff her on her third day which turned out to be a huge mistake. I thought she was going to gouge my eyes out the way she came after me. I had to smack her in the face. She didn't leave me any other choice. I put her back in the ties. She promised to stop after that and I was foolish enough to believe her so I let her out again. This time, she went berserk like an animal, running up the stairs to the door and pounding on it. She screamed for three hours without stopping. Paige kept going up next to her, talking to her in her calm, sweet voice, urging her to stop, but it was no use. She was determined. She screamed until she lost her voice, but she didn't stop there.

She ran down the stairs and started tearing stuff up. She flipped over her cot and did the same to Paige's. Paige stood off to the side in amazement. She'd never seen anyone act this way, but I had. She took all of the food Paige had placed on the nightstand and started throwing it. She tried to rip the toilet out of the ground and I had to step in because I couldn't have her messing up our place.

"Enough!" I ordered.

She didn't even look at me. Just kept spinning around the room, tearing chunks of foam off the wall and throwing them. She ripped my sheet down from the ceiling. That's when she went too far.

I grabbed her by the arm and whipped her around. I slammed her against the wall, pushing my face within inches of her. "Listen to me. You're going to knock this off and you're going to knock this off now." She glared at me like she was a wild animal, but I was stronger than her. She was smaller and weak from not eating. "If you hurt me, he will kill you. If you hurt Paige, he will kill you. If you don't act right, he will kill you. This shit is not a game."

My words sucked the fight out of her. I let go of her shirt and pushed her backward. She collapsed onto the floor in sobs. Paige ran to her side, kneeling down beside her. She put her arm around her. "Please, just calm down. I don't want him to hurt you." Paige cried right along with her and they clung to each other like old friends.

I went to work on rehanging my curtain.

ELLA

(THEN)

HATE HER. EVERY TIME she comes into our space, I want to stab her. How can she be a part of this? Maybe I should start eating so I can get strong enough to fight her, but the thought of food still makes my stomach heave. She doesn't understand that I'm not trying to be difficult by not eating. I just can't.

She goes upstairs every day now. He summons her over the intercom and she skips up the stairs all happy. She only smiles when she hears his voice. The only thing I can think of when I hear his voice is the way he said, "Excuse me, miss," when he pulled up alongside me.

A few minutes ago, he summoned her upstairs and after a while he called Paige too. A cloud of fear passed her face when he said her name. She walked to the landing and hesitated with each step she took. What do they do up there?

It's the first time I've been alone and I want to see what's in Sarah's room. I've come to think of it as her room as if the sheet is a real wall separating us from her. I hobble over there. She hasn't untied me again since I freaked out a few days ago. I'm hoping my legs will shrink from not eating and eventually, I can just wiggle out. I've been trying to loosen them every night after they go to sleep. I listen for the sounds of Paige falling asleep before I start. It's easy to know when she's out because she snores. I don't know about Sarah. I can't hear her, but it doesn't matter anyway because she can't see me.

I think I'm making progress. My ankles seem skinnier already and the ties feel like they have more give. I'm going to get out of them and when I do, I'm going to figure out a way to get out of this hole. There has to be some way.

I push back the sheet and hop through. She has a twin-sized bed pushed up against the wall, not the weird cots Paige and I sleep on. There's a fluffy, yellow comforter with a bunch of pillows laid on top of it, so much more comfortable than the flat pillows and thin, white blankets we get. Her room is filled with Rubbermaid plastic containers, even a few big ones with drawers in them. There's a tiny refrigerator and a small microwave on top of it. I rummage through the food in containers next to it. There's tons of cans of soup, but she hasn't shared those. All this time they've been trying to feed me crackers and bread, I could've had something warm. I hate her even more.

The walls are covered in pictures she's torn out of magazines. They're all landscapes. Exotic places that look beautiful. Oceans and islands. Waterfalls and mountains. I wonder if she's been to any of these places. Does he ever let her out of the house? Does she leave when she goes upstairs? What kind of a father makes his daughter help with his hostages? And what kind of a daughter is okay with this set up? Has she always been down here? Does she have a mom? Is there a woman upstairs? I'm going to ask Paige about it when she comes back downstairs tonight. She'll tell me. At least she's helpful.

I'm not sure how long they'll be upstairs so I start rummaging through all of her things as fast as I can. She's got stacks of black sweatpants and white t-shirts. It's what they wear every day. I'm still in my running shorts and Nike t-shirt. I've worn them for almost a week now. I've never smelled so foul. I'm sure it won't be long until I'm wearing the sweatpants and t-shirt too.

How do they stay clean? They never shower. As far as I know, there's no running water down here. They don't even brush their teeth. Well, Paige doesn't brush her teeth. For all I know, Sarah might brush hers.

There's other boxes with loads of coloring books. They're the new kind of coloring books for adults, but she's got kids' coloring books too. There's another container filled with markers, crayons, glue, and art supplies.

I find all sorts of goodies and things. Lots of books. The entire Twilight series and every Harry Potter book. I grab one of her Twilight books and I don't even like Twilight. I didn't see any of the movies, but I don't care. I just want to have something of hers. It's not fair that she has everything and we have nothing.

I hop back to my side of the room and tuck the book underneath my cot. She's not as powerful as she thinks she is. I lay back down on my bed, satisfied with my small victory and go back to doing what I always do—plotting my escape.

ELLA

(NOW)

I T FEELS GOOD TO HAVE MOM with me. I keep looking over at her just to make sure she's still here and feeling relieved each time she is. She talks to me weird now and I'm not sure I like it. It's the same voice she used when I was a little girl, like I'm a toddler again, as if somehow I've grown backward.

"How are you feeling, sweetie?"

"Can I get you anything, cupcake?"

"Things are going to be okay now, Ella Bear."

And it's always in a soft, low voice right above a whisper as if she talks to me too loud, something terrible will happen like I'm made of porcelain glass or something. I want to tell her to stop, but I don't want to hurt her feelings.

There's a knock at my door and everyone in the room turns to look. A short woman with wild, curly hair sticking up all over her head walks through the door. She's wearing a long flowing skirt that drapes all the way down to her ankles, stopping at her Birkenstock sandals. Blake and Phil rush forward to greet her, forming a semi-circle around her. They speak in hushed whispers and she nods at whatever they're saying. After they're finished, she walks over to my bed and stands beside it. She sticks out her hand, making the bangle bracelets on her wrist jingle.

"I'm Randy. I'm a victim's advocate with the FBI." Her eyes are dark, nearly black and framed by full eyebrows that arch up almost playfully.

I reach out and shake her hand. Mom comes around to meet her on the other side of the bed.

"I'm Jocelyn, Ella's mom. It's a pleasure to meet you." Mom smiles but her smile doesn't reach her eyes. Not like it used to.

Randy shakes Mom's hand. "I'm sorry to be meeting you under these circumstances."

"It's okay. I'm just happy to have someone here who can help us," Mom says.

Randy turns her attention to me. "How are you feeling?"

"Okay," I say just like I say each time anyone asks.

"Ella, would you mind if I talked to you by yourself?" She peers at me. Her gaze is so intense it's like she can see right through me.

I turn to Mom. Panic washes over me. I don't want her to leave. I just got her back.

"I prefer to stay while you talk to her," Mom says as if she can read my mind.

"I understand how you feel, but sometimes kids find it easier to talk to me without their parents," Randy says.

Mom stiffens. "There aren't any secrets between us."

"Ella, how do you feel about that? Are you comfortable with having your mom here? It's okay if you're not."

"I want her here," I say. I'm not sure I ever want her away from me.

"Okay, then." She tosses her hair over her shoulder and points to the end of my bed. "Do you mind if I sit here?"

"Sure. That's fine," I say sneaking a glance at Mom. She looks bewildered too.

She flips off her sandals and plops down on the bed, folding herself cross-legged on the edge. Her skirt fans out around her. "This is a lot to take in. Can I tell you a little bit about what my role is in all of this and explain what's going on?"

I nod.

"Basically, I'm here for you. That's the simplest description of my job. I work with kids who've experienced trauma. Kids just like you. My role is to help them navigate their world afterward. Sometimes the things that happen after something bad happens can be just as traumatic or even more traumatic than what they went through. I'm here to help you manage your emotions and not get too overwhelmed with everything going on around you. I can also answer any questions you have." She pauses, giving me a chance to speak. I don't have anything to say. Not yet, anyway. "Right now you're at Olive Memorial View Hospital in Simi Valley. Has anyone told you that yet?"

I shake my head. If anyone told me, I don't remember it. All I remember is the terror. The soul-sucking fear that he was only a few steps behind me and was going to grab me at any moment. Even after they'd locked me in the back of the squad car while we waited for the ambulance, my heart wouldn't stop pounding and I couldn't stop shaking. I kept picturing him shooting all of the officers then breaking the squad car windows and killing me. There were only a few officers at first and we were all alone on the road. Every sound made me jump.

"Do you know where Simi Valley is?"

"No."

"It's in California. Part of the San Fernando Valley. I'm sure you've heard of Los Angeles before, right?"

This time I nod. Everyone knows about Los Angeles.

"Well, Simi Valley is about thirty miles outside of Los Angeles."

Mom jumps in. "When can she go home?"

Randy turns to look at her. "It's difficult to say at this point. She'll be in the hospital for a few days to treat her injuries. She'll have officers standing guard over her room around the clock so you can rest assured she'll be safe while she's here. The FBI is on the scene and since it's a kidnapping case that crosses state lines with a minor, the local authorities will be turning the case over to them. They'll still be helping with the case, but the FBI will be in control of it from now on. They'll be the ones who authorize her to go home."

"Have they found the psycho who took her?" Mom's eyes flash with anger.

"Unfortunately, no."

The color drains from Mom's face. "Do they know who he is? Any idea where he is? Where he went? Who he knows? Is he connected with anyone? Do they have any leads?"

Randy raises her hand to stop her questions. "Take a deep breath. I know this is scary for you too, but it helps if you stay calm for Ella. The best thing you can do for her is to take care of her and let law enforcement take care of finding him."

"But, they'll find him, right? They'll find him?" I ask. "He's got to be coming back to the house soon. He can't stay gone forever."

He'd left us before but never longer than a few days. Sarah always seemed to know how long he was going to be gone. I don't know if he told her when he was leaving or if she figured it out on her own, but she never worried about him coming back.

"Has anyone told you what's going on?" Randy asks.

I look to Mom for answers. She's studying Randy intently, hanging on her every word.

"The only thing they told me when they called was that they found her and she was safe. I didn't ask any other questions except the fastest way to get to her." Her eyes fill with tears. She's lost a lot of weight. Her clothes hang on her and her cheekbones stick out. There are bags underneath her eyes.

This time Randy takes a deep breath. "The house was on fire when the officers arrived on the scene. It looks like he torched the place."

Panic claws at my chest. "Did anyone get out?"

"Yes, thankfully, the other girl made it out. She was there when the officers arrived. She's here in the hospital too."

"Was it Paige?"

Randy tilts her head. "Paige? Who's Paige?"

"One of the girls."

"There was another girl besides Sarah?"

My stomach flips. "Yes, Paige. She was there too. Did she make it out?"

"I'm sorry, I didn't know about another girl. Did you tell the officers that?"

"I asked the police officers about her."

"The ones in your room when you first got here?"

I nod, too scared to talk.

"Blake!" Randy calls out.

Blake cracks the door and pops his head through. "What's up? Everything okay?"

"There's another girl. There was another girl with them in the house." She runs her hand through her hair.

"You have to find her!" I scream at him. "You have to find Paige! You have to! Please!"

I can't stop screaming. Mom rushes to my side and wraps her arms around me. I throw them off me, pulling away from her. She tries to hug me again. I swat her hands away.

"Don't touch her," Randy says quietly.

Mom flips around. "Don't tell me what to do with my daughter," she snaps.

But she listens to her and leaves me alone. She stands twisting her hands in front of her. Tears wet her face. I pull my knees up to my chest and wrap my arms around them. My body rocks back and forth.

"Honey, Ella, it's going to be okay." Her voice is thin and desperate. "I'm right here. It's okay."

It's not. Not if Paige is dead. Not if I'm the one who killed her.

ELLA

(THEN)

PAIGE IS DIFFERENT WHEN she returns from upstairs. The smile is gone from her face along with the light in her eyes. She doesn't even look at me. She clutches her stomach as she shuffles to her bed and lays flat on her back once she's there, her hands by her sides, unmoving. Her body is stiff like she's in a coffin.

"Are you okay?" I whisper like there's someone who might hear us.

She doesn't respond. Just stares at the ceiling, unblinking.

"What happened?"

Again, nothing.

I stand motionless next to her. I want to reach out and hold her, but I can't with my ties. I've gotten used to my ties and stopped being afraid of them. Until now. I want them off me. I can't go another minute without moving my body freely. Once I ran a cross country meet with the flu and like I always do, I sprinted to the finish line, but when I got there and tried to catch my breath, I couldn't. I couldn't take in air and no air could escape. I felt like I was choking. They told me I hyperventilated. I feel the same way now except this time my coach isn't here to assure me that I'm going to be okay and Mom doesn't rush over to hold my hand and tell me to focus on the sound of her voice. Instead, it gets worse. I grow more frantic. My muscles stiffen, clenched towards my body and I'm shaking like I might be having a seizure.

I stare at Paige. She doesn't move. Why is she just lying there? She knows I can't breathe. I'm going to die if I can't catch my breath. I stop struggling. Just give in to it and relax into the darkness.

When I come to, I'm on my stomach, laying on the carpet between my cot and Paige's. She hasn't moved from her position.

"Sarah?" I yell.

I'm not sure why I call out for her. I never have before but I don't know what to do about Paige. Maybe she's acted like this before and Sarah knows what to do. Paige is the only thing that makes me feel normal and I don't know what I'm going to do if she doesn't snap out of it.

She doesn't answer. I move over to her room and peek behind her sheet in case she's ignoring me. Her space is empty. I hop back to Paige's cot and kneel next to her.

"Hey, are you okay? Please talk to me." I stroke her cheek with the back of my hands. "What's going on? You have to tell me. Maybe I can help you."

She finally speaks. "Nobody can help me." Her voice is flat.

"Please, you're scaring me. What did he do to you? What happens up there?"

"You'll find out soon enough."

"Paige, I'm begging you. Just sit up. Talk to me. Please."

She drags herself into sitting position. "Fine. You really want to know? He's a dirty old man who likes teenage girls. And not just any teenage girls. Special ones."

Special ones? I'm not special. There's nothing unique about me. I'm totally average. I don't get invited to any of the cool parties. None of the popular kids even talk to me. I spend my weekends reading, watching old movies, and helping Mom out in church on Sunday.

"What do you mean, special?"

"Virgins. He likes virgins. That's his whole deal. That's how this thing works. He takes us so he can be our first. It makes him feel special. Important or something. I don't really know. He's a freak."

All the energy gets sucked out of the room.

"But... but, I don't want to. I don't want to lose my virginity. He can't. He just can't." I shake my head.

No. I won't have it. I won't let him.

The dead look in her eyes is back. "You don't have a choice."

SARAH

(THEN)

'VE DRIED ALL THE DINNER dishes and put them away. The tea kettle whistles. I pull it off the stove and pour the water into his favorite mug. I plop his Chamomile tea bag in the water and wait for it to stew before spooning in the honey. Half a tablespoon. Never more than that. He doesn't like too much sugar, but he refuses to drink his tea without it and he has to have his tea to go to sleep.

I hear the sound of the shower turning off. He won't be long now. I set his tea at his spot at the table and take my seat, waiting for him. I decided earlier today that I was going to bring up sleeping upstairs again. Last time he dismissed me, refusing to even talk to me about it. But he'll be in a good mood tonight. He's never more alive than when he's brought home a new girl. His body hums with excitement and he practically skips when he walks. He arrives in his bathrobe shortly, his hair still wet from the shower.

"Thank you, darling," he says as he slides into his seat.

"You're welcome." I keep my eyes down.

"How is she doing?" He blows on his tea. It's still too hot to drink.

"Better today, I think. She still cries herself to sleep every night, but that's pretty normal. It's not the hysterical kind anymore and she ate a few crackers today. Finally. Paige coaxed her into doing it."

He looks pleased. "Good for Paige. I'm proud of her. I'm going to miss her."

Not me. I made the mistake of getting attached the first time he brought a new girl home. Her name was Tiffany and I was so excited. It was like getting the sister I always wanted even though she was older than me. We hit it off right from the start. We passed the hours in the basement reading to each other and making up stories. Sometimes we performed for each other like we were on TV. We created elaborate murals together and pasted them all over the walls. Pictures of trees and flowers. A great big sun shining down with a smile. We created an outdoor scene and spent hours looking at it, sharing secrets from our lives we'd never told anyone.

I cried for days after she was gone. Her absence left a gaping hole in my heart. I wrote her letters for the next year. I knew it was silly but I missed her desperately and had gotten used to talking to her. I still have the letters tucked away in one of my boxes somewhere. I used to pull them out and read them, but I don't anymore.

I've trained myself not to care about the girls or let them get close to me. It's easier that way. I won't miss Paige when she's gone.

He interrupts my thoughts.

"It's been over a week. I think it's time to bring her upstairs."

I nod. "I'll prepare things for her."

"I think I'd like to do it myself this time. I have a feeling about this one."

I sneak a peek. A wide smile is spread across his face. He looks dreamy like he's in another world. Why does he want to get things ready? I've been doing it for years. But sometimes he gets ideas in his head about the girls that I don't understand. Like Bianca. He'd been so excited because she was his first black girl. He'd searched for her for a long time. He was giddy when he'd gone to get her, but their first meeting hadn't gone well. Something happened. I don't know what and he didn't tell me. He never does. Sometimes the curiosity about how he is with them in the bedroom eats me alive and I have to work really hard at pushing it down.

The next night when I brought her upstairs, he didn't even bother to eat dinner with her. I'd worked really hard at figuring out how to make risotto that afternoon and was disappointed he didn't get the chance to try it. He left with her immediately. I never saw Bianca again. Sometimes it was like that.

"I have a request." I have to seize his good mood.

It's been a few months since I've asked for anything so I hope he says yes this time. I purposefully avoided asking him for anything because there's nothing I want more than to be out of the basement forever. I want to sleep in a bedroom that's mine. One with real walls and a door I can shut behind me.

"Yes?" I can tell by his voice that he's only half paying attention.

"I would like to sleep upstairs."

"Honey, we've talked about this before. You know how I feel about it." He shakes his head, sipping his tea.

"But I was hoping you might change your mind after you had more time to think about it. It's just so depressing down there." I almost leave out the last part because it sounds a bit whiny and he hates whining, but he hates it even more when I get depressed.

He reaches over to take my hand. His big hand encircles mine. His fingernails are cut short, perfectly manicured.

"You know that can't happen. I need you down there. You have to be my eyes." He traces circles with his fingertips on the top of my hand.

"I don't. Not really anymore. We have the cameras."

"I said no." He jerks his hand away.

I stare at the table top. I don't dare argue even though I'm fuming inside. I hate that he gets to make all the rules. It's not fair.

"Don't ask me again." His voice is harsh and stern. He gets up. I flinch, but instead of coming toward me he walks over to the sink and pours what's left of his tea down the drain. "It's time for bed."

I stand and push in my chair. He walks over and pats me on top of my head. "Now be a good girl and run along to bed."

I trudge down the stairs. The beeps sound behind me.

SARAH

(NOW)

STARE AT THE VICTIM'S advocate. I can't believe she actually works for the FBI when she looks like a hippie who sits around and smokes weed during her spare time in a garden with a Buddha statue. Her presence is so calm it's unnerving and she asks me permission to do anything. I'm annoyed with her already and she's only been in my room for five minutes.

"I just finished meeting with Ella and she told me about Paige. I told her what I'm about to tell you—we are going to do everything we can to find Paige. Do you think you could help us with that?"

What did Ella say about me? I want to ask, but I don't want her to think I care about what she thinks about me.

"I'll try, but I don't think I can really help. I was upstairs when the fire started."

"And where was she?"

"In the basement."

What do they know about our life? How much has she told her?

"When did you notice the fire had started?"

"I smelled smoke, but I didn't really think anything about it because I was too freaked out about the alarms going off. And then when the other alarms started going off, I just thought they were more house alarms."

"House alarms?" She raises her eyebrows.

"The house was wired. John set it whenever he left. If anyone opened any of the doors or windows, the alarms went off and sent a signal to his phone," I say, remembering the only other time the alarms had been triggered—the time I set them off. The memory makes me cringe. "We weren't supposed to leave."

"Is this hard for you to talk about?" Concern lines her face.

I shrug. "A little. Everything just happened so fast."

"So, when did you notice the fire?"

"I saw smoke coming from the back. That's when I ran out of the house too."

"But you stopped in the yard? Isn't that where the police found you?"

I nod.

"Why didn't you keep running?" She fixes her eyes on me.

I twist my hands together on my lap. "I didn't know what to do."

"Why didn't you go over the gate?"

I hold back the urge to laugh. "Have you seen the gate?"

"No, I haven't. Would you like to tell me about it?"

"It's huge." It was massive, encircling the entire property like we lived in a medieval castle.

"Ella got over it, didn't she? How'd she do it?"

"I have no idea."

I'd wracked my brain trying to figure that one out too. There was no way to climb it because it was made of sleek aluminum. You couldn't jump over either. John made it that way on purpose. He'd showed me all the pictures while it was being constructed. I often wondered what the neighbors thought about it.

"Did you think about going back for Paige?" She eyes me quizzically, her head tilted slightly to the side.

"I just froze. I didn't know what to do. I figured she'd make it out too."

"Weren't you worried that she wouldn't?"

"Of course I was worried," I snap.

"But you didn't go back to check on her?"

"No, I didn't. I already told you that."

"I noticed you didn't ask if she made it out," she says, pointedly. Her statement looms in the air.

I shrug. "I figured if she was dead, somebody would've told me." I don't want to talk about Paige. I change the subject to what's important. "Have you found John?"

She shakes her head. "We're still looking. We'll know more soon."

I wish they would hurry. I don't know how much longer I'm going to be able to stand this.

ELLA
(THEN)

SOMETIME IN THE AFTERNOON —at least I think it's the afternoon—Sarah comes downstairs with the scissors. They're the same scissors she used to cut my ties off last time. I'm so excited I can barely sit still while she snips, but my excitement is short-lived when she asks me to follow her upstairs. Since my talk with Paige, I've been hoping I might be different and he's decided just to keep me downstairs.

My legs and wrists feel strange without the ties binding them, but it's my fear that makes it difficult to walk up the stairs to the steel door I pounded on a few days earlier. It already seems like a lifetime ago. This time when we approach it, Sarah pushes it and it swings open. It clicks shut behind us, followed by the beeps that have become the soundtrack of my life.

I squint my eyes, blinded by the sunlight streaming in from the windows after having been in the dimly lit basement for so long. We're in a short entryway that opens up into an expansive hallway. I stand trembling, wringing my hands together. Sarah pulls me forward through the hallway and I scan the upstairs in shock.

In my imagination, I envisioned upstairs being rundown and filthy. In all the movies I've seen, the creepy bad guys always have disgusting houses. This place is beautiful, like a limestone museum. Everything is blindingly white. The walls. The ceiling. The marble floors. It's all pristine and perfect. Floor-to-ceiling windows line the open space. They sparkle and shine like they've never been touched, revealing a breathtaking view of mountains in the distance. The smell of lemon-scented bleach surrounds me.

Sarah stops and doesn't take me any further into the open space. I sneak a peek at the sprawling kitchen on the right. It's sleek and modern, so clean it looks like it's never been used, with granite countertops and stainless steel appliances. There's a huge central island ringed in cabinets. Barstools stand at attention around it.

The sound of footsteps moves toward us from somewhere in the house. My heartbeat explodes in my ears. I can't swallow.

Then, he appears.

"Hello, Ella. I've missed you," he says, his face breaking into a smile, exposing perfectly straight white teeth. He looks me up and down.

The world spins. I put my hand out to steady myself on the wall, afraid I'll fall if I don't. I break into a cold sweat. He doesn't look like a monster. He's handsome—the kind of man that makes women blush—not hideous like I expected. He looks like he stepped out of a business magazine. He's over six feet tall and dressed in a black suit, a stark contrast to all the white surrounding him. His short dark hair is neatly combed, every piece in place. His face is perfectly symmetrical. Distinct cheekbones and an angular jaw. Arched eyebrows form a perfect moon over his steel-blue eyes framed in dark lashes. His lips are pale and thin. His skin flawless. He's as impeccable as his house.

He steps toward me and with each step he takes, I move away from him until my back is smashed against the basement door and I can't go any further.

"There's nothing to be afraid of," he says. "It's time to get you cleaned up."

I don't move. I'm frozen to my spot. I furtively look around for Sarah, but she's gone. I don't see her anywhere. He grabs my arm. His fingers are cold. I jerk away.

"Please, just let me go home. I won't tell anyone. I promise. Nobody has to know. Please, just let me go."

He shakes his head. "It's time to clean you up."

"Why are you doing this to me? Please, just let me go," I whimper.

He reaches for me again and I move to slap his hand away. He catches my hand. His grip tightens around my fingers, crushing them. He moves into my space and presses his forearm against my chest. He pins his body against mine and his face contorts into anger.

"You do as I say. Do you understand me?" His words seep into my insides like ice water moving through my veins.

I nod, gulping down the sobs threatening to escape from my throat.

He releases me and pulls me forward, then places his hand on my back. "Move."

He shoves me forward into the house, quickly moving us through the living room and into another hallway. My eyes take in everything like snapshots. An L-shaped couch in front of a stone fireplace. More windows. Three doors in the hallway. All of them shut. He opens a door on the right and pushes me into a bathroom. He locks the door behind us.

I stare in horror at the claw-shaped bath tub filled to the top with bubbles. There's lit candles on the vanity and tall ones on candelabras next to the tub. Their flames cast an eerie glow against the white-washed walls. The room is filled with the scent of lavender. He points to the vanity and that's when I see it—a small gun.

"I'm not a violent man. I'd never do anything to hurt you, but I'll do what needs to be done if you get out of hand." He rubs his thumb across my cheek.

I cringe. "Please, don't hurt me."

"I'm not going to hurt you. I just want to get to know you." He smiles down at me. "Take your clothes off."

"Please. Please, I don't want to. I don't want to do this." I'm crying so hard I can barely speak.

"Take your clothes off." His voice has lost his even tone. It's laced with anger and threat.

I try to move around him. His body blocks the door. His crystalline blue eyes are cold now. They've turned to ice. His smile is gone and replaced with a sneer. I back away.

"Take your clothes off. I will not tell you another time."

I shrink before him. But I can't move. I know I should take my clothes off, but I can't do it. My arms won't work. I can't control them or stop my body from trembling. I've lost all control of myself. He grabs me and slaps me with the back of his hand across my face. The taste of blood fills my mouth. I reach my hand up to feel the sting. He grabs a chunk of my hair and snaps my head back.

"You will do what I say and I said to take your clothes off," he says through gritted teeth.

I nod frantically. He releases me and I stumble backward. I sob harder as I strip my clothes off. The harder I try to stop, the more I cry. I step out of my shorts and pull my shirt over my head. I stand in front of him in my sports bra and the same underwear I've been in since he took me.

"Everything." He narrows his eyes to slits.

I've never been naked in front of anyone besides Mom. I struggle out of my sports bra and gingerly pull my underwear down my legs. I stand in front of him with my arms across my chest. I've never been so exposed. Shame rises to my cheeks. I hang my head, refusing to look at him.

"Now, get into your bath."

I hurriedly step into the bath so he can't look at me. The water is hot, scalding my skin but I don't care. I slide underneath, sinking underneath the bubbles. I want to disappear. My heart thuds. I lay there for what feels like hours, too afraid to make eye contact with him to see what he's doing. His feet click on the tiled floor as he walks to the tub. He kneels next to it. All my muscles tense.

Before I know what's happening he picks up a washcloth and begins washing my back, stroking it up and down softly.

"I really wish you hadn't made me do that," he says as he continues washing my back. "I've been waiting for this all day. I couldn't stop thinking about you at work."

It's excruciating not to move as he touches me, but I don't dare.

"Let's lay back and work on that hair. You have such beautiful long hair. It's a shame to see it so dirty."

I force my body to lean back, staring up at the ceiling while he pours water over my head and begins lathering my hair with shampoo. It smells like flowers with a faint tinge of mint. After he's washed it twice, he fills it with conditioner and piles my hair on top of my head to let the conditioner soak in.

"Sit up," he says softly.

I do as I'm told.

He's back with the washcloth. This time he goes to work on my body. I burn with shame as he moves between my legs. I stare at the small tiles in front of me, focusing on counting each one. I keep losing track and have to start over. I multiply the numbers by three and then four. Over and over again as he scrubs. He rinses the conditioner out of my hair. Finally, he's finished and I'm scrubbed clean, but I've never felt so dirty.

ELLA

(NOW)

EVEN WITH MOM ASLEEP in the fold-out bed they brought in for her, I can't sleep. All day during the relentless questioning, all I wanted to do was go to sleep, but as soon as they dimmed the lights, I was suddenly wide awake. A new officer is standing outside my door and Randy assured me he wouldn't leave his post all night. She also promised to be back first thing in the morning.

Despite all the security measures around me, I still don't feel safe. I'm not sure I'll ever feel safe again. They still haven't found John. He's out there somewhere and as long as he is, I'll never be safe.

I did my best describing him to Blake and Phil. That part was easy. His face is forever etched in my brain. Tomorrow they're going to bring a sketch artist to the hospital and he's going to draw his portrait. Sarah and I are going to work on it together. It will be the first time I've seen her since we got here.

I feel sorry for her. I can't imagine what it's like having a monster for a father. I hope she gets the help she needs now that we're free. Maybe she'll be nicer to me now.

I can't stop thinking about Paige. I'm not sure what scares me most—that she didn't get out or that she's with him. But why would he take her and not Sarah? He'd never leave her behind. She was his daughter. His favorite. He called her his treasure. But if she's not with him, then where is she?

I refuse to believe she died in the fire. She had to get out. There were so many places to hide on the land. She might have even gotten over the gate in the back. The back of the property was pushed up against the hills. She has to be hiding in the hills somewhere. Waiting. Wondering. Just like I was.

They've already put together a team to canvass the area. Mom wanted to watch the news tonight, but Randy said it wasn't a good idea. She said we should stay away from the TV and the media. The media is already set up outside the hospital and people have been doing all kinds of crazy things to get inside. She told us they've been posing as doctors and nurses to get in or pretending to be visiting someone else just for a chance to see us. They've had to secure our entire floor just to keep people away from us.

Strangers have been dropping things off all day. They started coming this afternoon. My room is filled with flowers, balloons, and cards. It's weird to get things from people I don't even know. Mom goes through each card and she's started keeping a list of everyone's name and return address. She's committed to writing everybody a thank you note. At least all the stuff cheers up the hospital room.

I didn't let her close the blinds even after it got dark because it felt too claustrophobic. I like being able to see out my window even if my only view is another ward on the other side of the hospital.

The hospital is noisy even though it's the middle of the night. Every sound makes me jump. I hate my blanket. It reminds me of my blanket in the basement. It's thin and scratchy. There's nothing comfortable about it. Maybe John got our blankets from a hospital. I keep kicking it off but then I get cold. It's freezing in here. I should be used to it because John always kept the place cold, but I'm not. I'd give anything to be warm again.

I can't get comfortable no matter where I lay. My body aches from all of its wounds and the pain medication they gave me makes me itch. It feels like a thousand bugs are crawling all over my body.

I'm tempted to sneak out of my bed and peek in on Sarah because I know she's close. I just want to see what she's doing. Can she sleep? I'd do it if I could walk on my own, but I can't. They haven't given me crutches yet, but even when they do, I don't know how I'm going to walk with my leg in all these bulky bandages. The bites hurt worse than the break.

He wasn't kidding about the dogs. I always thought he just said it to scare us and keep us from trying to escape, but they were there just like he said and they were vicious. It'd taken sixty-two staples to put my calf back together. It's going to leave a nasty scar. A forever reminder of what I've been through. Not that I'll ever forget.

Mom keeps going on and on about putting this behind us, but she doesn't know what I've done or the things I've been through. There might come a day where my mind is able to forget, but not my body. My body will always remember.

SARAH

(NOW)

ISLEPT FITFULLY ALL NIGHT, moving between wake and sleep. I didn't want to sleep but they shot me full of medicine and it made me feel just like I did in the ambulance. They gave it to me after I started screaming at everyone to get away from me. I don't even know what happened or why I flipped out. I just did. Nobody was answering my questions and everyone kept getting in my space. They kept trying to touch me and I hate being touched.

My breakfast tray sits in front of me untouched. It's full of so much food and I never eat breakfast. I only eat at scheduled times and this isn't one of them. I stay on my eating schedule even when John is away. I made it a practice when he started going on runs. In the beginning when he'd go on runs, I'd gobble up all the food he left me by the end of the first day. I wasn't used to having food so I didn't have any control, but the hunger that came from the long days of starvation forced me into control. Now I do it automatically. Just in case. You can never be too sure.

Randy's already been back, dressed in another flowing skirt just like yesterday. She looked rested and refreshed like she slept well. She's going to be in the room with me and Ella when we work with the sketch artist. I've always been fascinated with people who can draw faces because they're so hard to get right. I used to try to draw them in my sketchbooks but nobody ever looked like I wanted them to.

I wish I had clothes to wear, but I don't have any. They put all my clothes in a plastic bag and I'm stuck in this hospital gown. It comes unfolded every time I go to the bathroom and I have to cinch it together with my hands when I walk. The officers promised not to look but I don't trust them. I hope they let me brush my teeth at some point today because it feels like fuzz is growing on them.

There's still no word about John. I've given them all the information I can. Now it's up to them.

There's a knock at my door. Everyone always knocks before they come in. I turn my head, expecting it to be a nurse bringing in more flowers since they've been bringing them in all morning, but it's Officer Malone. He's holding a Starbucks cup. Unlike Randy, he looks tired. There's bags under his eyes that weren't there yesterday and he's in the same clothes.

"Hey kiddo," he says with a smile. "How are you doing today?"

I shrug my shoulders. "Better than yesterday, I guess."

He tousles my hair. "Good, that's real good. We're going to have you back to normal in no time."

I wish I believed him.

"How do you feel about taking a little walk with me?"

"Where are we going?"

"The sketch artist is here. You girls are going to meet with him in Ella's room."

My stomach clenches. I thought I was going to have longer to prepare. I'm nervous about seeing Ella. I hope they haven't told her I've been freaking out. Officer Malone holds out his arm for me to take as I move off the bed. My knees are weak and my head spins when I stand up. It must be from the medication.

"Just take it easy," he says. "I've got you."

I lean against him for support. His chest is wide. His shoulders broad. I can feel his muscles around me. We step through our door and all of the nurses pretend not to stare but I feel their eyes on us as we shuffle down the hallway. We don't have to go far before he stops in front of another door. There's a uniformed officer standing outside her door just like the one who doesn't leave mine. He nods at Officer Malone before opening the door and letting us through.

Ella's room is packed with people and gifts. There's a woman standing next to her bed who must be her mom because she looks like an older version of Ella. They have the same facial structure with high cheekbones and a pointed chin. Rosy lips complement their thick chestnut-brown hair. Her mom's is streaked with gray and cut shoulder length unlike Ella's long, flowing locks. She even holds herself like Ella.

Randy's sitting in a chair in the corner with bright balloons floating over her head saying things like welcome home and get well soon. Blake and Phil stand next to her. Blake's arms are folded across his chest and Phil is tapping away on his phone. Both wear serious expressions on their faces.

I turn my attention to Ella and can't help but gasp. The entire right side of her face is covered in angry purple welts and bruises. Her right eye is swollen shut like she's been punched. Her hair is haphazardly sticking up all over her head making her look wild. Her left arm is in a purple cast and her other arm is lined with stitches creating a jagged ladder up her arm. Her eyes meet mine. She looks shell-shocked.

I finally speak, "Hi."

"Hi."

Her mom rushes toward me and surprises me by throwing her arms around me and squeezing tightly. "I'm so sorry, Sarah."

She says it over and over again as I'm awkwardly smashed against her. Her body is frail. I can feel her bones on my cheek.

When she finally pulls away, there are tears streaming down her face. Why is she crying for me? She doesn't even know me.

She leads me over to Ella's bed and pulls out the stool the doctors use for their examinations. Everyone is staring at us. I don't know who to look at or where to place my eyes so I stare at the linoleum floor. It's dirty and stained.

"It's supposed to rain today. I sure hope it does because my garden could use the water," Randy pipes up from the corner of the room.

"Yes, that's what I hear," Officer Malone says. "This drought just seems to be never ending. Can't wait for the day when I have grass again. I'm tired of getting my feet cut up if I walk outside barefoot."

Everyone laughs even though it's not funny except Ella and me. Neither of us are smiling. She looks as uncomfortable as I feel. Thankfully, we don't have to wait long until the sketch artist joins us. He looks like all of the other FBI agents. They're all in perfect shape and wear the same uniform—dress shirts tucked into pants so straight they have to iron them. None of them smile and they all have piercing eyes. You can't help but feel like you're under a microscope.

"Where should I set up shop?" he asks.

Blake steps forward. He's the person in charge. Everyone looks toward him for orders and direction. "I'd like to clear everyone who isn't essential out of the room. Randy and I will stay. I'd like to ask the rest of you to wait outside."

Ella's mom grabs her hand. "I'd really like to stay."

"I understand your fear of leaving her alone, but you'll be right outside the door if she needs you. It might be easier for them to work if there's not so many people staring at them. It puts a lot of pressure on them and we want them to be as relaxed as possible," Randy explains.

Ella's mom doesn't look convinced, but she follows the others out the door. It clicks shut behind them.

"This is Steve. He's going to be working with you girls on a creating a sketch of John," Blake says as Steve pulls a large sketch pad out of his briefcase. "We might be taking notes while you talk, but I want you to ignore us as best you can. Just pretend we're not even here."

"But if you feel uncomfortable or overwhelmed at any time, you just let us know and we'll stop," Randy says.

Blake shoots her a disapproving look.

I expected it to be lots of questions like yesterday, but for the most part, he just lets us talk. Before long, Ella and I are talking over each other, describing John's different features. He scribbles away while we talk, barely looking up. Every now and then, he flips the book around and asks us to comment on what he's done. By the time he's finished, he's come up with a penciled version of John. I'm stunned at how much it actually looks like him.

"Wow," I say, turning to look at Ella. "That's really good."

She's staring at the paper and into his face. She can't look away.

"It's him," she whispers. "That's him."

Steve doesn't look at us or say thank you before he packs up his stuff and leaves. What happens now that they know what he looks like? How does any of this work?

"How are you girls doing?" Randy asks.

"Excuse me, but I'm going to step away for second," Blake interrupts before we have a chance to answer her question. "Thank you for your cooperation. You did a great job." He shakes each of our hands.

"Can I have a minute alone with them before you send anyone back in?" Randy asks.

"Sure," he says. "I'll let them know you need a few more minutes with the girls."

"Thanks," Randy says.

She scoots her chair to the end of Ella's bed. "Sarah, why don't you slide your chair around this way? That way we can all see each other."

I move my chair so I'm on the other side of Ella's bed rather than sitting next to her. I stare down at her legs covered by the blankets, wondering what they look like underneath.

Randy leans forward, shifting her gaze back and forth between the two of us. "How does it feel to be in the same room with each other?"

Ella looks toward me. I'm not sure how she expects us to find words to describe what any of this feels like.

"It's weird," I say.

Ella nods her head in agreement.

"I know the two of you have been talking to a lot of people, but you haven't had the chance to talk to each other. Is there anything you'd like to say to each other?"

I want to tell her we're not close. We don't have conversations.

"I do," Ella pipes up.

My stomach rises in my throat. Randy nods, giving her permission to speak.

"Did you set the house on fire?" Her eyes flare with anger.

ELLA
(THEN)

FTER MY BATH, he towels me dry and wraps me in a white, fluffy bathrobe. I tie it tightly around me. He asks me to sit down on the toilet and begins brushing the tangles out of my hair. I stiffen at his touch.

"You have such thick, beautiful hair," he says, desire heavy in his breath.

Please, God, don't let him rape me.

"When someone pays you a compliment, you should always say thank you." Tension curls his words.

"Thank you," I mumble quickly before he can get angry again.

Once he's satisfied that my hair is combed thoroughly, he leads me out of the bathroom, back down the hall, through the kitchen, and into the dining room. It's an open layout so there's no separation between the two. There's a huge mahogany table large enough to fit at least ten people, but it's only set for two.

A table runner with an intricate geometric design runs down the center. Two tall candles burn in the center. Each place setting has matching folded napkins and polished silverware. Its spread with food in fancy covered trays. He leads me to the table and pulls out one of the tufted dining chairs for me.

"Right here, my dear," he says.

He takes the seat across from me and stares into my eyes. The angry man from the bathroom is gone and has been replaced with a perfect gentleman.

"You must be thirsty," he says. He reaches into the bowl in the center of the table and pulls out a bottle of wine. He fills my wine glass first and then his with red liquid just like the wine I used to drink at communion. "Normally, I'm against underage drinking, but tonight is such a special night, we couldn't let it pass us by without toasting the occasion."

He raises his glass. I raise mine with him.

"To us," he says.

I clink his glass. He takes the glass and swirls the wine around first before raising it to his lips. He takes a sip like he's taking a deep breath, closing his eyes for a second before setting his glass back down. "Delicious. What do you think?"

I'm still just holding my glass.

"Go on," he urges.

I do as I'm told. The wine doesn't taste anything like the communion wine. It's bitter and sour. I glance at the floor-to-ceiling windows lining the other side of the dining room, but we spent so long in the bathroom that it's gotten dark outside so I can't see anything.

"The house is on a full acre of land. It's quite the hike to make it to the gate. Did I tell you I have a security gate?" he asks, pointedly. "I had it specially built because I like my privacy. I don't want to have people just coming and going. You know they build amazing security systems nowadays, but even with the best security systems, you can never be too careful." He follows my gaze out the windows, squints his eyes. "If you look, you might be able to make out my two pit bulls, Rocky and Rambo. Not very creative names, I know, but I've never been good with names. They're vicious. I trained them well so they only respond to me. There's nothing I like more than taming a wild beast." He throws his head back and laughs. "I can't believe people actually keep them as pets. Mine aren't pets. They'd rip anyone to shreds who stepped foot on the property who wasn't me." He returns to looking at me, making sure I've read the meaning in his words.

I can't focus on anything while he eats. I'm too afraid of what happens when dinner is finished. He keeps trying to get me to try the chicken, even offers to serve me, but I keep saying I'm not hungry. My throat is too tight to swallow. My stomach upset. He chatters on while he eats, wiping his mouth with every bite. When he's finished, he drains the rest of his wine glass. I grip my chair tightly.

"Sarah?" he calls.

She appears like a ghost from somewhere else in the house and suddenly, she's in front of the table.

"Take Ella back downstairs."

I'm so relieved I almost start crying again. He calls me upstairs for the next three nights. Each night is the same as the first. He starts with a bath even though there's no way for me to get dirty locked in the basement all day, then brushes my hair, and puts me in a bathrobe. Every night when he sends me back downstairs I change into the black sweatpants and white t-shirts the other girls wear.

I've been refusing the food, but tonight it smells especially good. I don't want to eat it, but my body betrays me and as soon as I bite into the slow-roasted chicken, I can't help myself. I shovel it into my mouth as fast as I can. Before I know it, I'm devouring the mashed potatoes. They're not the kind that come from a box. They're the real deal—the kind you only make at Thanksgiving. The gravy is even more delicious and the string beans nearly melt in my mouth. I eat until I think I might be sick and guilt washes over me when I've finished.

He likes to talk while we eat and tonight is no different. He rambles on about the deer he saw on his drive to work. It's not long before he switches gears and starts in on what's going on in the news and politics. He loves to talk politics and there's nothing I hate more than politics. I just pretend to listen and feign interest.

"Am I boring you to death?" He doesn't wait for an answer before continuing. "How about we talk about something you're interested in? Are you happy to have a break from all of your school work?"

I shrug.

"Well, it must be nice to not have to worry about finishing up your history project. You were really having a hard time with that, huh?"

My history project? How does he know about my history project?

I shrug again.

"Honey, when someone asks you a question, it's impolite not to give them an answer."

He hasn't gotten angry with me since the first night and I'm not giving him a reason to get angry again.

"I guess," I say.

"How about Jaycee? Have you been missing her?"

All the food I just ate threatens to come back up. He sees it happening.

"Ella, darling, do you miss Jaycee?"

"Yes, yes I do," I force myself to respond.

"At least she's not going to have to worry about finishing in second place at your state finals meet next month. It'll be nice for her to come in first for once. The two of you have such a fierce competition, it must make it difficult to stay friends." He smiles at me with his perfect straight, white teeth.

It hits me like I've been punched in the gut. I'm not just some teenager he grabbed when he saw the opportunity. He picked me on purpose. Somehow the fact that it isn't random makes it worse.

He must've been following me. That's how he knew I'd be running that evening and almost to the end of my four miles, at the spot where I take out my earbuds so I can run the last mile in silence. I run the same route every time.

Did he take me for ransom?

He couldn't have. If he knows me then he knows my family and we don't have any money. Mom can barely afford to pay the bills every month. She's worked two jobs for as long as I can remember.

"Why are you doing this to me?" My voice quivers.

He leans across the table and takes my hand. "I'm doing this because I care about you."

ELLA
(NOW)

BLAKE AND PHIL HAVE been grilling me with questions for what feels like hours. I've told them everything I can think of that might help them. How John knew everything about me before he took me—my family, friends, where I lived, the color of my bedroom walls, my teachers, and my favorite books. He loved to ask me questions over dinner like he was genuinely interested in getting to know me.

"And you're sure you never saw him before the night he took you?" Blake asks even though he's already asked me the question.

"No," I say again. "I'd never seen him before."

"Not just in passing even? Sometimes it's hard to remember. Think back to any strange encounter you might have had in the months or weeks leading up to it," he presses.

I was a normal teenager before he took me. I was happy and my life was ordinary, but they act like I have a deep, dark secret

I'm trying to hide. They're obsessed with boys I was involved with at the time and even though they don't come right out and say it, I know they think I had a boyfriend I didn't tell Mom about. They don't understand that she'd be the first person I'd tell if I had a boyfriend.

We keep running the same circles. Did I notice anything unusual about the night I went missing? Had I noticed anyone following me? When did I see John? What color was the car? The make? The model? Was I able to make out any of the numbers on the license plate? Could I sense the direction we were going in the car? Was he alone? Was I sure he was alone? Did I ever see anyone else? Could I think of anyone who might want to harm me?

They keep asking about Paige too. It hurts so much to talk about her, but I make myself do it. They still haven't found her and every time they come in my room, I hold my breath and hope they're going to have good news about her, but they never do.

She was the only bright spot in that house. She made me laugh and kept me from crawling into myself and never coming out. She was impossible to ignore because she talked all the time, constantly and incessantly. The silence was too overwhelming for her and she had to fill up the hours with words like if she just kept talking she could ignore what was happening to us.

She loved telling stories about her family. I know almost as much about them as I do my own family. We had a lot in common. Her dad left when she was a baby too. Unlike mine who'd disappeared two weeks after I was born because he never wanted to be a father, hers left to be with another woman he'd been having an affair with throughout her mom's pregnancy. At least her dad still paid child support even if she never saw him. My dad has never given Mom a penny. He barely signed my birth certificate and left to get a pack of cigarettes and never came back.

Both our moms had found religion since tragedy has a way of bringing people to God. Paige's mom remarried a pastor at their local church. It wasn't long before she had two twin brothers she adored. She never tired of telling funny stories about them. Last year, her family had rented an RV and spent the entire year traveling around, working and volunteering in various countries throughout the world. She said it was life-changing. As part of her homeschooling, she wrote essays about the things she learned on the road—about the orphanages she'd been to in Romania, the fields she'd helped plant in Tanzania, and the schools where she'd taught English. She'd done so many interesting things, like feeding koalas at a zoo in Australia, family work-camping at Jellystone Park, and picking vegetables for sale at a marketplace in Pike's Peak. Halfway through the year, she'd fallen in love with travel and serving people. She wanted to become a missionary nurse when she was old enough.

"I had this dream that my husband would be a doctor and I'd be his nurse. We'd be this power couple serving parts of the world where nobody else wanted to go." Her eyes filled with sadness as she spoke. "All that's over now. Nobody is going to want me to be their wife now."

I tried to cheer her up that day, assuring her that her future husband would understand she hadn't willingly given up her virginity, but we both knew it was wishful thinking. Once you're dirty, you can't ever get clean again and we'd both been defiled.

"There is one thing that might be important," I say.

They perk up immediately. They've grown just as tired of the question loop as I have.

"We were both virgins," I say. My cheeks burn with shame and humiliation.

"How do you know?" Phil asks.

I clear my throat. "Well, because, I know I was a virgin and Paige told me she was too. She told me all the girls he took were. I think it might be why he took us."

Most of the time Phil does a great job of maintaining a neutral face and not showing any emotion, but a cloud of sadness crosses his face and he shakes his head in disgust.

SARAH

(THEN)

ELLA'S BEEN UPSTAIRS with him for a long time. Last night he told me he wanted to cook for her himself tonight. He didn't need me to do it. I'm fuming. He used to cook for me, but I can't remember the last meal he prepared. We never even get to eat together anymore. He always eats with one of them.

I don't like being down here with Paige while he's up there with her. It's not supposed to be this way. It makes me feel like I'm still one of them and I'm not. I'm different. I'm special. He tells me that all the time. He calls me his treasure, but sometimes I wonder if he tells them the same thing.

I've thought about listening at the bedroom door when they go in there, but he'd find out and punish me. I don't know how often he reviews the surveillance video so I don't dare risk it. Instead, I do the dishes and clean the kitchen. I set out his clothes for the next day and get his tea ready for when he's finished. At least he still sits with me for tea after he sends whoever it is downstairs for the night.

"Sarah?" Paige calls out.

"What?"

"Do you mind if I come talk to you?"

"I'll come out there." I don't like them coming into my space. I hate even being around them. I stand in front of the sheet with my arms folded across my chest. "What?"

"I'm sorry to bother you," she says. "But, I really just wanted to talk."

I hold back the urge to roll my eyes. Paige probably would've grown up to be a therapist. She used to ask to talk to me all the time when she first got here. She'd say she had an important question, but it was always something trivial. Just an excuse to talk and not be alone. But tonight she seems different and on edge. She's having a hard time getting her words out and formulating sentences.

"I just... I just want to... I'm..." She's trying not to cry. She always chews on her cheek when she's trying not to cry and I can see her doing it now. "What happened to Rachel?"

Rachel was here when Paige was in Phase One.

"I don't know," I say.

She doesn't believe me. I can tell. It's not the first time she's asked.

"Really?" Her eyes beg me for answers.

"Paige, I've told you this already. I don't know what happened to her."

"And Erin?"

I didn't know she knew about Erin. Rachel must've told her. Rachel was the one who replaced Erin.

I shrug my shoulders. "I don't ask him questions."

"Please, Sarah."

"I'm not having this conversation with you again. I don't know, okay? I don't know. Now, unless you have something new that you want to talk about, I'm going back to my room."

I turn to leave.

"Wait," she calls.

I stop.

"What does he do when he's finished with us?" she says super-fast, each word tripping over the next.

I should've known this was coming. It was only a matter of time. They always figure it out. Every single one. I did the same thing when I was the only one and John brought home Tiffany. I remember what it was like to be her and the moment it hit.

"I like to think we get to go home," I say.

I give her hope because it's the nice thing to do. Just because I'm unattached doesn't mean I'm cruel.

SARAH

(NOW)

OFFICER MALONE HAS BEEN keeping me company all day but he leaves me alone when Blake and Phil come in for more questions. Maybe if they spent more time looking for John and less time asking me questions, they might be able to find him. They stand in front of my bed, a formidable wall in front of me.

"We want to follow up on some of our questions from yesterday," Blake says. "Is that okay with you?"

I say yes, but only because I can't say no even though they're presenting it like it's a question.

Blake is carrying a folder. He opens it and rummages through. Finally, he finds what he's looking for and hands me a photograph. "Do you recognize this man?"

I take it from him. It looks like a mug shot. The man in the picture is staring at the camera wild-eyed. His hair is greasy and messy. His lips form a straight line and he sneers at the camera like he wants to attack it.

"Nope," I say and hand the picture back to him. "I've never seen him before."

Blake doesn't take it back from me. "Take another look."

I humor him by staring at the picture longer this time. There's still no flicker of recognition.

"Sorry. I wish I did, but I just don't."

Blake takes the picture from me. He doesn't put it back in the folder. He grabs a chair, slides it over to my bedside, and sits. He slaps the picture on my bed and points to it dramatically. "That man right there, Sarah? That man is your father."

I shake my head. "That man isn't my dad."

"He's your dad. His name is Enrique Manuel." His eyes are locked on mine.

I shake my head harder. "No, he isn't. John's my dad. I already told you that."

He pulls another picture out of his folder. He sets it on top of the picture of the man. "Take a look at this one."

It's a picture of a girl standing with her arms in front of her, hands clasped together like she's nervous. She looks about ten years old. Skinny legs peek out from underneath a red dress with small printed butterflies. Her eyes are partially hidden by her dark hair. She's half-heartedly smiling at the camera. There's a white board behind her. There's something familiar about the dress but I can't place her face. She might be one of the girls John brought home, but I can't be sure.

"She looks a little bit familiar, but I can't say from where."

"I need you to tell me the truth. I'm giving you an opportunity to tell the truth." He taps his fingers on the pictures.

"I'm sorry. I wish I could help you, but I just can't."

He pulls another picture out of his folder. This time he throws it down on top of the others. "How about this one? What about her?"

It might be the same girl, but I can't tell. Her head is hanging down, her hair obscuring all of her face. She's holding out both her arms. Dark bruises run the lengths of them. Some of them look new, bright purple and red. Others faded and old, muted yellows and greens.

"No. I don't know her either."

He grabs the stack and holds the picture of the man out in front of him. "This man is your father." He flips through to the first picture of the girl. "And this girl? This is you. Now, do you want to tell me what your name really is?"

"Sarah. My name is Sarah Smith." I clench my fists.

"Sarah Smith?" His voice rises. "And your dad is John Smith? Come on, do you really think we're that dumb? Stop playing with us."

"I'm not playing with you!" It comes out louder than I wanted it to.

"Did you really think we wouldn't find out? Like we'd somehow run around spinning our tails chasing after the millions of Sarah and John Smiths out there in the world? Why are you trying to help him?" He scoots closer to me. His breath smells like stale coffee.

I scoot as far back as I can, pulling my blankets up to my chest. "Leave me alone. Just leave me alone. Go away. I want you to leave."

He doesn't move. Doesn't even flinch. "Did he tell you to tell us that was his name? Do you know his real name?"

"His name is John," I say through gritted teeth.

"Nope. I don't believe his name is John any more than I believe your name is Sarah." He fixes his eyes on me.

He needs to shut up. My heartbeat explodes in my ears.

"In fact, I already know what your name is. You see this picture?" He holds up the one of the girl covered in bruises. "This is you—Petra Manuel. It was taken at Belmont Children's Services. It was the third time you'd been removed from your home. Do you remember why they took you away from your dad that time?"

I glare at him. I want to shove the pictures down his throat.

"He beat you up. Again. Your fourth grade teacher was the one who called social services that time."

I lunge for him and grab the pictures from his hand. I rip them into pieces and throw them at him. "Get out! Get out! Get out!"

He doesn't move.

"Help me! Please, somebody help me!" I scream.

Officer Malone bursts through the door. I shake my fingers at Blake. "This man is crazy. He's crazy! Get him away from me! Please! He's trying to hurt me! Please!"

Officer Malone rushes to my side. I grab him, pulling him close to me. The metal of his badge pokes into my arm. I jerk on his shirt again and again, "Please, make him stop. Make him stop."

I'm crying now. Animal sounds escape from my body. I flail against him, pounding on his chest, and scream at him to help me. The lights whirl around me. They're too bright. I can't see. There's lots of movement around me. Everything moving too fast. The nurse is in front of me, peeling me off him. I swat at her. She comes closer and I try to bite her, sink my teeth into her arm like a dog. Now I can't move. I'm surrounded. They hold me down. A sharp sting pinches my leg. Everything relaxes and goes still.

ELLA

(THEN)

'M STARTING TO THINK I'm going to get lucky and he's only interested in our twisted dinners. Paige says he should've tried by now, but he still hasn't. I hope there's something about me that he doesn't like. Maybe I'm not his type. I'm afraid to hope but the more days that go on and he doesn't make a move, I'm beginning to let myself believe it might be possible.

Our dinners aren't really even that bad. He asks me lots of questions about myself and seems genuinely interested, like he really cares what I have to say. It's getting easier to just play along with him. I'll do anything to keep him from touching me.

I hate the baths, but I don't fight them because they end quicker if I don't fight. I've learned how to put my mind somewhere else. I'm getting good at it. I start by counting the tiles systematically from the top down. Then, I group them in threes and see how many times I can multiply them by four in my head. Once he moves down to my privates, I imagine myself being able to leave my body. Like the real me is this teeny-tiny person inside my brain that can step out and go somewhere else. Sometimes I walk on the bubbles. Other times, I dive under the water and swim near the drain. I do laps back and forth across the length of the tub. I'm usually still swimming by the time he pronounces me clean.

The rest of the night is easy. The food is delicious and I hate even admitting it to myself, but I've grown to look forward to it even though I don't want to. Throughout the day, I catch myself imagining what I'll eat that night. Last night when he brought Paige upstairs instead of me, for a second, I felt disappointed. I was going to be stuck eating peanut butter and jelly sandwiches while she got to eat whatever amazing concoction Sarah created. As soon as I realized I was disappointed, I was flooded with disbelief and felt like I'd sold part of my soul to the devil.

I can't believe I'm adapting to this place and it scares me. I don't want to get used to it here. It's been nineteen days since he took me. Almost three full weeks. Pieces of my old life feel like they're slipping away from me. The other night I woke because I'd dreamed about Mom and broke out in a cold sweat because for a minute I couldn't remember the sound of her voice.

I used to think about her every day all day long. It was all I thought about. How she was feeling. Where she was. Did she think I was dead? Where was she looking for me? How was she making it through? I spent lots of energy trying to reach out to her with my mind and let her know I was okay. Paige told me that she does the same thing with her mom.

The other day when we were swapping stories about our lives, Sarah stormed out of her room like she does sometimes when we're irritating her.

She pointed at each of us. "Stop talking about what it used to be like. Nothing from before matters. Forget all of it. It only makes this harder. Seriously, do yourselves a favor."

I wanted to slap her and scream at her to shut up. Replaying the memories are the only way I keep them alive. I will not forget who I am or where I come from. My mom. All my friends.

The things I like to do. The way our house smells. That's the thing that terrifies me the most. More than him. More than what happens upstairs. The forgetting.

ELLA

(NOW)

THEY'VE SHIFTED FROM focusing their questions on John and turned toward asking about Sarah. I don't understand why. I just spent another hour with Randy and it was all she wanted to talk about too. I haven't seen Sarah since we met with the sketch artist. I'm tired of the questions and sick of being in the hospital. It's starting to feel as confining as the basement.

"Mom, can we go outside and go for a walk?" I ask. They've been promising to get me a wheel chair so I can move around easier but it's been two days and nobody's brought one yet. I think they like keeping me in this bed, but if I stay a minute longer, my head might explode.

"I don't see why not," she says.

She has to be as bored as I am. She never goes further than the hallway outside my room. They keep trying to get her to go down to the hospital cafeteria and eat, but she refuses. She has them bring a tray up to the room for her just like they do for me.

"I'm not sure that's a good idea," Randy says.

"I think it might do her good to get some fresh air," Mom says.

I can tell she's getting tired of Randy always acting like she knows what's best for me or the right way to talk to me.

"Paparazzi are swarming outside. They're all over the place and the police don't want her giving any statements to the media."

"So, we'll put her in a disguise," Mom says, matter-of-factly.

It sounds like a good idea to me.

"Please, can we go, Randy?" I ask.

"You don't need to ask her permission," Mom snaps. "She's not in charge of you and besides, it's not like you're under arrest or something. They can't keep you in this room forever."

"I–"

Mom interrupts her, "We're going outside. You might have been in these kinds of situations before, but I know my daughter."

I smile. My mom might be small, but she doesn't take any crap from anyone, especially when it comes to me. Never has.

"Honey." She looks at me. "I'll be back."

For the first time, she leaves the room and doesn't just stand in the hallway to wait. I'm so excited to be away from all of this. Tension fills the room after she's gone. Randy stares out the window.

"Your mom really loves you and she's just trying to do what's best for you," she says without turning around. "But she doesn't understand that I have experience in these situations."

"Do you have any kids?" I ask.

"I do," she says. "Two of them. They're both grown now. In fact, last month I became a grandmother."

"Maybe you should start thinking like a mother, then, and not like a therapist all the time."

I'm shocked by my words. I'm never rude to adults. Ever.

"If I thought like a mother, I wouldn't be able to do my job and my job is to help you." She still hasn't turned around.

"How's that any different than my mom? All she's trying to do is help too."

"I understand–"

I cut her off. "Please stop saying you understand. I'm so sick of hearing you say that. I can't handle it anymore. You don't understand."

"It makes sense that you would feel that way."

"Oh my God—that's like saying you understand. Have you ever been kidnapped by a freak? Have you?"

She shakes her head. Still as calm as ever. For some reason, it just makes me madder.

"Then don't tell me what it's like. Don't tell me you understand how I feel. Just shut up!"

I don't even know why I'm so angry. It's not even that big of a deal, but I'm filled with rage and it feels good to scream at someone. I want to hurt her. Make her cry. Do something to shake her up and make her stop acting like everything is okay. Nothing is okay. Nothing about this is normal.

"I don't want to talk to you anymore. Just get out of my room. Go talk to Sarah. Maybe you can help her," I snap.

SARAH

(THEN)

PAIGE HAS BEEN ON edge for days. She's barely talking and when she does there's an underlying anxiety in her voice. She can't shake the fear from her voice.

I get it. I've been exactly where she's at except I was all alone in the basement. There was nobody but me and the place certainly didn't look like it looks now. There was no toilet. Only a bucket. They complain that this one smells bad but they have no idea. It used to smell like a dirty Porta Potty. I didn't have a bed, only a bunch of blankets laid out on the floor and nobody was there to bring me food. I starved for days waiting on John to bring me something to eat. I had nobody to talk to. Nothing to do. They have each other and books, games, and art they can work on. It took a long time for me to earn those things, but he just gives them to them now.

When he came home one night with a girl I'd never seen before, I was elated to have someone with me. I wouldn't leave her side. I clung to her like I was a stray puppy. I sat up with her all night long, trying to soothe her even though I wasn't allowed to untie her. I rubbed her back while she sobbed and promised her it was going to be okay. I told her she'd get used to it and after a while it wouldn't seem so bad.

It didn't take her long to trust me and tell me her story. Her name was Tiffany and she was fourteen. She was from Minnesota and worked at a department store at the Mall of America. She was walking to the bus stop after work when a man stopped and asked her for directions to the airport. It was the last thing she remembered before waking up in the basement with me.

Her dad was a Southern Baptist pastor and I'd never met someone who was so religious. She prayed constantly. She talked about God like he was a real person and thought he talked to her back. She'd say things like, "Today when I was praying, God told me I'm going to get through this."

The only thing she wanted from John was a Bible. She begged me to ask him for it. He looked at me like I was crazy when I asked, but he handed it to me at our next dinner. She grinned like it was Christmas and hugged it to her chest when I gave it to her. She read it out loud for hours every day. The wording was so weird. There were so many words I'd never heard before, but I liked the stories, especially the one about the guy who built an ark and put all the animals inside it. I made her read it to me again and again.

She was a great singer too. She'd grown up singing in her church choir and had a voice that gave me chills. She taught me all her favorite hymns and didn't care that I'm incredibly tone deaf. We didn't only sing gospel music. She liked regular music and we sang popular stuff too, arguing over whether Twenty-One Pilots or One Direction was a better band.

For weeks, it was just us. I went upstairs with John, but she never did. I started to think he might have just brought her there to be my friend so I didn't have to be alone, but one night, he called for her instead of me. We both froze.

Things changed between us after that. She was never the same and neither was I. We tried to pretend like nothing had changed, but something had shifted and we both knew it.

For a while he took turns. One night it was her. The next night it was me. But then she started going upstairs more and more and I was left in the basement. It didn't take me long to figure out he was replacing me and I seethed with rage. I didn't understand how he could do that to me after what we'd been through and everything he'd done to me. I'd given him the most intimate part of me and now that'd he'd taken it, he didn't want me anymore and was just going to toss me aside for another girl. How could he?

I was plagued with questions. What would happen next? Would he just let me wither away and die in the basement? What if he gave me back to my dad? He couldn't. He wouldn't. He'd bought me for a price, how could he just return me like I was some used-up gift?

I wasn't going back with my dad. No way. John might have hurt me but it wasn't anything like what my dad had done to me. John's pain had a purpose, but my dad was a monster. I was never going back there and wasn't going to spend the rest of my days living in a basement either. I'd find another way.

And I did. Because I'm smart. I don't care that my teachers said I was a slow learner and had difficulty paying attention. It wasn't true. I paid plenty of attention to the things that mattered.

ELLA
(NOW)

THE SUN FEELS AMAZING on my face. I want to soak it into every pore. I hungrily gulp in the smell of fresh air. Mom is a genius. She bought me an oversized hat at the gift shop and pair of sunglasses. She tucked my long hair up under my hat and threw on my shades. She did the same with herself.

One of the officers was nice enough to take us through the service department in the cafeteria and through the kitchen in the back so we wouldn't be seen. There was an outside area behind the kitchen where maintenance workers took their break and nobody would be looking for us. It's surrounded by a gray chain link fence encircling the dumpsters and recycling bins, but I don't care. It feels so good to be outside. I savor the feeling, trying to let it seep into my soul and erase the darkness.

"I wish I could tuck you into your Baby Bjorn and carry you close to me everywhere I go just like when you were a little girl,"

Mom says. "I'm just so glad to have you back. I never thought I'd get you back. They told me the more time that went on, the more likely it was you'd never be found. It was so awful. After a while, they stopped looking for you and started looking for a body. They never came right out and said it, but I knew." Her eyes are wet. "I never gave up hope, though. Never. It's such a miracle you're here."

She gazes up at the sky and I know she's saying a silent thank you to God. She tried to pray with me on my first night back and I asked her not to. So far, she's respected my wishes. I'm done praying to God.

"I was starting to think I wasn't ever going to come home either," I say. Yesterday, I found out I'd been gone for four months. In the beginning, I counted every day. I kept track because each day that passed meant I was one day closer to being found, but as the days added up, I stopped counting. It was too depressing.

She crouches in front of me and places her hands on both of my knees. "Whatever happened in that house, and I know it was terrible, it doesn't have to wreck you. You're strong and you'll get through this. I know it probably doesn't feel like it right now, but things can go back to normal. They really can. We can both use this as an opportunity to be grateful for everything we have in life." Her face radiates hope. "We're going to do whatever it takes to put it behind us. Whatever it takes."

Her words don't reach me. The hope doesn't penetrate. John took pieces of me I'll never get back.

"You don't know what I've done." I swallow the lump of emotions in my throat.

She still thinks I'm the same person. Like nothing has changed, but the Ella she knew died in the basement.

She cups my face in her hands. "Nothing you've done can ever change the way I feel about you. Do you hear me? Nothing." Her face is solemn, concern making her forehead tight.

My secrets eat at my insides. I try to smile but it's a crude imitation. She pulls herself up and stands beside me, resting her hand on my shoulder.

We sit in silence, enjoying being out of the hospital. It's a relief not to have to talk, but I still feel nervous and jittery. I jump at every sound and have to keep reminding myself that there are police officers watching us from the doorway even if I can't see them. They'll pounce if John appears, but even though I know they're there, it doesn't stop me from continually scanning for any sign of him.

SARAH

(NOW)

WHEN I COME TO, I'm flat on my back, lifeless. My body numb. I can't move my arms. They're tied up with something. I struggle against them. The straps bite my skin.

No! No! No! Not again.

A cry slips past my lips.

Officer Malone's dark face appears in front of mine. His eyes are a deep brown and so soft. "Shh, shh," he says, running his hand through my hair. "You're in the hospital. Don't be afraid."

But I am. I'm strapped down. I try to kick, but I can't do that either. I arch my back just like before, trying to free myself.

"Just take a deep breath. I'm right here." Randy appears next to him.

I'm breathing so hard, I feel dizzy. My head is rolling on my neck.

"We can take the straps off you, but you have to promise not to hurt yourself. The doctors had to put them on for your safety."

I look down at my arms. They're covered in chaotic red scratches like I've been attacked by an angry cat. Did I do that to myself? I don't remember.

"Please, take them off me," I whimper.

The two of them stare at each other. Officer Malone gives her a nod and she begins working on one side while he works on the other. Within seconds, I'm free. Relief washes over me. I can breathe again. I sit up in my bed, pulling my knees up to my chest.

"I'm sorry I wasn't here this morning when Blake and Phil talked to you. I wish I was. Can I sit next to you?" Randy asks.

I don't want anyone to touch me. I shake my head. She stays in her spot.

"Do you remember what you talked about?" she asks.

I stay mute. I'm done talking to any of them.

"When kids go through trauma, they do incredible things to survive their situation. Sometimes it means their brains create different stories and other realities to help them cope, elaborate fantasies to make something horrible make sense." She leans forward, her skirt fanned around her. "You were only twelve when John took you. Young. Impressionable. I imagine he terrorized you and made you one hundred percent dependent on him for everything because that's what people like him do. He probably withheld water and food and offered them as rewards for good behavior. It's what people do who need to control you and John very much wanted to control you."

She doesn't know anything. I was special. John loved me.

"You aren't alone in what happened to you. I've worked with lots of girls who've been taken by predators and manipulated. Do you remember Mindy Steward?"

Of course I do. Everyone knows about Mindy Steward. She was the girl kidnapped by some homeless man and lived near her home with him for nine months. She never tried to escape even when she could have. I'm nothing like her.

"I was part of the team that worked with her after she was returned to her family. There are hundreds of other girls just like her. And you. People like John use systematic forms of abuse to chip away at your reality until eventually, you stop believing you were kidnapped and start to believe their lies." Her face is as relaxed as her voice.

It takes great control not to interrupt her and set her straight. She's totally wrong. John never lied to me. He always told me the truth.

"I know it's probably very confusing for you and doesn't make sense, but girls often end up developing feelings towards their kidnappers and forming a bond with them. The attachment grows stronger the longer they're held captive. It doesn't mean you're crazy or a bad person. Blake should've explained all of this to you this morning and I'm sorry he didn't." She frowns. "If he had, it might have made it easier for you to understand what he was saying and lessened the emotional impact. Unfortunately, the detectives can get so focused on the case and catching the bad guy that they forget about how to treat the victims."

I sit up straighter. I'm not a victim. I'm special. He told me that many times.

Officer Malone has kept quiet, but he speaks up when she's finished. "She's right, you know. You should trust her. She can help you work through all of this. She's done some amazing work with other girls. I can vouch for her since I spent all last night googling her."

Randy glances over her shoulder at him and laughs. "Thank goodness my Facebook settings are private."

He smiles back. "Will you let her help you?" His eyes plead with me.

I look away. I don't need any help. There's nothing wrong with me.

ELLA

(THEN)

"**TONIGHT WE'RE GOING TO** do something different," he says after Sarah finishes clearing our plates.

Ice water shoots through my veins.

He snaps his fingers and Sarah appears from the kitchen. She stands at attention before him like she always does whenever he calls.

"Sarah, dear, I need you to go on downstairs."

"Yes, sir," she says.

He dismisses her with a flick of his hand.

No—I want to scream—don't leave me alone with him.

I've never been alone with him. Even though Sarah and I never speak to each other upstairs, I always know she's somewhere in the house even if I can't see her. She scurries away and I hear the beeps as the basement door closes behind her. I feel him staring at me. I don't look up. I stare at my hands, twisting them together on my lap.

"Come, dear," he says standing up and pushing in his chair.

"I don't want to," I whimper. It's the first time I've told him no since our first meeting in the bathroom. It's dangerous, but I'm more afraid of what comes next then getting slapped.

He walks over to my chair and grips my arm. His fingers are always so cold. I push back my chair and stand. My legs are shaking. He wraps his arm around me and moves me through the living room and down the bathroom hallway. Instead of going into the bathroom, he opens another door on the other side. It's a bedroom. Fear erases every thought in my head.

"Don't be afraid," he says.

He pulls me through the door. My legs are moving but I can't feel them.

The door shuts behind us. He locks it.

Like every other room in the house, it's lined in windows on one side. The long drapes are closed. The king-sized bed is the centerpiece; its tufted headboard pushed up against the back wall. A plush white comforter matches the fabric hanging from the windows.

"Please don't do this. Please, don't." I start to cry.

He puts his arms around me, holding me tightly, rubbing circles on my back. "It's okay. Everyone is scared when it's their first time. It's perfectly normal."

I sob harder. My entire body convulses against him.

He speaks in a whisper, his lips moving on the top of my head. "I'll be so gentle. You'll see. I'll talk you through the whole thing."

I will my legs to kick him, run—to do something, anything—but I can't make them move. Everything moves in slow motion.

"Please don't hurt me," I sob.

"I'm not a violent man. I've already told you that. I only do what needs to be done." It isn't his words. It's how he says them that makes my stomach curl.

My teeth chatter like I'm cold, but I'm not cold. I'm hot. Flushed, dripping with sweat. Everything is blurry. The fluffy white comforter and lace pillows swerve in front of me. He releases me.

"Go on," he motions toward the bed. "Don't be afraid."

I can't move. He turns me around and stands behind me. My arms are at my side. Frozen. I can feel his breath on my neck. His fingers reach around me. Playing at my bathrobe tie.

This isn't real. It can't be happening.

My robe drops. I'm naked. Exposed. I tremble.

"See, I told you it's not so bad." His voice is deep. One I've never heard before. "I can see you're starting to get excited already."

I want to throw up. Scream. Turn around and smash his head in. His gun is on the nightstand next to the bed, his threats burned in my brain. I do nothing. Nothing except shake and cry.

"Why don't you have a seat on the bed while I get undressed?"

It's not a question. It's a command and I do as I'm told. I sit on my hands to keep them from shaking. He stands in front of me, devouring my body with his eyes. I can see what he wants to do to me. He begins unbuttoning his shirt. Button by button. Slow, methodical. I've never seen a naked man before. I close my eyes tightly.

"Open your eyes," he snaps.

His shirt is off. He's worked his way to his pants. He's standing there in a pair of red silk boxers.

"Lay back on the bed."

"Please, no. Please, no." It's all I can say over and over again.

I shake like I'm having a seizure. I'm sobbing so hard snot drips down my face and into my mouth. Thick globs. I try to swallow the sobs, but it only makes me cry harder and more difficult to breathe.

His face turns to disgust. Anger clouds his eyes. The gentleman from dinner is gone. He grabs my bathrobe from the floor and throws it at me. He can't even look at me now.

"Put your fucking clothes back on," he sneers.

I scramble off the bed, grabbing my robe, and throw it around me. I pull the tie as tight as it will go. What will he do to me now? I didn't want to make him mad, but I did.

He pushes the intercom button in the bedroom. I hadn't noticed it before. It's right by the door.

"Sarah, come get her and take her downstairs."

ELLA

(NOW)

RANDY'S WAITING FOR us in the room when we get back from being outside. She doesn't even mention how I yelled at her earlier.

"How was it?" she asks.

"Wonderful," Mom says. Her face is flushed with color from being outside.

Phil is here by himself. It's rare to see him without Blake. He's always watching and studying, but he mostly stays out of Blake's way and lets him do all the talking. Sometimes I forget he's there. He waits to speak until after Mom settles me back in bed.

"I wanted to update you on where we stand with the case," he says.

"Have you found him?" I ask.

Finding John is the only thing I care about in the case. Everything else is insignificant. I'm not going to be able to relax until he's caught.

He shakes his head. "We haven't been able to locate him yet, but we're following up on some leads. First, John isn't his name—"

"His name isn't John?" My mind reels.

"No."

"Why would he make up a fake name?" I ask.

"To be unable to be identified. John Smith is designed to be as non-descript and generic as possible. If you search for John Smith, you'll get millions of profiles. It would take forever to narrow down the John Smith you're looking for. He probably uses lots of different names and none that would ever stand out." He takes out a notepad. It's the same type of legal pad Blake always writes in. "We do have some leads on the property, though. The house on Spaulding Avenue belongs to an Eric Sorenson. We're looking into Eric Sorenson's background to see if he is the person we're looking for, but we're fairly certain he's not going to be a match. We've been showing the sketch you girls created around the community. The good news is that there are many people who recognize him. He's been seen numerous times at the grocery store and Target. We're interviewing everyone that had any contact with him. The bad news is that most of them report knowing Eric Sorenson and he's not the same person."

"But it's good that people saw him, right?" Mom asks.

"Yes." He nods, looking pleased. "It gives us something to go on and helps us to figure out his daily activities and lifestyle. And also that he wasn't scared to go out in the community, which means he still might be in the community somewhere. Many times these types of perpetrators have a God complex and think they're above getting caught. They like to flaunt themselves. We've also begun developing a profile of his victim type and we're researching other open missing persons' cases that fit the profile."

"What's his profile?" Mom's face tenses, drawing wrinkles in her forehead.

She's wondering the same thing as me. Why did he pick me?

"It seems he targets teenage girls who don't have a biological father in their lives. Ones whose fathers are either dead or play no part in their life. It's likely he sees himself as fulfilling a fatherly role. In addition, the girls tend to come from religious families. It might be that he thinks of himself as a religious man or he has a past with religion that's hurt him in some way. Either way, we're following up on a couple of cases we think he might be involved in. It's still too early to tell, but we're making progress. Petra is our strongest lead."

"Who is Petra?" I ask.

I don't remember Paige or Sarah ever mentioning her. Sometimes Paige talked about the girl, Rachel, who was in the basement when he first took her. She mentioned a few other names Rachel talked about with her, but nobody named Petra.

"Petra is Sarah's real name. Petra Manuel. Her father is Enrique Manual and he's incarcerated at Middleton Correctional Facility in southern California."

My mouth drops open. "Are you serious? You mean John isn't her dad?"

"Yes, John isn't her father. At least not her biological father. She's maintaining that he's her father, but he's not. Petra was born in southern California to Destiny and Enrique. Her mom died of a drug overdose a few weeks after she was born. Petra was raised by her father but came under the investigation of child services numerous times over the years for neglect and physical abuse. She was removed from his home many times and placed in foster homes, but was repeatedly given back to Enrique." He takes a deep breath before continuing. "Unfortunately, she's one of the kids the system failed and she fell through the cracks. Her paper trail ends when she was twelve. We've spoken with her sixth grade teacher who remembers her. She took a special interest in her and was always trying to help her. She didn't think anything of it when Petra quit coming to

LUCINDA BERRY

school because she was frequently truant and after a few months had passed, she figured they'd just moved. We suspect that's when John kidnapped her because shortly after that Enrique was arrested and awaiting trial so she couldn't have been with him. It's possible Petra was abandoned and living on the streets. That might be when he grabbed her."

"That doesn't fit with the profile you were just talking about," Mom points out.

"You're right, but for now, we're operating under the theory that Petra might have been his first victim. He may have used her as sort of a trial run. We see that frequently in cases like these. Men who exploit children often hone their skills and develop their preferences over time. But again, it's still very early in the investigation. I just want to make sure you know where we're at."

"That's so sad about Sarah. I mean Petra," Mom says. She looks like she might cry.

"Ella, did Petra every talk about anything that led you to believe she may have been taken by him too?" he asks. "Ever anything about her past that hinted at a life without John?"

I search my memory. I can't think of her as Petra. It feels too weird. To me, she's Sarah. It's not like I never tried to talk to her about things, but she always acted like she was annoyed with me and had so many other important things to do than talk to me or answer my questions. She treated me like I was her annoying younger sister even though we're the same age.

Paige and I tried to include her in things. Every time we played Scrabble or Spades, we asked her to join us but she always said no. She didn't speak to us at all upstairs. It was as if she didn't even know us. She waited on us silently, bringing us our food and setting it carefully on the table, preparing our meals for us and clearing them when we were finished. She only spoke to John. Never us. I asked Paige if she was the same way when she was upstairs and she said yes.

Even though she didn't talk to us much, Paige and I talked about her all the time.

"Do you think he has sex with her too?" I asked Paige.

130

She turned up her nose. "I don't know. That's so gross if he does."

"Have you ever seen her go into the bedroom?"

She shook her head and moved over to sit on my bed with me. She put her face close to mine and whispered even though Sarah was upstairs and there was no way she could hear us. "But Rachel told me the girl she was locked up with told her that she heard from Lyla or something like that that she used to. And if she did, well... you know what happened if she did."

"She was always afraid of him," I tell Phil. "Even though she pretended like she wasn't, she was. I could tell."

"Did he refer to her as his daughter?" he asks.

Now that he mentioned it, it dawns on me that he never called her his daughter. He only called her by her name. Never anything else. She never actually said she was his daughter, either. And I always thought it was weird that she called him John rather than Dad, but nothing about our situation was normal. The story of her being his daughter was one of the many stories passed down from girl to girl.

"No, he never did and she never called him Dad," I say.

"Then, what made you think she was?" he asks.

"Paige told me just like Rachel told her and the girl before her told her. It's kinda how things worked."

He rubs his temples like he has a headache. "Blake is on his way to meet with Enrique and we're hoping he'll be able to provide us with some valuable information. He might be the key that opens up this investigation."

"Have you notified Sarah's family?" Mom corrects herself. "I mean Petra. They'll probably be a huge help trying to figure things out."

"Unfortunately, nobody came forward. She was never reported missing."

"Nobody reported her missing?" Mom is horrified. "How is that even possible?"

"I don't know how to say this delicately, but Petra was not a child that was wanted by her family even before she went missing. We were able to make contact this morning. It went about as well as we expected." He clears the emotion from his throat. "Her mother, Destiny, was estranged from her family because of her drug use. She was in and out of rehab for years. We contacted the family but they hadn't spoken to Destiny for ten years before she died and they want nothing to do with any of this. Enrique's mother passed away four years ago and her husband is in a nursing home with late-stage Alzheimer's. The rest of his family is spread out all over Mexico. We're still trying to reach them, but I don't expect there will be a warm reception there either."

Mom wipes her tears. "I just feel so sorry for that poor girl."

I should feel sorry for her too, but I don't. She always walked around like she was so much better than us. She looked at us like we were pathetic, as if we were somehow to blame for our situation. It was easy to think she was right when I thought John was her dad because she was born into it and didn't have a choice. Plus, I blamed myself for getting stolen too. I knew better than to talk to strange men. Mom had drilled it into my head since I was a toddler. But I was wrong. She was just like us.

SARAH

(NOW)

THERE'S A KNOCK at my door. I expect it to be Randy but it's Ella's mom. What is Ella's mom doing in my room? She hesitates in the doorway, afraid to come in.

"Hi, Sarah," she says. "I don't think we've officially met. I'm Ella's mom, Jocelyn."

"Hi," I say.

She's still hovering in the doorway. "How are you doing?"

"I'm okay."

"Good. That's good. It's been a crazy few days, huh?"

I nod. Crazy doesn't even begin to describe it.

"Ella's having a pretty hard time with all of this. I figured you might be too."

"It's tough."

She's the first person I've admitted that to. I don't know why I tell her the truth. I just do. It feels right.

"Do you mind if I come in for a minute?"

"Sure."

She walks slowly into my room. She looks around at all my gifts—the same gifts Ella keeps getting. They haven't stopped coming. Soon, there's not going to be enough room for them. I have chairs in my room, but she doesn't sit in any of them. She stands next to my bed, shifting her weight back and forth. She keeps clearing her throat.

"Listen, I don't want to get into your personal business. I respect your privacy. I do. And if you want me to leave, I will, but I just couldn't stop thinking about you being in this room all alone."

"I'm not exactly alone," I say, motioning to my door where the officers stand guard.

She laughs. It lifts some of the nervous tension in the room.

"You know what I mean. It's got to be hard not having a family member here with you." Her voice catches. "You've got to feel so scared and alone. I just want you to know I'm here. I know I'm a total stranger, but I'm here if you want to talk or anything like that. Although, you're probably over talking as much as Ella is. Feels like all they've been making you girls do is talk. So, even if you just want to sit in silence, I'll sit with you. You don't have to be alone."

It's the kindest thing anyone has ever said to me. Sadness wells up inside my chest.

"Would it be too weird if I gave you a hug?" she asks.

I nod because I can't speak. I motion for her to come closer. She wraps her arms around me and pulls me close to her chest. She rubs my back gently. I crumble in tears. I can't help myself. It's been so long since anyone held me like this.

It makes me think of John even though I don't want to. Back before everything changed, he'd hold me while I cried and promise things were going to be okay. He used to go through every one of the scars on my body whenever he bathed me and say, "I'm kissing away every bad thing that's ever been done to you."

I weep silently into her shirt. Her body odor is sweet. Not pungent like a man's and I drink it in. She doesn't say anything for the longest time. Just keeps holding me. Finally, she moves back a bit. She puts her hands on my cheeks. They're so soft. I've never felt skin so soft. She tucks my hair behind my ears.

"You're a survivor," she says. "You've walked through hell and you made it. All by yourself. But you don't have to keep walking by yourself anymore. I'm here and I'm not going anywhere."

ELLA

(THEN)

"IT'S OVER," I tell Paige.

"What's over?" she asks looking up from her book.

"Him being nice to me and not wanting anything."

"Oh." She exhales slowly and closes her book. "I'm sorry."

I start to sob. He hasn't raped me yet, but it's coming. He tries each night after dinner. He makes me undress and lie down on the bed. He starts kissing and touching me. I try not to cry, but I can't help myself. Each time I cry, he gets angry and stops. My crying makes him not want to touch me and he loses his erection. I should feel happy that I keep dodging it, but I don't. I'm terrified of making him mad and he grows more and more furious each time I can't keep my emotions under control. I'm afraid of what he'll do to me if he can't have me.

It's why I'm here. I know that now. My days of pretending like I'm just a prisoner he likes to have dinner with are gone. He has one goal. Always has.

I start to cry. "What's he going to do if he can't... if he can't..."

I can't speak the words, but I don't need to. Paige knows what I'm talking about.

She comes over to my bed and holds my hand. "I don't know, but I don't think you want to find out."

I want to die, close my eyes and never wake up.

"Here's what you have to do." She motions for me to come closer. "You just pretend you're somewhere else. You have to make your brain go away. Switch it off and think about something happy."

"Does it work?"

"Sometimes. Not always."

"Does it hurt?"

He always says he'll be gentle. He promises to go slow.

"Yes." Her voice is barely a whisper.

I start dreading each day more than ever, even more than my first week. I cringe each time his voice calls out over the intercom and relief washes over me when he calls Paige instead of me, but then I'm wracked with guilt because I know he's hurting her. I cry for her until she comes downstairs again. I try to lay next to her on her bed and comfort her but she pushes me away, tells me not to touch her.

Whenever he calls my name, I've started throwing up in the toilet before I go upstairs. Sarah gets super annoyed with it. She says he doesn't like to wait. I can barely eat because I'm sick to my stomach but I've discovered the effect wine has on an empty stomach. It dulls my senses. Blurs all the edges.

I've started drinking more and more at dinner. If I drink enough, it's like I'm sleepwalking. He notices how much I'm drinking because he's the one who fills my glass, but he doesn't say anything. By the time he's ready to move into the bedroom, my head is swirling and I'm unsteady on my feet.

Tonight he has to practically carry me there because I drank so much. I don't shake while I drop my robe. My hands are steady. My fear is still there but it's outside of myself where I can't touch it. I lay back.

Just pretend you're somewhere else, I tell myself over and over again. I picture myself in my bedroom at home, but I know what's about to happen and I don't want my room, even if it's only in my imagination, to be tainted with his filth. I switch to picturing myself at the beach, but that doesn't work either. I can still feel his hands on my body, pinching, pulling, and prodding. I can still hear his moans in my ear as he gets more and more excited. His hot breath on my neck. His slobbery kisses all over me.

My head is spinning. The room is tilted on its side. Before I know it, vomit is in my throat and it spews out of my mouth uncontrollably. I turn my head to the side, gagging and heaving. I can't stop. It just keeps coming. He slaps the back of my head and yanks me up by my hair.

"Now you've done it," he hisses through gritted teeth. "You've pissed me off."

"I'm sorry. I'm so sorry." My words are slurred. "I was trying. I was really trying this time."

"You don't understand how patient I've been with you," he says. He wipes at my red puke with his shirt. His face is filled with disgust and revulsion. "I can't have any of this. This is not how it works. You've got one more try."

Terror rushes through my body. "What happens if I can't?"

He doesn't answer.

SARAH

(THEN)

H E'S GIVEN UP HOPE ON Ella. I've seen it happen before. Sometimes the girls just can't get it together. They can't do what they need to do to make him happy. When they can't, he gets rid of them. He has an appetite for innocence and a very short attention span. It's not a good combination.

It doesn't matter to me, anyway. He'll replace her with somebody else if things don't work out. At least her end won't be as painful as some of the others. He has more compassion for the girls who are too afraid to give him what he wants than the ones who lie to him. He goes into one of his rages if he discovers they're not pure. Then, he has no mercy.

He's already planning his next one if this doesn't work out. It's why I know its nearing the end for her. He skips bringing either girl up for dinner and spends it on the Internet, scouring social media profiles to find the perfect one. I don't understand why girls are so dumb. They put a target on their back with their constant check-ins, telling the world where they're at and opening up private lives for anyone to see.

But I cherish our nights alone. He asks for my opinions on their pictures and I'm honest. He can tell when I'm lying anyway so there's no point. Besides, he's the one who cares what they look like. Not me.

We eat dinner together. I get to be the one to sit with him rather than having to serve him. It's so much better this way. I talk to him about my day. The things I did around the house. The shows I watched on TV.

I love being in the house alone. When it's just me, I pretend it's all mine. I plop on the couch with the expensive chocolates he brings back from work trips and flip through the channels, settling on whatever show I want. Sometimes I take a nap in one of the bedrooms. Never his bedroom or the one he uses for the girls. Always one of the spares. My favorite one is the red room. Just one red wall against the contrasting white. The bed is like sinking into heaven. The windows are next to the trees that bloom small orange flowers year-round. During the spring, it's covered in bees and the same family of robins come back each year. It's my favorite room and the one I'd choose as mine if he'd ever let me move upstairs permanently.

Someday, he will. Everything always takes a long time with him. It was ages before I got the freedom I have now. I had to prove myself first, but I've never let him down. Not once. I always do what I say I'll do and I follow his directions. It's not always easy. He is picky and can be finicky about things. Like one day he insists that the black mugs go on the second shelf, but the next day, he's angry because they belong on the third. The towels in every bathroom need to be lined up perfectly. That was my first lesson in how particular he is.

One day they were uneven, just slightly off, but enough for him to notice. He took away my food for three days and didn't let me out.

I've studied him for a long time, though, and I've learned to read his moods like I read my favorite books. I can tell by the slightest twitch of his eyebrow if he's getting angry or by how far apart his strides are in his walk if he's had a bad day and I plan accordingly. I anticipate his every move. Every need. I try to meet them before he even has to ask.

"I'm so proud of you," he'll say when I surprise him with what he wanted without him even having to ask like I've read his mind.

I always beam. I love when he tells me he's proud of me.

He confirms what I already suspected as we sit down to eat.

"I don't think Ella is going to work out. I think she's one of those," he says.

I take a sip of my wine, dabbing my mouth afterward with a napkin just like he taught me. "Really?"

"Yes. She just can't get past her fear."

"That's too bad. Have you tried the chicken yet?"

He takes a bite. "It's great. Really juicy."

I beam. "I tried a new recipe. I saw Rachael Ray do it the other day."

"I'm going to give her one more try, but I think we're going to have to start preparing for her to be gone."

I nod. "I understand. Will you let me know so I can get things ready?"

He smiles at me. "Of course."

ELLA

(THEN)

SHOULD JUST LET HIM kill me. Get it over with. End all of this because what do I have to live for? Let a man brutalize me so I can stay his prisoner? I hate the thought of him killing me. I'd rather just kill myself. Maybe I should. But what about my mom? I know she's still out there searching for me, but it's been over two months and I'm losing hope that they'll ever find me. It seems silly to hold on, but I know she'd never give up. Ever. She'll never stop looking for me so don't I owe it to her to stay alive?

Would she want me to stay alive if she knew I was living this way? And when he's done with me, when he's had his fill, then what happens? What happened to the other girls? Does he let them go? That's the question nobody knows. It's a story whose ending nobody has despite all the tales passed down. What if he lets me go free when all this is over? What if this is the rite of passage to my freedom?

My head spins with all the questions. The questions that have to be answered because either way, it's all going to be over soon. He's put me on a timetable. I can either make the decision myself or leave my fate in his hands.

I think about praying. It's what I've done for every other decision I've made in my life. I've always asked for wisdom and guidance. Or strength. Whatever I needed for the situation. I used to think God provided it, but I don't think so anymore. If God can let something like this happen, then God's a horrible person and I want nothing to do with him.

The next night when it's my name he calls over the intercom, my stomach flips. I swallow back the taste of bile in my throat. My legs are lead as I follow Sarah up the stairs. The bath is quick tonight and he barely pays me attention. His thoughts are somewhere else.

And then it hits me—he doesn't let us go. If he did, I would've heard countless stories about it in the news and there's never been anything. No stories of girls kept in basements and released once he was done with them. The media would be all over it. It's not like he's only done this a few times. We'd all be on the alert for a serial rapist, but we're not, which means nobody knows about him and if nobody knows about him, then nobody knows about us.

He kills us. That's what he does.

He doesn't speak during dinner. He's never been quiet while we eat. He taps away on his phone. It's as if I don't even exist to him anymore.

"Did you have a good day?" I clutch my glass of wine.

He shrugs his shoulders. Doesn't even make eye contact.

"What are you reading?" I ask. I'm obsessed with getting him to talk to me. Look at me. Anything.

"Nothing special."

My hands are shaking so hard it's difficult to bring the fork to my mouth, but I have to eat something to counteract the wine. I can't make it through this night without the wine and I can't throw up on him like I did last time.

There's too much silence. I stumble over my words trying to fill it. He's annoyed. Annoyance is one step away from his anger. I have to do it. I can't give up and die here. If I die here, he gets away with it. He can't get away with this. He just can't.

"Are you done yet?" His voice is clipped. Eyes are dark.

"Yes." I put down my fork and take one last huge gulp of my wine.

He doesn't have to push me into the bedroom. I plod along with him behind me, each step getting closer to the inevitable. I fight the waves of panic pummeling me.

He shuts the door behind us and locks it like always.

I look into his eyes as I drop my robe in front of him. I force myself to make eye contact, to look deep into his eyes like people do when they're in love at the movies. I don't flinch. I don't look away. I don't cover my body. The flecks of silver glimmer in his eyes. A smile slowly tugs at the corner of his mouth.

I step back to the bed and lay down. His eyes devour me. I want to move so badly it makes my muscles twitch, but I force myself to stay still. And then he's on top of me. I lay motionless, but I don't cry. I bite my cheek to keep the tears inside. The taste of blood fills my mouth. I swallow it. Keep biting. I turn my head to the side. Stare at the blinking red light from the camera above the door staring back at me. What will he see in my eyes when he watches this later?

And then it's happening. I fight the urge to kick. To scream. Hit. Bite, scratch. Claw. White hot pain sears me like a knife. My insides are being torn apart. I want to scream. Instead, I moan. It only makes him more excited.

Pretend you're dead, I chant in my head. *Pretend you're dead.*

When it's over, he lays me on my side and rests my head on his lap. He strokes my hair, softly petting me like I'm a kitten. "See, that wasn't so bad now, was it?"

ELLA

(NOW)

'M TIRED OF THE STALE AIR in here. The fluo-rescent lights. The meals on trays. I just want to go home. I still can't sleep. It doesn't matter how many pills they give me. I'm exhausted, but wide awake and it's brutal.

"Mom, are we ever going to leave?" I ask when she returns with tea for both of us. Decaffeinated for me. Caffeinated for her.

"I talked to Blake about it this morning. He said as long as the doctors clear you, we should be able to go either tomorrow or the next day. They're not sending us home alone, though. It looks like one of the officers will be coming with us and probably Randy too." She frowns. She grows more and more annoyed with Randy every day. I can't blame her. She has something to say about everything Mom does and she rarely agrees with her.

"Ugh," I groan. "Can't they find us someone else?"

"Apparently, she's the best there is," Mom says.

Randy has started trying to get me to talk about the rapes. She says it will help me begin to move past it, but I don't want to. I'm not telling her the details of what he did to me. Not now. Not ever. I haven't told Mom either and I won't. It would crush her. She knows he raped me. That's enough.

"There's something else I want to talk to you about," Mom says.

"What?" I ask.

"Sarah."

Even though her real name is Petra, we still call her Sarah. Mom's been going back and forth between our two rooms ever since Phil told her Sarah's real story.

"What about her?" I ask.

"I'm thinking about asking if we can bring her home with us."

I sit straight up in bed. "Are you kidding me? No way!"

I'm not bringing that girl to my home. Not after everything she did. It's bad enough that I've had to share Mom with her these past few days. I'm not sharing my home. She'll contaminate it. I'm trying to leave all of this behind me, not bring it with me.

"Honey–"

"Don't call me honey!" I snap. I've already told her that. She can call me Ella Bear, but no other terms of endearment. No Honey. No Sweetie. No Darling. Nothing. He's stolen those words. I'm never getting them back.

"Sorry, I forgot. But before you get upset, just hear me out. That poor girl has nothing. Nobody. When I was talking to Phil this morning about where she'll go after here, do you know what he said?"

I shake my head. I want to cover my ears. I don't care where she goes. She's not my problem. I want to forget everything about her.

"They're going to have to put her back in foster care. She'll probably just float through the system until she's eighteen. I just don't feel right about sending her into foster care. Those places can be so terrible. She needs someone to love her. To give her a safe place where she can work through everything she's been through." She sounds close to tears.

If it was Paige, I'd say yes without a second thought, but Sarah? No way.

"Will you please just think about it?" Her eyes are pleading. I can see she's made up her mind already. "It might be nice for the two of you to work through things together. You could be each other's support network."

"What'd Randy say?" I ask.

"She doesn't think it's a good idea."

"Then, you should listen to Randy. She's the expert," I snap.

She frowns. "I thought you'd be more excited about it. You've always wanted a sister."

That part was true. Yes, I wanted a sister, but not someone who pretended to be a psychopath's daughter. Not someone who could've helped us escape any time she wanted to, but chose not to. Not someone I had to fight off just so I could try. No way. It's not happening.

SARAH

(NOW)

'M AFRAID TO LOOK AT the pictures. Last time I looked at their pictures, they told me I was someone else. Blake and Phil keep calling me Petra no matter how many times I tell them my name is Sarah. They don't care. They insist it's who I am. At least Randy calls me what I want to be called.

This time the pictures are of teenage girls. There's hundreds of them.

"Who are these girls?" I ask.

"They're all missing children," Blake says.

He's not kind to me anymore. He treats me like a criminal. I don't blame him for it. I've done unspeakable things. Things I'll never tell anyone, but I wasn't always this way. I didn't set out to become what I've become. I didn't have any other choice. Everything changed after Tiffany.

I was devastated when he picked her over me. I didn't understand how he could have said all those nice things to me and then just throw me away like I meant nothing to him. I'll never forget the night I became a different person.

It'd been three months since Tiffany arrived and one week since he'd called me upstairs. I hadn't eaten in three days. Back then, he didn't let us keep any food downstairs. I'd been relying on the scraps he allowed Tiffany to bring down with her each night after he was finished with her. I stunk. I hadn't bathed in just as long.

I knew my end was near when he called me upstairs instead of Tiffany and didn't give me a bath. He always bathed me before touching me. Instead, we stood in the hallway outside the basement door and he handed me a water bottle.

"Drink this," he said.

I took the bottle. The seal had already been opened.

"C'mon, Petra. Drink," he said.

I shook my head. I was trembling.

He sneered, "Don't make this any more difficult than it needs to be."

I wasn't going to make it that easy to get rid of me. Not after everything we'd been through and the things he'd promised.

"No." I'd never defied him. Not once. I'd done everything he'd ever asked, complied with every request.

He couldn't hide his shock or disdain. He twisted my arm. I cried out in pain. "Do it." He raised his fist at my face.

"I don't want to leave!" I blurted out.

He froze. He brought his arm down in defeat. "What are you talking about?"

I spit the words out as fast as I could. "I don't want to go. I want to stay here. I know you're trying to get rid of me. I know there's probably something in this water and if I drink it, I'll fall asleep and wake up somewhere else. I don't want to go back home. Please don't make me. I want to stay here with you. I'll do anything. Anything." I stress the word *anything* and then unleashed the plan I'd been thinking about all week while I lay in the dark basement alone. "You need someone to help you. I–"

He interrupted me. "I don't need anyone to help me. You just need–"

This time I cut him off. I only had a small window of opportunity. I wasn't losing it. I kept going, talking just as fast. "I could make your life so much easier. Easier on you and the girls. I can get them ready. Prepare them for you. I can make it so you can have them sooner. You won't have to wait as long. And I can cook and clean. Not just in the basement but up here. I'll learn how to cook. I can be like your personal assistant. Think about it. How much easier would your life be if you didn't have to work out so many of the details? You never have to hide anything from me because I already know what you do. I just want to help you do it better."

The fight left his body. He stared at me for a long time. "I'll think about it." He motioned to the bathroom door. "Go take a shower. You stink."

I had been so elated to stay and he started calling me up to speak with him, but not at night. The evenings were reserved for Tiffany but he called me up during the day. I never even knew he was around during the day. I'd always assumed he was off working whatever important job he had. I felt special because I got his daytime hours.

We started talking about our arrangement and what it would entail. He agreed to a trial run. He said if it didn't work out he was going to have to let me go, but he'd give me a chance. It was all I wanted. Just a chance. He only had one condition.

"You have to prove I can trust you completely," he said.

"Of course," I said. I didn't even have to think about it. "What do I have to do?"

"You'll see," he said. "I'll be watching everything you do. Everything. I'm going to get cameras set up in every room upstairs. If there's anything even hinting at betrayal, you're gone. You understand?"

"Yes."

"I don't want to hurt you. Really, I don't." He pointed to the gun on the table next to him. "I don't want to use this, but I will if I have to. Are we clear?"

I nodded.

"Speak up. I can't hear you."

"I understand." My voice cracked.

"Good." He poured himself another glass of wine.

I thought about those first conversations as I shifted through the piles of photographs on my lap. There are so many different smiling faces. Most of them look like school pictures. I recognize a few of the girls—Tiffany, Erin, and Michelle. I hand the pile back to Blake once I finished.

"Sorry," I say. "I wish I could help you but I don't recognize any of the girls in these pictures. I've never seen them."

ELLA

(THEN)

'M IN SO MUCH PAIN it hurts to open my eyes. I'm disappointed I didn't die in my sleep. I thought he'd give me a break and let my body rest since I was in so much pain, but he didn't. Instead, he started called me up during the day and at night. He rapes me multiple times every day as if I'm a new drug he can't get enough of.

"It won't always be like this," Paige says. "He slows down after a while."

She tries to get me to roll over to face her, but I scoot further away on my bed. I don't want her to touch me. Her incessant chattering, usually a good distraction that helps me not feel alone, grates on me. All I want is for her to be quiet and leave me alone. I want to sleep away my days. His depravity has seeped into my insides and moves through my veins. I want to crawl out of my skin.

I've stopped dreaming when I'm asleep. It's started to feel like the outside world doesn't exist. The moments when I'm awake are filled with fantasies about killing him or myself. I envision grabbing one of the long knifes from the wooden chopping blocks in the kitchen and slicing him open, then ripping his heart out and smashing it onto the perfectly white, clean floors and stomping on it until it's pulverized. When I think about killing myself, I imagine plunging the knife into my gut and the sweet release it would give me as it bled out the evil he's put in me. I play the scenarios over and over again.

The only thing I look forward to is the wine he fills my glass with every night. He doesn't care how much I drink and I've learned how to handle my liquor quite well. I don't throw up anymore.

I cry all the time, even in my sleep. My pillow stays damp from my tears. Paige tries to comfort me but I refuse to be comforted. There's nothing she can say to make this better.

Last night he dressed me up like a Catholic school girl and put my hair in pigtails. He wasn't satisfied until he could get the part perfectly straight and both sides even.

"You look beautiful," he said when he finished.

He held up a mirror so I could admire his handiwork. I didn't recognize my face even though I look the same. Nothing has changed, but I'm not her anymore. I'm not the girl who stared back at me. I don't know who I am.

He got out an old-fashioned camera and took pictures. He made me pose for him for hours while he snapped away. I moved like a robot. Turning this way and that. Bending over. Opening my legs so he could peek up my skirt. When it was finally over, and he'd taken me again, he pulled me next to him.

"You're so special," he said as he stroked my hair. "It was nice to see you enjoying yourself tonight."

I didn't speak. Having to lay next to him while he cuddles me and speaks to me lovingly are harder than the moments when he's violating me.

I made the wrong choice. I should've let him kill me.

SARAH

(THEN)

'M SO EXCITED I DON'T know what to do with myself. I didn't think the day would ever come. Yesterday morning when he called me upstairs to talk to him while he was getting ready for work, he told me he'd changed his mind and I could move upstairs. I can't believe he changed his mind. He rarely ever does.

I'm going to be free of the basement for good and we're finally going to be a real family. He's even going to teach me how to use the intercom so I can summon the girls myself. Tonight when I go to sleep, I get to sleep in my princess bed, that's what I've always called it, and it's going to be mine. All mine. A room with four walls and a door. He says I can lock it at night if I want to, he even prefers that I do.

I start going through my things in the basement. I'm not taking much of it with me. I don't want anything that will remind me of the darkness down here. Only the things I hold dear. The food and the kitchen things will stay because the girls will need those. They'll have to figure out how to ration things themselves because it's not my problem anymore. They'll learn soon enough what happens if they eat all their food in one day and it doesn't take long to figure out the water situation—you drink too much of your water and you run out of water for the toilet. Paige will know that one, though. She's smart.

I carry out a box filled with coloring books and crayons. Paige is reading and Ella is curled up in her bed. She's been that way for weeks. She's nearly catatonic. I've seen it happen sometimes. By now, I feel like I've seen everything happen at least once.

"Hey," I say. "Do either of you want this stuff?"

Paige looks up, instantly suspicious. Ella doesn't move.

"What is it?" she asks.

I set it on her bed and pull off the lid, thumbing through the things quickly. "It's all my coloring stuff."

She stares at me in disbelief. She knows I never share.

"Why?" she asks.

"I don't need them anymore," I say. A smile stretches across my face.

"Why don't you need them?"

"I'm moving upstairs," I say. I don't even try to hide my excitement.

"Are you serious?" she asks. "Ella, did you hear that? Sarah's moving upstairs."

No response. The girl might as well be dead, but she's not. When John calls her tonight, she'll rise from the dead and go to meet him.

"Do you want them or not?"

"Sure." Paige takes them from me hesitantly like she's waiting for me to snatch them back.

I skip back behind my sheet and spend the rest of the afternoon sorting things. At some point, Paige asks if she can come in my room. Normally, I'd say no, but today I'm too happy to care. Besides, this room is no longer my sacred space.

"What's up?" I ask.

"After you go upstairs, do you think I could have your room?"

ELLA

(NOW)

I SHOULD BE HAPPY that I finally get to leave the hospital but there's no joy in going home because Sarah's coming with us. I'm so mad at Mom I can't even look at her. She's convinced I'll get used to it and that it will be good for me, but there's nothing good about bringing the nightmare home. I've done everything I can think of to prevent it. I've begged, cried, kicked, and screamed. I even thought about threatening to kill myself, but I couldn't do that to Mom no matter how mad I am at her.

For once, I'm on Randy's side. She's tried to talk her out of it too, but Mom won't change her mind.

"I couldn't live with myself knowing I had the power to keep that girl out of the system and give her a loving home, but I chose not to," she said, her jaw set with determination.

That shut Randy down. How could she argue with logic like that? She's coming to talk to me about it again today right after she finishes her session with Sarah.

At least I get to take a shower today—a real shower. They've been giving me sponge baths because of all my stitches, but today, the doctor said I can take a shower. I hobble my way into the bathroom on the crutches they finally brought me yesterday. I'm still figuring out how to use them without rubbing my armpits raw.

"I'm right here if you need me," Mom calls out as I shut the door behind me.

So far, I haven't looked at myself in the mirror when I've used the bathroom, but today, I look. My face is grotesque and I barely recognize myself. I trace the bruises along my left side, remembering how hard I hit the concrete—the loud smack it made. I didn't even have time to think about how much pain my face was in, though, because within seconds, one of the dogs sunk his teeth into my leg. I shudder at the memories and shove them down.

I brush my teeth and my hair falls forward as I spit. I pull it up into a messy bun on top of my head to keep it out of the way. I catch my reflection again in the mirror and the images tumble through my brain intrusively. John pulling my bun out and combing through it with his fingers to splay it out on the pillow. I don't want to see. Don't want to remember, but the pictures won't stop. Me sitting on the toilet while he brushed it. The way he twirled it in bed after he raped me. I hate my hair. Every inch of it.

"Mom?" I call out.

"Yes?" She's at the door immediately. She treats me like I'm a fragile infant. She didn't even want me to take a shower by myself.

"Can I have a scissors?"

There's a long drawn out silence while she thinks about it.

"Why do you want a scissors?"

"I'm going to cut my hair."

She flings open the door. "Ella, you can't cut your hair. You love your hair. You've always loved your hair."

"I told you to stay out of here. I want to do this alone and I want a scissors." I cross my arms on my chest.

Randy is behind her now.

"Are you feeling like hurting yourself?" she asks.

"No! I'm feeling like cutting my hair, dammit!"

Mom looks like I slapped her. She's never heard me swear. It's not something I used to do, but there's a lot of things I do now that I never did before.

Randy places her hand on Mom's arm. "I think if she wants to cut her hair, perhaps we should let her."

"I'm not giving her a scissors," Mom says. "No way. She's too fragile."

"Fragile? You think I'm too fragile?" I laugh bitterly. "If I was going to kill myself, I would've done that a long time ago."

Mom glares at Randy. She can't get angry at me so she directs her anger at her instead. Randy wins the battle with her eyes. Mom leaves the room and returns with a scissors. She hands them to me.

"We're going to stand here and watch you with these. Just in case. It will make your mom feel better," Randy says.

"Fine," I huff, taking them from her.

I grab a chunk of my hair and cut. It falls on the linoleum floor. I snip another and another. It feels wonderful. I can't stop. Before I know it, I'm grabbing chunks and hacking frantically. Piles line the floor.

"Ella, that's good. Maybe you want to stop," Mom warns.

I ignore her. I can't get it off my head fast enough. I cut until it's as close to my head as I can get and I can't cut anymore. I look in the mirror. There's still hair on my head.

"I want a razor," I announce.

Mom sucks in her breath. "Ella, no." She looks behind her at Randy. "Randy, tell her no. She can't shave her head."

Randy shrugs. "Why not?"

Mom looks at her like she's agreed to me selling crack. "Why not? Because only cancer patients and crazy people shave their heads."

"Or maybe she just wants to get rid of her hair," Randy says, refusing to get riled like she always does.

I turn to look at her. She gets it. This time, she gets it. Relief washes over me.

"I can't watch this. I can't," Mom says.

I start to laugh. I laugh so hard it brings tears to my eyes, and then suddenly, I'm crying.

"Please, just get me a razor." I sob uncontrollably.

Mom doesn't know what to do. She's looking at me like she's never seen me before. "Okay, honey, okay. I'll get you a razor." Her voice quivers, full of uncertainty.

"Stop calling me honey!" I scream so loudly I'm sure Sarah hears me down the hall.

She's crying now too and scurries away. Randy just stands there, motionless while great heaving sobs shake my body. She grabs one of the chairs from my room and brings it into the bathroom. She slides it behind me.

"If you feel like you're going to fall, just sit on this," she instructs without touching me.

I collapse into it. I want to curl up into a ball, but the bandages on my leg get in the way.

"He loved my hair," I say through my sobs, not sure she can even understand me through my tears. "He loved it. I have to get rid of it."

She nods. This time she doesn't say she understands. She just stands behind me while I cry until Mom comes back with an electric razor. I snatch it from her hand. I plug it in and exhale as the final pieces of my hair fall away.

SARAH

(NOW)

'M GOING HOME WITH ELLA and Jocelyn. It feels so weird. When Jocelyn first posed the idea to me, I rejected it immediately. I have no interest in living with Ella and I'm sure she feels the same way about me. But after she left, I thought more about it. Where would I go when I leave if I don't live with them? Randy talked to me about foster homes or group homes for teenagers and they sounded horrible. I can't imagine anything worse than living with a bunch of teenagers who've spent half of their lives in and out of juvenile detention centers.

And really, it will be so much easier for John to find me if we're together. I know he's looking for me as hard as they're looking for him. Sometimes I feel him watching me. Sure that some night I'll turn around and he'll be slinking into my room or one of these times, there'll be a knock at my door and he'll stick his head through with his finger up to his lips reminding me to keep quiet as we tiptoe out the door. But he's not going to try anything when all these cops are surrounding me. He'll bide his time until they've loosened their grip and then he'll get me. He has to. He promised.

ELLA

(THEN)

SARAH'S GONE. SHE'S MOVED upstairs with him. Paige is elated because she's moved over to her bed. She ripped the sheet down so there's no separation between us. She was afraid I'd be mad she took her spot and promised she wasn't going to turn into Sarah. All she wanted was to sleep in a real bed. I don't blame her. She offered to take turns sleeping in it, but I don't care.

Nothing matters. My despair is like a cancer eating away at my insides, destroying more and more parts of me every day. I have nobody to blame but myself. This is all my fault. All I had to do was ignore him when he pulled up alongside me in his car. I replay the scene again and again just like I did when he first took me.

I was running my four-mile loop. The same route I run most days except when I'm training for a long run, then I increase my distance. But Mom and I didn't have another marathon scheduled so I was only doing four miles every night. I ran the route so many times I could run it with my eyes closed.

I'm a creature of habit when it comes to running. Most long-distance runners are. We have systematic rituals of how we do things. When we drink water. How we drink it. The clothes we wear. Some of us listen to music while others don't. I'm one that listens to music. My playlists are carefully designed and prepared.

I always listen to music during the first few miles and vary my songs depending on my mood. No matter how I'm feeling though, once I'm about a mile from the end, I pull out my earbuds and run in silence. I like to just be present with my body and feel how my muscles have worked themselves out. I like how open and free my mind is. Sometimes I run just because it's the only time my brain is clear. There's not a thought in my head. I just listen to the sound of my feet pounding the pavement. No matter how bad my day might have been, I always feel better after I run. It uncoils me.

I was nearing the end of my run, so I'd slipped my earbuds off and was inhaling my first breaths of clarity. His voice called out to me in the darkness.

"Hey, miss, excuse me."

A car slowed next to me. It might have been a black car. Maybe not, though. It was dark. I would've paid more attention if I'd known what was about to happen. I don't know what made me stop. I never stop. It's not like people never call out to me while I run. It happens all the time. I ignore them even if they're yelling out encouragement because that's what you do. But I stopped. All I would've had to do was keep running. That's it. A two-second pause changed my entire life.

I turned to look at him. I couldn't make out much of his face but he was smiling. It was a nice smile. Not the smile you'd expect to see on a monster.

"I'm so sorry to bother you, but my wife and I live over on the next block and our dog, Cricket, just got out. She's a small black poodle. Have you seen her?"

I took a step closer to look at the picture he was holding on his phone. Why did I do that? I hadn't seen any dogs. Why would I have to look at the picture? I was within arm's reach of his window. Something shocked me. I remember a jolt of paralyzing pain and then another harsh pain on the back of my head before everything went black.

When I opened my eyes, I was locked in a trunk. The space was tight and small like a coffin, a metal ceiling inches from my face. My hands were tied behind me and my feet were bound together at the ankles. My head throbbed. My body tingled. The orchestrated chaos of classical music filled my ears. The level of terror was indescribable. There were no words. No thoughts. Only sheer panic as I screamed, twisted, kicked, and writhed.

Suddenly, gravel crunched underneath the tires. The car stopped. The cover was lifted. A man's face above me. I pitched myself forward, screaming like a wild animal. He shoved me back in, but I struggled against him. I hurled myself out of the trunk again and landed flat on my face on the gravel. A heavy boot pressed against my back. The gravel burned my cheek. I arched my back and lifted my head. He slammed my head down with the other boot. I cried out in pain.

"Help! Help! Help!"

A sharp sting on my thigh and my muscles melted. I couldn't help it. Then, darkness again.

I was in the basement the next time I opened my eyes. I knew it was my fault then and I have the same sickening realization every time I open my eyes now. I did this. All of it. And when I had a chance to end it, I didn't. He's capable of killing me. That much I know for sure, but I was too afraid to let him. I chose to become his sex slave. I did this too.

SARAH

(THEN)

LOVE LIVING UPSTAIRS. It's exactly like I always dreamed it would be. Even better. I don't have to pretend the house is mine or that I belong here anymore. It is mine—all of it. It's worth every test he put me through. I try not to think too much about the things I've done because I had to do what I had to do to prove myself to him. There was no other way.

I spent every day trying make myself useful to him and wracked my brain for anything I could do to become indispensable to him. I scrubbed and polished the house. I made sure there wasn't a speck of dust on anything or a droplet of water on the floor. I made every bed even though the only one ever slept in was his. I remade them all, making sure there wasn't a wrinkle on any of the comforters and that the pillows were perfectly arranged.

I washed the bedding from the room he took Tiffany into and replaced it with fresh sheets every morning. I sprayed the comforter with lavender to give it a hint of freshness. I primped the flowers arranged on the nightstand. They looked real, but they weren't. There weren't any real flowers allowed in the house.

All the dishes were scrubbed. I made sure there weren't any water spots. I wiped every counter. Sprayed all the appliances to make sure they gleamed like they were brand new. I pushed in each chair at the dining table so there was an equal distance between each. Four inches on each side. Eight inches apart. I used a tape measure to make sure. I had it down to a science.

I ironed all his clothes. Not just his shirts and his pants. I even ironed his socks and boxers. I organized his closets and drawers. Everything hung straight, the blacks and whites separated.

I obsessed over cooking shows. It was the one area I struggled. I didn't know how to cook. I'd only ever heated things up in the microwave. I didn't know how to use the stove, especially not his with all the strange buttons and knobs. I took scrupulous notes from Rachel Ray and Bobby Flay as if I was preparing for a huge exam. I was sure each time he ate one of my overcooked vegetables or hard-as-rock chicken that it was going to be over for me. After he spit out what I had cooked one night, I spent the next hour promising him I'd do better until he finally told me to shut up and go back downstairs.

It took a while, but I got better at cooking and it wasn't long before I was actually good. I started catering every meal toward his preferences. If it wasn't something he liked, I never made it again. I had lists for every meal that I kept arranged in alphabetical order.

At first, he only let me upstairs for a few hours and only when he was present in the house. I wanted to jump around the house dancing the first time he left me alone, but I kept my routine. The blinking red lights strategically placed in all the rooms were a constant reminder that he was always watching. I stared at the huge glass doors leading out to the patio. I'd return to them again and again, wondering what the alarm would sound like if I pushed open the door. How long would it take for him to arrive? Did he really have pit bulls outside in the yard? Why didn't I ever see them?

Even though I wasn't going to leave, I couldn't stop the thoughts. The door intruded on my work all day so I forced myself to stay busy and stop looking at it or imagining what it would feel like to breathe fresh air again. How long had it been? One year? Two? I wasn't even sure anymore. I kept reminding myself I had nowhere to go. There was no home to return to.

When he got home that night, he didn't say anything to me. Just gave me a nod but we both knew I'd passed his test. My ultimate test was with Tiffany a few nights later.

He pulled me aside before he summoned her upstairs and handed me a small plastic baggie filled with white powder. "I want you to put this in Tiffany's water tonight before you serve her."

I nodded. I knew it was only a matter of time before he got rid of her when he'd brought home a new girl two weeks ago. My hands shook as I dumped the contents of the bag into her water while he bathed her. It was the same powder he'd probably put in my water the night he tried to get rid of me. What was going to happen to her when she drank it? I told myself I wasn't a part of whatever he was planning. I was only following orders. It could be Tylenol or some other medication. Maybe it was an aphrodisiac. He might have something special planned for them tonight that I didn't know about. It was possible.

It was hard to keep my composure while I served them. I watched as she drank, never taking my eyes off her. I held back the urge to slap the water out of her hand. We'd spent months living together and even though my loyalty was with him, it didn't change the fact that she'd been my friend even if we ignored each other now.

At first nothing happened. She picked away at her pork chop dribbled with marmalade. She hated pork. She'd been a vegetarian before, but he forced her to eat meat because he said she needed the protein. She nibbled on the string beans as he chattered away about his day. I watched as her lids grew heavy and she slunk down in her chair. I snuck a peek at him. He watched in fascination as she slumped further and further down.

Eventually, she slid onto the floor with a loud thud. I gasped. I couldn't help myself. It just slipped out. Was she dead? Did he kill her?

His feet clacked on the floor as he walked around the table to her body. He kicked her shoulder with his toe. She didn't move. "Petra, I want you to stand and watch her while I run and get changed." His tone was even and calm.

I nodded. Too nervous to speak. What would I do if she came to while I stood over her? Even worse, what if she was dead and I was standing in the dining room with a dead body? I couldn't help myself. I crouched down and brought my face next to hers. I felt her breath on my cheek. I looked at her chest. It was still moving. I breathed a sigh of relief. I just wanted it to be over and for him to get her out of my sight. I didn't want any part of it.

It wasn't long before he returned dressed in a sweat suit like he wore on the weekends or whenever he worked out in the gym. He squatted down, picked her up, and slung her over his shoulder. He struggled to gain his balance under the weight of her.

"I need you to open the door for me," he grunted.

I moved around him, trying not to touch either of them. It felt surreal to put my hand on the doorknob and turn. I waited for the alarm, but nothing sounded. He must've turned it off.

"Shut it behind me," he said as he stepped outside.

I slammed it shut quickly after they left. I stood motionless for a minute, trying to erase what I'd just seen and done. I forced myself to move. I cleared the table and did the dishes. I finished the dishes and then did them all over again. I had to do something with my hands to keep them from shaking.

"C'mon," he said from behind me.

I jumped. I hadn't heard him come back inside.

"What? Huh?" I stammered.

He pointed toward the door. "I tied the dogs up. You'll be fine. Now, hurry up."

I followed him outside onto the patio like I was in a trance. The sun was setting. We walked down a few steps. A long black Lincoln town car sat idling in the driveway. He opened the passenger door for me. I got in, sliding in on the leather seats.

I sat on my hands so he couldn't see them shake. I crossed my legs and twisted my ankles around each other to steady my legs.

The headlights cast an eerie glow down a long driveway that seemed to go on forever. Trees lined each side of the car. The driveway ended at a steel gate. He reached above me and pushed a button on my visor. The gate slid open and he made a left onto the street.

He was the perfect driver as we wrapped around winding curves. We passed other gated homes. Ominous doors hid their inhabitants just like us. We twisted through them until we reached a gas station on the corner where he made another left. I stared out the window at all the lights until they blurred together. He switched lanes and entered a wide freeway. Once there, he turned on the radio filling the car with classical music.

He drove for hours. He didn't speak. Didn't look at me. I kept sneaking glances at him. I couldn't read his face. I'd never seen this one. It was focused, unmoving. He stared ahead. His lips pursed in a straight line.

Where were we going? Where was he taking me? What about Tiffany? The same questions ran on a repeated track. The city lights disappeared behind us. This time when he turned, it was onto a bumpy service road that led to a gravel road. We took one gravel road after the next. I lost all sense of where we were. In the beginning, I kept track just in case I needed to find my way back, but I was lost. Finally, he stopped.

He got out first, walked over to my car door, and let me out. We were in the middle of a desert. All I saw for miles was flat land with a few silhouettes of cactus. The moon was hidden by wispy clouds and even though the sun was down, it was still hot. I wrung my hands together. My heart pounded in my head. He opened the back door and pulled out a long shovel, then reached in again and pulled out another one. He handed one to me. He started walking into the night so I followed, trying not to trip. We only walked a few feet before he stopped.

"Dig," he said pointing to the ground.

I started to cry. "No, please. Please, don't do this to me. You can just leave me here. I'll probably never find my way back into the city anyway. I won't tell anyone anything. Ever. Please, you've—"

He interrupted me, "Dig."

I sobbed as I began digging my own grave. I cried harder with each load. I couldn't believe that after all I'd done, it was going to end like this. No one would ever find my body. No one ever looked for me anyway, but somehow, people not knowing I ever existed was even more painful.

He helped me dig. My palms burned within a short period of time. It wasn't long before they blistered, but I kept shoveling. My shirt stuck to me with sweat. Sweat poured from his forehead and after a while, he took his shirt off. Still we dug. It was exhausting. The heat was blazing even though it was pitch black. The headlights formed our only light.

He went back to the car and came back with water. He took a drink and gave it to me. I gulped hungrily this time, hoping he'd given me whatever he gave Tiffany. I wanted to fall asleep before I died or be dead before he threw me in the hole we'd dug. I couldn't think of anything worse than being buried alive.

He sat to take a rest while I continued to work. I waited to feel something, but all I felt were my muscles screaming at me. It felt like I'd been digging for hours. He joined me after his break and jumped down into the hole. He started shoveling dirt and sand out of the hole, and over his head. He wiped the dust and sweat off his forehead and climbed out when he was satisfied it was deep enough.

He tossed his shovel to the side. I stood holding mine. As he walked back to the car, I plotted how I would smash him in the back of his head with my shovel when he turned around and steal the car. I had to make sure I hit him hard enough to knock him unconscious or he'd be on me in no time. I tried to catch my breath as he popped the trunk and prepare myself for what I had to do. He grabbed a backpack and strapped it on.

He yanked Tiffany from the trunk. I had no idea she was in there. She was screaming and crying, but couldn't move because her arms and legs were tied. She spotted me. Her eyes were filled with unimaginable terror.

"Sarah! Sarah! Sarah!"

I stood rooted to my spot.

"Please let him kill her first. Please let him kill her first," I pled to a God I didn't believe in.

He threw her onto the ground. She screamed again.

"Shut up!" He pulled out duct tape from his backpack and slapped it across her mouth, tearing it with his teeth. Her eyes bulged out of her head. She kept screaming underneath the gag, but her screams were muted. She crawled along the ground, trying to get away.

He reached into the backpack again and pulled out a gun. He ran after her and stamped on her back with his tennis shoes, smashing her into the ground. She flailed about, whimpering the most distressed cries I'd ever heard.

"Petra, get over here," he said. He motioned for me with the hand holding the gun.

I walked in slow motion over to them. I stared at him in horror.

"What did you think I'd do with her? Send her back home to mommy and daddy? Did you really think that's how this played out?" He snorted, threw his head back, and laughed.

He handed the gun to me. I took it because I didn't know what else to do. My hands were shaking so much I was afraid I'd drop it. He had her pinned to the ground with his feet. He pulled her head up by her hair, snapping her back. He pointed at me with his other hand.

"Shoot her," he said.

Everything froze. Still. I shook so hard I could barely stand. Tears streamed down my face. I didn't realize I was crying.

"No," I whimpered. "I can't do it."

"You said you'd do anything for me." Tension curled his words.

"Please, don't make me do this. I'm not a murderer. Please. I don't know how to shoot a gun. I've never even held one before." I was sobbing as loudly as Tiffany. I couldn't help myself. "I don't know how to shoot a gun."

"Get over here!"

I stepped toward them. He grabbed the hand holding the gun and moved it so the barrel met the back of her head. "There's nothing to it. Just pull the trigger."

"I can't. I can't. I can't." I babbled incoherently.

He snatched the gun from me and I fell to the ground, burying my face in my hands. Suddenly, the gun was at the back of my head, pressed against me. Pee pooled between my legs.

"Oh my God, no, please, don't. Please, don't. I'll do it. I'll do it!" I screamed.

"Last chance," he said.

I stood up, swallowing the sobs in my throat and took the gun back. I didn't breathe. He pulled her head back up again. I placed the gun against the back of her head, closed my eyes, and pulled the trigger. The shot rang out into the night.

I cried the entire way home. He kept saying he'd never been more proud of me and wanted to give me a new name because I was a new person. We were leaving Petra in the desert, buried along with Tiffany, and I was now Sarah. He picked Sarah because it meant princess.

"We're family now," he said.

I often think back to that night—the night that changed everything. I could've shot him instead of Tiffany, but I couldn't kill the only person who ever really loved me. If I had, I wouldn't be living like I am now in this beautiful mansion surrounded by beautiful things.

ELLA

(NOW)

PAIGE'S PARENTS ARE HERE. Their flight got in late last night. They want to see us before we leave to go home. I wonder if it will be her stepdad or if her real dad decided to come too. She talked about him a lot. She always wanted to know if he was looking for her; if he cared she was gone or felt so little for her that he didn't want to be bothered with it.

They're coming because yesterday they found human remains at the crime scene. That's what they call John's house now—the crime scene. It will be awhile before the results come back from whatever lab they have to send them to, but her parents want to be close. Mom says she understands but it seems a bit creepy to want to be close to bones.

I want to know where Paige is as much as they do. I hope she's alive. If the bones are Paige's, then the search can finally be over. There'll be some answers. But the answer means she's dead. There's no way for this to have a good outcome. Either she's dead or she's still missing.

I don't want to meet them. Sarah refused but Mom insisted I do. She says she'd want the same thing if she was in their position. Sometimes I wish her heart wasn't so big. I rub my hand back and forth across my shaved head. I love the way it feels even though I look like a freak.

Randy walks into the room with a man and woman. The man towers over the woman and he's got his arm wrapped around her waist. She looks like she might fall over if he didn't. Edges of pain cut into her face. Her eyes are swollen as if she's cried the entire way here. She can't hide her horror when she sees me.

"Oh my God." She brings her hand up to cover her mouth.

Mom steps in front of me. "She shaved her head herself. He didn't do that."

Paige's mom looks her up and down.

"I'm Jocelyn." Mom shakes her hand.

"I'm Melanie," she says.

"Why don't we all take a seat?" Randy ushers them in the rest of the way.

Everyone is staring at everyone, but trying to pretend like they aren't.

"Are you Paige's real dad?" I break the awkward silence.

"Ella! Don't be rude," Mom jumps in.

Melanie forces a smile. "No, it's okay. This is Paige's stepdad, Victor."

Victor nods as if to say hello. He's wearing a red flannel shirt that bulges over his waistline tucked into a pair of jeans. His eyes are hidden behind wire-rimmed glasses. He forces an awkward smile revealing crooked teeth with a slight gap between the front two. I'm glad his smile isn't perfect.

"Does her real dad know she's missing?" I ask.

Melanie looks at me through hollow eyes, tunnels of spent emotion. "He does."

"So, why isn't he here?" I ask.

"Ella. Stop," Mom admonishes.

I turn to look at her. "What else are we supposed to talk about?"

Melanie waves her off. "It's okay. Really, it is." She clears her throat. "Did Paige talk about her real dad a lot?"

"She talked about them both," I say even though she talked more about her real dad. I don't want to make Victor feel bad.

Paige never had anything bad to say about Victor. He was really good to her and she thought of him as her father. He was kind and loving and never made her feel second place even after her twin brothers were born, but there was a hole in her heart where her real father should be. It doesn't matter how good you have it or how much other people love you. It doesn't change the fact that your real dad left you and the person who birthed you doesn't care enough about you to be in your life. It leaves a mark even if you don't want it to. Paige and I had the same wound. We all did. It's why John liked us and what made us so attractive to him.

"We notified him when she went missing, but... but..." Her voice trails off.

Victor finishes what she can't. "He never even checks to see if we've found her."

I hear Mom's sharp intake of breath. Victor reaches out to hold Melanie's hand. I watch her knuckles turn white as she squeezes him.

"That's just awful," Mom says.

I don't like how she says it. She says it like we're somehow different and I have a dad who shows up for me. Mom didn't even have a way to contact him and let him know I was missing. He signed off on all his parental rights when I was three months old, and we've never heard from him since. Mom didn't even bother to try to find him after I went missing.

"Can you tell us about Paige?" Melanie asks, every word clothed in desperation.

"Didn't the detectives tell you?" I ask.

I can't imagine they haven't filled them in on every detail. If they're anything like Mom, I'm sure they haven't left them alone. Even though they check in during the day, Mom is constantly texting one of them to see if there's anything new to report.

"The detectives have filled the Pratts in on all the details of the case. I think what they're asking for is any personal information you could give them about Paige," Randy explains.

"Yes, yes, that's what I mean. What was she like? How did she handle it? Were you close? Did you see her? Were the two of you allowed to talk? Was she in pain every day?" Her voice cracks at her last question. "I'm sorry. I just have so many questions."

"It's okay," I say. "Paige was a really sweet girl. We lived through a lot of pain. I'm not going to lie—he did terrible things to us. But, she never lost her sweetness. No matter what. She was kind and always thinking of ways to make things easier for me."

Paige possessed a special ability. She was able to take everything he'd done to us and lock it into a separate compartment. She needed time alone on her bed to put it in its place, but once it was there, she left it there. I wish I'd been able to do it too, but I couldn't. I couldn't tuck it away and keep it separate. It infiltrated every part of me. Nothing was untouched.

"She held on to who she was and spent lots of time reading. I don't know if she read before, but it was her favorite thing to do in the basement and she loved to talk."

Melanie bursts out laughing. She's crying at the same time she's laughing. "Yes, my girl loved to talk. Keep going. Please, keep going."

"She told me all about you and her brothers. She shared all the adventures you had last year and how she pictured herself in the RV to fall asleep at night. She said she remembered what the stars looked like out of the small window on top and that she could actually put herself back there."

Mom is hanging on every word just like Melanie. This is the most I've talked about the basement and what it was really like, how we really were down there. Most of the time I don't want to talk about it because it's too hard, but I do it for Paige. She'd want me to and I know how much she loved her family.

"We played lots of games. She was the reigning Scrabble champion. I think her vocabulary was so amazing because of all the books she read. I taught her how to play Spades and she taught me how to play Kings in the Corner. She spoon-fed me soup when I was too depressed to eat. We didn't have much down there, but everything we did have, she shared even if it was her last cracker."

They're both weeping now.

"We would've been friends if we'd met on the outside. She was a good person."

Melanie stands and throws herself on my bed. She hugs me tightly, shaking and sobbing. It's not me she's hugging. I know that. She's hugging the parts of Paige that she left in me. I let her hug me until Victor gently pulls her away from me.

"I can't thank you enough for taking the time to meet with us and share your stories," Melanie says.

"You're welcome." It's a weird thing to say but I have to say something.

Her parents and Mom step outside to have a private talk without me present, probably to talk about the case. As they shut the door behind them, all I can think about is how she won't be thanking me if I'm the one who got her daughter killed.

SARAH

(THEN)

H E'S STARTED TO TALK ABOUT babies and creating a family of his own. My heart skips a beat each time he brings it up. It's been so long since we've had sex. Years. For a while after Tiffany, he developed a renewed interest in me. He couldn't get enough of me once he knew the lengths I was willing to go for him, but it was only a matter of time until he returned to what he likes the most—innocent, virgin girls.

I've never pictured him as the family type. He's never even mentioned children of his own. He's always said he hates kids because he grew up surrounded by them. I can't imagine how I'll keep the house clean once we have a little one running around, but I'll figure out a way. Maybe he'll even let me bring the baby outside. Our kid will have to go out in the real world because there's no way he'll keep him or her locked up here too. It's too cruel to do to a child.

Maybe he was just waiting for me to become an adult so he could bring me out into the world. It won't be long until I'm eighteen. Lots of older men go for younger girls all the time and I can definitely pass for twenty especially if I do my hair and put on make-up. He might even let me buy a new wardrobe. I can't imagine he'd let his wife run around in the real world in sweat pants and t-shirts. It's been so long since I wore anything with color. Sometimes I think about asking for dye just so I can color my shirts, but he'd never let me.

I've started imagining what room I'll use for the nursery. For a while, I'll want to keep the baby with me. I can get one of those cute little bassinets you put next to the bed. I've been watching *A Baby Story* on TLC ever since he brought it up. I'm learning all sorts of things about babies. I'm definitely going to breastfeed and I'm only going to prepare organic food.

I'm going to have someone to love who's all mine and I can't wait.

ELLA

(THEN)

I HATE WHEN HE'S ROUGH and not because it hurts even though it does. I'm used to the pain. It's because the more he hurts me, the tighter he holds me afterward, the sweeter he is and the longer he wants to talk. Tonight, he was particularly rough and he's had me wrapped in his arm for over an hour. It's hard to lay still as he rambles on and on. He's been babbling about fathers. Not his own, but becoming one.

"I think I'm ready for it. To be a dad. It's not like it'd be the first time I put a baby in somebody, but this time, I want to keep it. I wasn't ready before and you have to really be ready to be a father or else it's just not fair to the kid. But I'm ready. I think I'm going to be a great dad..."

He keeps going, but I'm only half-listening. I've gotten good at faking attention while he goes off on his ridiculous tangents. Last night, he talked about how he'd make a good president.

"Also, the timing's never been right and I haven't found anyone I could see myself creating life with. Until now. Until you, Ella. I want to create life with you."

I snap back to reality.

"What do you think about that, sweetheart?" He kisses the top of my head softly.

I want to throw up. My mind reels. Blood pools my insides. He can't be serious. He's not making any sense. He's already a father. He has Sarah. It's just another one of his crazy ideas.

But he doesn't drop it the next night or the night after. He's convinced he wants to get me pregnant and that we'll be a great family. Just the three of us. He hints at moving me upstairs with him where Sarah can help me take care of the baby when it arrives. I don't know why I haven't thought about him getting me pregnant before but the thought has never crossed my mind even though it's always been a possibility.

The next night after he's finished with me, he makes me lay with my legs straight up against the wall. He says it helps the sperm reach my eggs. He doesn't let me take them down even after my legs are stiff and achy. He rubs my cheek and plays with my hair while we wait. When I'm finally allowed to stumble downstairs, I collapse on my bed. I want to cry but there's nothing left. I've run out of tears.

ELLA

(NOW)

"IT WAS NICE TO FINALLY meet them in person," Mom says after Paige's parents leave. They'd talked a lot over the phone in the last few days. "I can't imagine what it must be like to have your daughter missing for nine months. You were only gone for four and I thought I'd die."

She says it was like being tortured every day. She's already told me about everything she did to look for me. She knew something was wrong immediately when I didn't come home after my run. I wasn't someone who veered from my routines. I always did my evening run, came home and showered, then watched TV with her for about an hour before going to bed. I was in bed at 10:30 with lights out by 11:00. If I didn't get my seven hours of sleep, I was a zombie in school the next day.

She called the police immediately, but they'd blown her off at first. They assured her I'd probably ran into a friend or forgotten to tell her about something else I had to do that night.

"Teenagers aren't always real responsible," they'd said.

"You don't know my daughter," she'd replied.

She still harbored guilt about not forcing them to look for me immediately. It wasn't until almost midnight when I still hadn't come home that they started to listen to her. Even then, they didn't take it seriously or even consider something bad might have happened to me. They focused on whether I had a boyfriend, was into drugs, or had a secret teenage lifestyle she didn't know about. They talked to all my friends and interviewed my teachers the next day. Even though their searches didn't turn up any secret boyfriends or hidden addictions, they weren't convinced someone took me.

"Teenage girls go missing all the time," they told her. "Most of the time, they come home on their own."

She was horrified at their nonchalant response and took it upon herself to alert the media that her daughter had disappeared. Unlike the police, the media grabbed on to the story immediately which forced my disappearance into the spotlight. She appeared on every TV station that would have her, created a Facebook and Instagram account for me, and raised money through our church to build a reward fund for me.

The authorities couldn't ignore her anymore. They helped organize search parties and went knocking door-to-door. They created human chains and covered every inch of space they could in our small town, extending out into the base of the mountains and thick forests. She told me how she walked my four-mile loop hundreds of times, even crawling at certain points to get a different vantage point, scrutinizing for any sign or clue she might have missed.

She never went back to work. Still hadn't. It was a full-time job leading the search for me. She printed out thousands of flyers and plastered businesses and poles with them. Her flyers were neon yellow with "missing" in capital, bold letters. She wanted them to stand out from the missing pet flyers. She stood on busy intersections handing them out to people as they passed. At one point, she'd even stood on different corners with a huge sign with my name and picture on it along with a number to call if they had any information.

There'd never been any real leads. People from all over the world called in tips all the time saying they'd seen me, but nothing was ever substantial. It was as if I'd vanished into thin air. It was every parents' worst nightmare.

But her nightmare is over now. It's what she keeps saying since Paige's parents left. As sad as she is for them, she can't hide her gratitude that I've been found any better than they hid their jealousy. They asked me all kinds of questions. Every question they could think of except the one that mattered the most. Why did I get out and Paige didn't?

SARAH

(NOW)

BLAKE AND PHIL CALL ME Petra every time they talk to me no matter how many times I tell them it's not my name. It's like they're trying to rub my face in it. I don't like their tone of voice or how they look at me.

Today, they want to know when I started living upstairs. I hate that Ella has already told them so many things. Stuff they don't have any business knowing. She needs to keep her mouth shut. She thinks she's safe now so she can just blab whatever she wants but she has no idea.

"Was it before or after Ella lost the baby?" Blake asks.

My stomach coils at the mention of the baby. I don't bother telling him we've already been through this. They like to ask the same question numerous times. They think they're smart, like if they ask it enough times and in different ways they'll trip me up and get me to tell everything.

"Before," I say. "She was upstairs when she got pregnant."

"How did you feel when she got to live upstairs?"

How did they think I felt? I was furious. I'd slaved over him for years and then she shows up, stays in the basement for a few months, and suddenly she gets to live upstairs? It wasn't fair, but I'm careful not to show my anger.

I shrug. "I didn't care."

"Really?" Phil raises his eyebrows in mock surprise. "Hadn't he just moved you up there? You must've felt at least a little angry that she got to move up there so quickly."

"No. It was fine." I force my voice to be flat.

Phil looks over at Blake. Today, he's the silent one. He studies me, trying to read my body language and searching for clues in my eye movements.

"When did you know she was pregnant?" Phil asks.

"After she took the test."

"Did she show it to you?"

I shake my head. John showed it to me. He came running out of the bathroom waving it in his hands.

"We did it, Sarah! We did it. We're pregnant." He skipped around the kitchen like a little kid while I stared in amazement. I'd never seen him let his guard down and certainly never act giddy. What had she done to him?

When she came out of the bathroom, she wasn't smiling. Her face was flat. Eyes dull and emotionless. It was the same expression she wore every day as she drifted through the house like she wasn't even there. I couldn't stand her. What did he see in her?

"That's so great," I said feigning a smile, pretending to be happy for him.

"I think it's a good idea to put her on bed rest while she's pregnant. I want to make sure nothing happens to this baby. You're going to have to take care of her while I'm away. Can you do that for me?" he asked.

I close my eyes, forcing the memories back under. Blake's eyes are on me. His gaze never falters.

"How did you feel when you found out she was pregnant?" Phil asks.

"Disgusted." It's the truth and I grew more disgusted with her as the days went on.

"Were you jealous?"

I narrow my eyes. How dare he ask me that? How could I be jealous of her? I'll never be jealous of her. She might think she's special. That she was his chosen one, but I was more important to him than she'd ever be. It didn't matter that she was having his baby.

"Not at all. Why would I be jealous of her? She was going to get all fat and ugly."

It was why he'd chosen her to carry the baby instead of me. He didn't want to damage my body. He wanted me to stay beautiful. I couldn't have any ugly stretch marks or saggy hips. Her body would be forever changed after the baby. Everyone knows you never get your body back no matter how hard you work at it or how much you pretend. I hadn't understood why he'd chosen her when he announced he was going to get Ella pregnant, but it didn't take long to figure out it was because he needed me to stay pretty.

We could've raised the baby like she was our own. It wouldn't have mattered if she carried it. Lots of women had other people carry their babies. She was simply our surrogate and after the baby was born, we'd get rid of her. But then she went and ruined everything.

Now we're here and I have to talk to these stupid investigators every day who aren't any closer to finding John than they were before. They told me when they arrived today that Enrique finally agreed to talk to them. Blake has been to see him twice but he refused to speak to them about anything. Now he's saying he'll talk as long as they can get him extra privileges in prison. Maybe even decrease the number of years he has to spend there. He's such a loser. He's going to fill their heads with lies and they're even stupider because they're going to believe him.

I can't wait for this to be over. I miss him so much. The only thing getting me through the days is knowing how much he misses me too. Sometimes at night, I can feel him thinking about me. That's how strong our connection is and it doesn't matter what they do or how hard they try to break me because I'm unbreakable.

ELLA

(THEN)

HE'S OBSESSED WITH GETTING me pregnant. I've become his pet science project. Every morning he makes me take handfuls of vitamins. Things that are supposed to be good for the baby. Something called folic acid. He doesn't know I hide them under my tongue and spit them out in the toilet later. I'll do anything I can to prevent this from happening.

He put me on bedrest upstairs. I'm in one of the guest bedrooms down the hallway, but I don't know what kind of a guest you lock in their room with a padlock. I'm not allowed to get out of bed unless it's to go to the bathroom or do my daily exercises. He has Sarah do prenatal yoga with me that's supposed to prepare my body for pregnancy and makes me listen to CDs about my cervix opening. I recite the pledge of allegiance during them. It's the only thing I know by heart. Everything else I used to know seems to have left my head. There was a time when I would've recited my Bible verses, but those days are gone. I'm on a special diet too. Completely organic and full of protein.

"It's important that you get more protein," he says at every meal.

I throw it all up when I'm allowed to use the bathroom after dinner. The worst part is that I no longer get to drink wine at dinner. I'm stuck with milk because it's supposed to be good for my bones and I miss my wine. I stare at his glass longingly as he drinks. Sometimes I think about sneaking a bottle into my room.

He has a heightened interest in me. He's increasing the odds of getting me pregnant by increasing the number of times he has sex with me every day. I hate it. Without my wine, I've lost my insulating bubble. I focus on not getting pregnant. I imagine my cervix closing up. Each time he plants his seed in me, I focus on rejecting it, hoping my mind is powerful enough to make it a reality. I close my eyes and imagine his poison leaving my body.

Every morning I take a pregnancy test. Each time it comes back negative, his face crumples in sadness. Until today.

Today it came back positive. But I will not have this thing growing inside me. I refuse. I will not bring his devil child into the world. I have a purpose now. A reason to live and I thought all my reasons were gone. I have to find a way to kill this thing.

ELLA
(NOW)

T'S BEEN SIX DAYS. Six days and I don't feel any freer
than before. I'm locked in this hospital room. They said we
could leave yesterday, but then came up with some excuse
about the plane not being ready. We don't get to fly home on a
regular plane because they don't want the public to see us. They
don't want the media to know where we are even though I'm
pretty sure my house is the first place they'll look. They say they
want to stay one step ahead of John in case he's still looking for
us, but that doesn't make any sense either because he already
knows where I live.

They've figured out how he knew everything about us.
They scoured through Paige's and my Facebook and Instagram
accounts. They have fancy tech people who look at people's

profiles and they found a guy we were both friends with on Facebook and who followed us on Instagram. He didn't use the same name but they connected him to us through his IP address. Strangers follow me all the time on Instagram just like everybody else so I wouldn't have even paid him attention. I'm much more selective on Facebook than Instagram, so he must've seemed harmless or connected to someone I knew or I wouldn't have friended him.

He pretended to be a sixteen-year-old boy named Marcus on my accounts. He said he went to Westbrook, the private high school two cities over from mine. He posed as a track star and had the pictures to prove it. I probably thought he was cute and we had similar interests so I accepted his request, but I don't remember doing it. I didn't have any other contact with him.

He posed as a fourteen-year-old boy when he connected with Paige. He pretended to have followed the blog she kept while they were traveling abroad and was interested in their missionary work. He said his parents were missionaries as well. They'd even private messaged each other a few times.

It's also how he knew we were virgins. Vowing to stay a virgin is a big deal and we had posted pictures of our purity rings with the status update signaling the classic Christian promise, "True Love Waits," after we'd had our commitment ceremonies. I'd been wearing mine when he took me, but I threw it in the toilet bowl not long after he kidnapped me. Paige took hers off too, but she still kept it in her nightstand drawer.

The sickest part was that he'd been on the Facebook pages our parents created for us after we went missing. He'd even reached out and sent them condolences. He subscribed to be notified of any updates. Even though the FBI monitored the pages, there'd been nothing about him that stood out. Everything had checked out.

Blake told me he'd most likely learned our routines from status updates we posted and any check-ins we did. He didn't have to tell me that my runs on Nike Running that automatically posted to my page were a map leading him right to me.

They've tracked down two other missing girls they think he's involved with. One of them was named Rachel and even though I never saw her, she sounds like the one Paige said was there when she first got to the house. I didn't recognize the other one.

None of it makes me feel better. All he's done is confirm what I already knew. All of this is my fault.

SARAH

(NOW)

BLAKE AND PHIL walk in together. Both wear serious expressions. I've never seen either of them smile. Officer Malone just left and he's not going to be back again today. I hate meeting with them alone. Officer Malone is good at making them back off when I need it.

"We want to talk to you about what we learned after meeting with your father." Blake wastes no time getting started. "He was able to provide us with some valuable information to help with the case. We're hoping you'll work with us and help corroborate his story."

"Some of this might be difficult for you to hear and bring up painful emotions. If you start to feel overwhelmed, just let us know and we'll call in Randy," Phil interjects.

I don't like where this is headed. They only bring in Randy for the serious stuff.

"Your father informed us that four years ago, he met this man." Blake hands me a photo.

I'm so tired of looking at photos. Yesterday, they made me look at all these different girls' Facebook pages to see if I recognized anyone. I told them no like I always do. I sigh and take it from him. I look down and John's face stares up at me. His hair is longer and he looks younger but there's no mistaking his crystalline eyes and perfect smile. I can't hide my shock.

Blake points at the picture. "That is the man you girls call John. The one you repeatedly try to claim is your father despite the scientific evidence that he's not. By the way, Enrique Manuel is your father. The paternity test confirmed it." He pauses.

I shake my head wildly.

He continues, not waiting for me to gain my composure. "His name isn't John Smith. It's Derek Hunt. We pulled this picture from an old real estate company he used to work for when he met your father. He befriended your father when he was panhandling outside of the Waseca shopping mall. Do you know why he stopped? Why he took such a sudden interest in him? Derek doesn't seem like the kind of man who really gives a shit about other people so why would he even care?" He doesn't wait for an answer. "He stopped because he was panhandling with his daughter. You—his daughter."

"He says you were twelve at the time, is that right?" Phil asks.

I glare at them. I want to hurt them.

"Is that right?" he repeats.

"Leave me alone." I clutch my blanket, digging my nails into it.

"Your father says Derek was loaded. He drove a Mercedes Benz and started coming by every few days and giving him a hundred dollars each time. That's a lot of money to give a panhandler. I bet he spent all of it on crack, huh? What'd your father do with you while he was smoking crack?" Blake studies my reaction.

"Get out!" I shake my finger at the door. "I don't want to talk to you anymore."

They don't move. Blake continues like I haven't even spoken. "One day, he rolled up and had a proposition for your dad. He wanted to buy you, take you off his hands. All your dad had to do was name the price. Did he ever tell you what he paid for you?"

"Shut up!" I don't want to hear any more. They don't understand.

"Two thousand dollars. Your father sold you to Derek Hunt for two thousand dollars." He shakes his head, looks disgusted. "The sad part is I'm willing to bet Derek would've paid him anything he asked, but your dad was too high to even notice."

Phil steps in and tries to reach for my hand. I jerk it away and slide up against the hospital wall behind me. I curl myself into a ball. I'm trapped. I can't get away from them. The room is getting smaller.

Blake is relentless. He won't quit. The conversation isn't over unless he says it's over. "Do you want to know what I think is the saddest part of the whole story? Your father, the man who birthed you, only made one condition on the entire deal. Do you remember what it was? I don't know why I'm even asking you questions. You don't answer them and when you do, you certainly don't tell the truth. Well, your father's only condition was that Derek never bring you back."

"I didn't want to go back!" I explode, unable to hold it in any longer. "I hated that man—my sorry, worthless excuse for a father. Do you know what he did to me? Do you?" I stick out my arms, covered in round burn scars. "These—these right here are the cigarettes he put out on my arms just because he felt like it." I whip my covers off my body, pull up my gown, and expose the jagged scars covering my legs. "And these? These are the marks from the belt he beat me with if I spilled my milk. If I was lucky to even have milk to drink. You think John starved me?" I throw my head back, shrieking in laughter I don't recognize. "Try not eating for weeks at a time. Nothing. So hungry that you actually go outside and eat dirt just so your stomach will have something inside of it. John was the only person who ever gave a shit about me. Ever!"

Blake clasps his hands together in front of him as if he's holding back the urge to clap. "That's it. Now we're finally getting somewhere."

ELLA

(THEN)

'VE STARTED PUNCHING my stomach during the day when he's gone. I have to be careful about it. I can't let Sarah see and I have to do it away from the cameras. I lay under the covers on my side, plumping them up with pillows so that when I punch myself in the gut, he won't be able to see. I can't do it hard enough to leave bruises. He'll notice them right away and wonder where they came from. I don't think I'm hitting hard enough to kill this thing inside of me.

I've spent the last week plotting ways to get rid of it. I've thought of everything—faking a fall, slamming against a night stand, shoving the bed post into my gut—but none of them were feasible because he'd know exactly what I was doing and probably kill me for it. But yesterday I finally came up with the perfect plan. It's a risk but I have to try. I'll never forgive myself if I don't.

The TV is on which means he's at work. I have a better chance of not getting caught if I do it while he's at work. I swallow my fear and slide out of bed before I lose my nerve and walk over to the closet, making sure to keep my expression blank because I don't know which angle the cameras have in this room. I open the closet door. There's three white robes hanging and a stack of empty dry cleaning hangers at the edge of the closet bar. The wire kind. My heart skips a beat. It's a sign. It has to be. I take a step inside the closet, hoping he can't see me if I'm inside. I grab one quickly and stuff it into my robe. Then, I step back out of the closet.

"Ugh," I say out loud. "I'm so sick of wearing bathrobes. I wish there was something else for me to wear." I want him to think I was looking for other clothes in the closet. I plod back to my bed doing my best to look disappointed but my heart is racing. I'm so excited it's hard to lay still.

The next two hours drag, but I have to wait until enough time has passed. Nothing about this can look suspicious. Nothing. My closet trip can't be connected to my bathroom trip. I wait another hour just to be safe before summoning Sarah.

I have a bell on my nightstand like we're from the 1940s and I ring it. It takes her awhile to come. She never responds slowly when John is here. She appears immediately when he calls for her. She doesn't unlock the door.

"What?" she asks from the other side of the door.

"I need to go to the bathroom."

She lets out a deep sigh. "I was right in the middle of Survivor. They're just about to vote."

"Please? I don't think I can wait. I really have to go."

I hear her fumbling with the lock and then she pushes open the door. "Fine, just hurry up. I want to see who they got rid of last night."

She doesn't lock the bathroom door. They never do. But it's shut. I hear the sound of her footsteps padding back into the living room to watch her show. I drop my robe. My heart is pounding. Blood surges through my veins. My senses are on high alert. I frantically unwind the top of the hanger. I pull the wire into a straight line making sure to hold the loop at the bottom so I have something to hold on to.

I grab a towel and stuff it into my mouth so I have something to bite. I stand with my legs spread apart and get down into a squatting position. I take a deep breath as I push the wire inside me. I grit my teeth against the towel. Sweat pours down my face.

It's now or never.

I jab. Sharp pain shoots from my center and radiates throughout my body. I'm panting. I jab again, moving it around inside me as bright lights shoot off in my head. Twisting and turning. Scraping my insides. I almost fall over. I steady myself on the sink with my other hand. I'm in so much pain I'm afraid I'll pass out. I can't pass out.

One more. One more time just to make sure.

I stab myself again. The pain makes my stomach come up in my throat. I lean over and hurl into the toilet. I try to stand up. I can't stand straight. The pain in my center makes me hunch over. White spots dance in front of my eyes. I have to move fast. I don't have much time.

I let my brain take over, pulling the plug connecting it to the pain in my body. I lift the lid on the back of the toilet. I tuck the hanger in behind the coils. It's the only spot it will be safe. Then, I flush and wash my hands.

"Sarah, I'm done," I call out, forcing my voice to stay even.

It hurts so bad I can't breathe. I will myself to stand upright. It's only twelve steps to my bedroom. Twelve steps. I can make it twelve steps.

She opens the door and eyes me quizzically.

"You don't look good," she says.

"I don't feel good," I respond.

She hurries me back to bed, anxious to get back to her show. I hold back the urge to moan or hold my stomach while we walk. I pull the covers up over me, bringing them up to my chin. I don't move until I hear the door lock. I let out the breath I've been holding. I grab my pillow and put it over my head like I'm suffocating myself and scream into it like a wild animal. Firecrackers explode on my insides.

I turn on my side, folding myself into the fetal position. I rock and force myself to breathe. *It's all going to be over soon*, I chant in my head again and again, trying to calm myself.

It isn't long before I feel water between my legs. I pull the covers back. Crimson red stains my crotch.

"Sarah! Sarah! Something's wrong!"

SARAH

(THEN)

ELLA'S FRANTIC SCREAMS pierce the air. I run to her bedroom and throw open the door. She's curled up on her bed, the covers thrown to the side. She clutches her side. And that's when I see it—the blood pooling underneath her.

"Oh my God. Oh my God," I say.

She looks up at me. Her eyes are filled with pain. "Do something," she begs. "I need a hospital. Please, take me to a hospital."

I don't know what to do. I race to her side and put my hand on her head. She's clammy and covered in a sweaty film. The smell of copper fills my nose.

"I don't know what to do," I say.

"Just do something," she cries. Her tears intermingle with her sweat. Her eyes are wide. Her face contorted in pain.

"Um... um..." I scan the room.

I need John. He'll know what to do. He's got to help her. I run back out the door.

"Sarah! Sarah! Where are you going?" Her screams are desperate.

I fling open the front door. The alarm blares. He always told me if I triggered the alarm, it goes straight to his phone, and I'd never get away because he'd be here in five minutes. I hope it's true. I race back to her room. The alarm wails in my ears.

"What's happening?" she asks.

"I set off the alarm. It's the only thing I know that will bring him home," I say.

Her arms are wrapped around her stomach. She's moaning like a wounded animal, deep sounds coming up from her throat.

I run out and into the kitchen. I fill a bowl with water. Not too hot. I don't want to burn her. I grab towels and carry everything carefully back into her bedroom. I wet the towel and bring it to her forehead. I wet another and place it around her neck. I don't know if it will help, but I have to do something. I rub her back like I've seen them do on TV when someone is in labor. Her entire body is rigid. Every muscle contracted.

"Is this too hard?" I ask.

She doesn't respond.

I rush around the other side to look at her. Her eyes are open. Pupils wide and dilated. All the blue has disappeared. I wave my hand in front of her face. She doesn't even blink. I take her face in my hands, staring into her face.

"Ella, it's going to be okay. John is on his way. He'll know what to do. You're going to be okay."

The alarm stops.

"Sarah!" John's voice pierces the air.

I run into the hallway, pointing like a crazy person into the bedroom.

"It's Ella! Something's wrong with Ella! You have to help her!"

As soon as I say Ella, he starts to run. He's pushing past me before I even finish my sentence. He rushes to her side. There's no mistaking the blood. I've never seen so much blood. The pool grows larger and larger. He looks like he's afraid to touch her.

"Ella. Oh, Ella," he whispers, his voice thick with emotion.

"We have to do something," I say. "We've got to help her. She needs a hospital."

"We can't take her to a hospital."

"But she needs one. She's having a miscarriage."

He's just staring at her, his eyes as unfocused as hers.

"John!" I yell at him. "We have to do something." I keep repeating it until he snaps out of it.

"Okay. Okay." He runs his hands through his hair over and over again. I've never seen him lose his composure. "Help me lift her out of the bed."

He lifts her to a sitting position. She yelps. He puts one of his arms around her and pulls her to her feet. I race to her other side, putting my arm around her too. Her head flops against my shoulder. She's in too much pain to walk. We drag her through the bedroom and into the bathroom, leaving a bloody trail behind us. She alternates between moaning and crying.

"Fill the tub," John orders.

I turn the knob, plug the drain, and let the water fill.

He picks her up in his arms like she weighs nothing and carries her like an overgrown baby into the tub. He sets her down softly and carefully into the water. Blood rises up from between her legs. There's pieces of meaty flesh in it. Globs of her insides and what's left of the baby. I take a deep breath so I don't vomit.

John looks horrified. He stares at her like it's the first time he's seen her. I grab the glass from the sink and fill it with the water still pouring out of the faucet. I fill it and dribble it down her back. I do it rhythmically again and again.

"We should take her to the hospital." I try to persuade him one last time.

He just shakes his head.

"Do you have anything you can give her? Anything to help with the pain?"

He leaves without speaking.

"I'm sorry this is happening to you," I whisper to her while he's gone. I don't care if we're not friends. Nobody should have to go through this. "I wish I could help you. I do."

I reach out and grab her hand. She lets me hold it. Her hands are limp and lifeless. Her face is as white as the walls. "It's going to be okay. You're going to get through this."

John returns. He hands me a small pink pill. I take the glass I've been using to pour water on her back and fill it with cold tap water from the sink.

"Ella, open your mouth," I say.

She opens her mouth mechanically. I place the pill on her tongue. It sits there. She doesn't do anything. Her mouth is still wide open.

"Close your mouth."

She closes her mouth.

I bring the glass of cold water to her lips. "Swallow the pill with this." I pour the water into her mouth. It spills out, but she swallows. The pill goes down with it. "Get her another one. Whatever that is. She needs more of it."

We follow the same routine with the second pill. It looks like she's swimming in the Red Sea that I used to read about in Tiffany's Bible. It's disgusting. I drain the water from the tub, scooping up the pieces of her that are too big to go down the drain. I toss them outside the tub. I'll clean them up later.

I refill it again, making it hotter this time. I ease her back so she's not sitting upright and so rigid. Her muscles are beginning to relax. The pills must be working. They don't do anything for the pain in her eyes, but her body uncoils. I crouch next to the tub and rub her back until the water runs cool again.

ELLA

(NOW)

MY MOM STILL DOESN'T KNOW I'm the
one who killed my baby. She's against abortion no
matter what and she'd be horrified if she ever found
out I'd gotten rid of the life inside me. She thinks he did it. It's
better that way. I wasn't surprised when the doctors told me
I'd never be able to have children because there was too much
damage inside me. Randy made her leave the room because she
was crying so hard she couldn't get herself together.

I'm glad I can't have children. I don't want to bring a child
into this world. I used to think the world was a good place.
Now I know it was only a fairytale. Bad things happen and they
happen all the time. They're everywhere. You can't stop them.

Blake and Phil ask about the baby too. What happened to it?
How far along was I? I told them I don't know and that my baby
is circling in his pipes somewhere.

This afternoon they told me John's real name. Derek Hunt. I keep rolling the words around in my brain. Derek Hunt. I have no connection to it. He will always be John to me. Randy says it's okay if I don't use his real name just like I don't call Sarah her real name.

She also told me about what happened to Sarah. John didn't steal her. Her dad sold her to him. They all think she was his first victim and his kidnapping spree started with her. She was his guinea pig. The one he tried things out on until he worked up to taking other girls.

She won't tell me a lot about the details of what her life was like before. She says it's Sarah's choice to tell me and I should give her space. All she would say was that she was horribly abused and neglected by her father. It crushed Mom's heart all over again. If there was any chance of her not coming home with us, it's gone now.

Mom is as determined to save her as she is me. She's already working on different therapists and survivor groups we can go to when we get home. She doesn't understand that some wounds run too deep. She's convinced all we need is love and time. Oh, and God. God's grace will heal us too.

I don't have the heart to tell her my faith in God was the first thing I abandoned in the basement. In the beginning, I prayed so much I even did it in my sleep, begging for protection, guidance for the people trying to find me, and to watch over Mom. God had always been as real to me as the bed I slept in at night and the walls of my house. I'd carried my Bible in my backpack since kindergarten. He was my compass, always my due north. His job was to love and protect me from harm.

As time went on and things grew worse, it seeped in what I fool I'd been to believe. At first, I saw it as a test of faith. I'd always been taught God tested your faith, but it wasn't a test—it was torture. It boiled down to two options: God was real, present, and directly involved in our lives like I'd been taught or nothing I'd been taught was true and God wasn't real. He was either there and did nothing to help me or he didn't exist. I quickly decided there couldn't be a God because no God who was supposed to love me and had the power to intervene in my life would do nothing to save me. I didn't have to be scared of going to hell because of my unbelief. I was already there. I lived in it every day.

I want something to hold on to, but there's nothing there anymore. I feel like I'm flying or falling, never steady or planted on anything solid. I'm unstuck from the world around me. Now I just float in empty, vast darkness.

SARAH

(NOW)

"**H**AVE YOU EVER HEARD of Patty Hearst?" Randy asks.

I shake my head. I've refused to speak since my meeting with Blake and Phil.

"I want you to know you're not alone and there's other people who've been through what you've been through. There's even a name for your experience."

She talks about me like I have some kind of disease. I'm disappointed in myself. I promised John I'd never tell and keep all his secrets. I took my life before and locked it in a vault. There's no key, and even if there was, I wouldn't open it, but they keep insisting on prying it open. They'd gotten under my skin talking about my dad this morning. I screwed up and let my emotions get the better of me, but I won't allow it to happen again.

"Do you want to hear about Patty Hearst?"

It doesn't matter if I do, she'll still tell me. I don't respond.

Just like I predicted, she begins talking. "Patty Hearst was a nineteen-year-old girl who was kidnapped in college. She was kidnapped at knife point by a terrorist group. When they first took her, they kept her locked in a closet and blindfolded for weeks. They only let her out to eat. She didn't have any other contact with the outside world. She had to rely on the people who'd kidnapped her for everything. Much like John did with you."

He was only trying to train me. Girls have to be trained.

"They threatened to kill her numerous times. Eventually, they raped her. Repeatedly." She draws out the word *repeatedly* for effect.

I will myself not to react to the words she's throwing at me. It's what she wants me to do. Just like Blake and Phil. It's not going to work this time.

"After a while, they started letting her out for brief periods of time, but always with the threat of death unless she did what they said. Do you know what happened to her eventually?"

I pretend I don't care, but there's a small part of me that does.

She studies me for a few moments before continuing. "They gave her a different name. Tania instead of Patty. They indoctrinated her with their beliefs about the world and over time, she started believing them as her own. She even went so far as to start committing crimes with them for their cause. She robbed banks at gunpoint and was involved in shootings where people died. She tried to blow up a bank. She continued to pledge her allegiance to them even after she was arrested. It wasn't until weeks after that she was able to talk about what really happened. Patty Hearst had what psychologists refer to as Stockholm Syndrome and she's not alone. Neither are you. We see it play out again and again. Children are even more vulnerable to it than adults. And no matter how grown up you might think you are, you were still a child when John took you from your father. We also call it Survival Identification Syndrome. Do you know why?"

I don't trust myself to speak. I shake my head.

"We call it that because bonding and identifying with your captor is actually a very strong survival technique. People get so beaten down, tortured, and brainwashed that they believe there's no way out. They stop believing they'll be let free or escape so they create a new story for themselves and force themselves to believe it. It keeps people alive when they're terrified of their captor but completely dependent on them at the same time."

I'm not like the people she's talking about. I never wanted to escape. I didn't want to go back home because there wasn't a home to go back to. When my father and I weren't living on the streets, we lived in filthy crack houses or disgusting storage sites. We never had any plumbing and lived like savages. The only reason my father kept me after my mother died was to collect the benefits from the state and use me as a prop when he begged for money or to sell me out to his friends. That was it.

"I know what it was like for you with your father, Sarah." Her eyes meet mine.

At least she calls me Sarah. Blake and Phil refuse to. I hold my breath for what's coming next.

"I've read your social services file and hospital reports." She flips through the papers in the folder on her lap. "The first report was made when you were two-years-old. You had two broken ribs and a black eye. They removed you from him then. But your foster home wasn't any better, was it?"

She moves to sit next to me on my bed, getting closer to me than I would like. She always does that like she thinks being physically closer to me will bring us closer together emotionally.

"You're a really smart girl, Sarah, and I know you think I'm only talking to you so I can get information from you. That I'm out to get you. Punish you or see what kind of help you gave John, but I'm not." Her voice softens even more. "I'm actually here because I want to help you. Those guys?" She motions to the door where Blake and Phil are probably posted along with whatever law enforcement officers are out there. "They want to solve this case and will do whatever they have to in order to get the job done even if it means hurting you. And yes, if you're thinking they only pretend to care about you so they can get information, you're probably right. It's the downfall of doing what they do. If they got attached to every victim, they'd never be able to do what they need to do. But me?" She places her hand on top of my hand. "I care about you. Nobody should have to live through the things you've lived through. All you've ever known is abuse and betrayal. And you know what? Tracking down John will stop him from hurting other girls, but it's not going to do anything for you. It's not going to heal you and it's not going to help you find your way back to reality, but I can. I can help you, but you have to let me."

For a second—only a second—I almost start to talk and tell her everything.

ELLA

(THEN)

THE THROBBING PAIN WAKES me again, only slightly dulled by the pain pills they keep giving me. The last twenty-four hours are a blur. I can't believe I made it, but the constant pain is a continual reminder that I did.

That filthy thing is gone. It's no longer inside of me. My plan worked. John has no idea I did it to myself. He's barely been in to see me, but Sarah hasn't left my side. Every time I open my eyes, she's there. Putting a cool washcloth on my forehead. Rubbing my feet. Adjusting my bedding. She brings me my pills and washes them down with water. She spoon-feeds me her homemade chicken noodle soup.

We don't talk. Not a word.

I'm still bleeding. It hasn't stopped, but it's nothing like it was before. Every time I close my eyes, I see myself in the tub surrounded by red water. I wake up feeling like it's still covering me. I don't know if I'll ever get it off.

SARAH

(THEN)

IT'S BEEN FIVE DAYS since she lost the baby. She lays in bed all day staring at the ceiling. She barely blinks. I've cleaned the bathroom four times and scoured everything with bleach. I cleaned the tiles around the tub with a tooth brush, but every time I'm in there, I look down and am sure I see a speck I missed so I do it again.

I burned all the bedding in the fireplace. John gave me permission. He said he didn't want anything to do with it.

"Just get rid of all of it," he said.

I want to throw out everything in that room. The bed. The mattress. Even the carpet. I want to strip everything bare. I understand why she lays there like she's dead. I wouldn't be able to be in that room either. I keep wondering. Did the baby die in the bed? In the bathtub? Or did it come out in pieces? Some of it left there and some of it left in the drain?

Everything feels contaminated now and it's still there no matter how much I clean. Nothing bad happens in the house. It's why the girls never come upstairs until we can be sure they won't do anything. He never gets rid of the girls here either. All the killing happens outside. That's how it works. Upstairs is clean.

Now it's everywhere. I breathe it in. I feel like I'll choke on it.

I can't even sleep. All I do is dream about dead babies. They scream at me like they're being tortured. They won't leave me alone.

It's not like I killed the baby. It wasn't my fault. I didn't have anything to do with it, but it still feels like my fault somehow.

Everything is falling apart and slipping away. I feel fractured. I'm trying to follow my routines, but nothing feels right. It's all slightly off like I'm tilted one degree to the right of my equilibrium spot.

John isn't any help. I've never seen him like this before. He hasn't said anything about what happened. Nothing. He doesn't ask about her or me. He hasn't brought up Paige. He might have even forgotten she's down there. The poor girl. It's been over a week since she's been upstairs. What's he going to do with her? He never keeps them this long after he's done with them and she's been expired for a long time.

None of this makes sense. I don't know what to do. How can I make things right again?

ELLA

(NOW)

W E'RE FINALLY LEAVING. I'm going home. It's still hard to believe. They gave me a weird boot to help me walk so I don't have to use my crutches anymore. I keep waiting for someone to come in the room and tell us plans have changed.

Mom spent all morning scurrying around and delivering my flowers to other rooms in the hospital. She doesn't want to throw them away. She's taken the cards down from the elaborate collage of well wishes that she taped on the walls and put them in a box to take with us. She's only halfway through her thank you cards and hasn't wavered in her commitment to responding to every one. The walls look barren without them. The balloons have all been deflated and carried out with the trash. Our bags are packed. We're just waiting for Phil to show up because he's going to escort us home.

Sarah walks in with Randy. I haven't seen her in a few days. She looks nervous as she stands clutching a small bag close to her. It's weird to see her dressed in regular clothes. She's wearing a pair of jeans that are two sizes too big and a pair of flip flops with a big flower on the toe that must be from the gift shop on the second floor. Her t-shirt hugs her small frame. Her hair is pulled back in a ponytail.

"Hi," she says cautiously.

"Hi," I respond.

I still can't believe we're going to live together. Mom's talking about enrolling her at my school. She's been out of school since sixth grade so she's going to be in special classes and working with a tutor to get her caught up. Mom talks like I'm just supposed to step back into my old life like nothing's happened. She says the sooner I get back to normal activities; the sooner I'll start feeling normal again.

Mom arrives within a few minutes. She throws her arms around Sarah and gives her a squeeze. Sarah puts her arms around her like she's not quite sure what to do with her hands and pats her awkwardly on the back. It's weird to see them together.

The nurses and doctors all gather for our send off and clap as we walk down the hallway. Mom nestles herself between Sarah and I. FBI agents surround us with one leading the way and others trailing behind. They're taking us through the back way to an exit in the rear of the hospital, hoping to avoid the media which has kept a dedicated camp outside the hospital along with hundreds of other people obsessed with our story and getting a look at us.

They push open the heavy doors and within seconds, we're swarmed by microphones, flashing lights, and voices. They stand waving their cameras and microphones in the air like an angry mob at a rock concert. The officers form a protective circle around us, pushing them backward as they press in on us.

"Ella! Ella! Can you tell us where he held you?

"Do you have any suspects in custody?"

"How many girls?"

"How'd you escape?"

The questions surround us, one on top of the other. They fire their questions at us like bullets. I look down, covering my face with my arms. Sarah waves at the crowds, flashing smiles like we're celebrities on the red carpet. The officers usher us into a large black SUV with tinted windows. I'm breathing hard and my pulse pounds. They swarm the car like bugs, banging on the windows. It's so loud. There's arms everywhere. Sarah starts to roll down one of the windows on her side.

"What are you doing?" I yell.

Blake leans over and rolls the window up. The windows and doors lock. I jump at the sound. "Not a good idea," he says to her.

There's so many of them. They're everywhere. The car can't go anywhere without driving over them. And then I hear it. The sirens. I cover my ears and rock. Randy places her hand on me from the seat behind us.

"Just breathe," she reminds me. "It's just the police coming to break up the crowds and escort us out of here."

I can't breathe. There's too many people. Too many lights.

I close my eyes, trying to steady my breath. Before long, we're moving, edging our way through the sea of reporters and people. It takes ten more minutes until my breathing returns to normal and my heart stills. I don't open my eyes again until we've picked up speed and are cruising down the highway. I stare out the windows at rolling canyons and bright red rock formations jutting into the sky. Sweeping views of Simi Valley get further and further behind us as we speed down an expansive five-lane highway.

We're headed to Los Angeles because we're flying out of LAX. I always wanted to visit Los Angeles. It was on our list of places to visit, but this isn't how I imagined doing it. Sarah is staring out the window too, her eyes wide, taking it all in. The driver upfront turns on the radio as we turn onto the next freeway and classical music fills the car.

I freeze.

"Turn it off! Turn it off!" Sarah screams.

The driver fumbles to turn off the radio.

Mom places her hand on top of mine.

"It's going to be okay," she says. "We'll get through this."

SARAH

(NOW)

THE DRIVE IS LONG and makes me feel sick. Disoriented. There's too many people in one car. I don't like it. Ella doesn't either. She looks as uncomfortable as I feel. She's been leaning into Jocelyn with her eyes closed for the last hour but I don't think she's sleeping. Her body is too stiff.

I watch as we pass through terminals. I've never been on a plane before and it makes me nervous. All of this makes me nervous. We drive around lots of loops, each loop making my head spin even more. Finally, the car stops.

Blake comes around and opens all our doors for us. We're standing on a wide runway with the airport behind us. Planes roar over our head. I cringe. It's so loud. Everything is so loud. Ella's covering her ears. Jocelyn holds her up.

There's a small plane in front of us. We've got our own private plane because they didn't want to put us on a plane with so many people. They're still trying to keep us a secret, but I'm pretty sure our cover's blown. I hope the reporters got my picture and flash it on the news. I want John to see where I am. He needs to know I'm still with them. He knows where Ella lives. I wonder how long it will take for him to come get me. I still don't understand why he didn't follow through with the plan. I did my part and I have to trust him to do his. He knows what's best. He'll figure this out. He always does. I just have to be patient and stay strong.

A small door opens on the plane and stairs fold down. We trudge up the stairs in a single file line. There's twelve seats on each side and a tiny aisle down the center. Ella settles in next to Jocelyn. Some of the officers take seats behind her. Everyone is so much nicer to her than they are to me.

"How about here?" Randy points to the seats across from them.

I slide into the cramped space, taking a seat next to the window. The windows are a tiny hole and I can barely see out. Everyone is busy doing something, bustling around the plane. It's taking forever. The air is stale. There's a weird whirring fan above my head and I don't like it. It tickles my neck. I adjust my seatbelt again. It feels too tight. The doors close and we're sealed in. The plane begins to move. I grip my armrest.

"Are you okay?" Randy asks.

I nod my head, but I'm lying.

Ella begins to whimper. Jocelyn is holding her again, whispering things in her ear. As the plane moves faster and faster, Ella begins to cry harder and louder. The plane picks up even more speed and suddenly, we're lifted off the ground. Ella starts screaming. I wish she'd shut up. It doesn't help. Her screaming only makes it worse.

Randy leans over, trying to calm her down, but it's like she can't hear anyone. She's trying to unbuckle her seatbelt and get out. Jocelyn holds her down, but she's fighting against her. She's totally losing it.

I feel sick. Everything is moving so fast around me, but I'm still. The pressure of the plane is going to split my body in half. I'm so dizzy. I close my eyes, but it only makes it worse. Nausea assaults me, making me gag.

Randy reaches over and grabs a small brown bag in front of me. She hands it to me. "Are you going to be sick?"

I don't speak. I'll puke if I open my mouth. Each one of Ella's screams makes my stomach heave and my head spin. There isn't enough air in here. We're going to run out of air. My stomach heaves again. This time I can't keep the contents down and I put the bag over my mouth just in time. I wretch again and again. Suddenly, everyone is unclicking their seatbelts and moving fast around me. Some of them are attending to Ella.

"Give her this. Make her take this."

There's so many people around her I can't see what they're doing.

Randy hands me a pill. "This will help you relax."

I'm afraid to put anything in my mouth because it might make me throw up again but I do it anyway. She hands me a bottle of water to wash it down. I only take a small sip. My stomach is so weak. I lay my hands on my stomach, trying to calm my twisted insides. I stare straight ahead at the seat in front of me, focusing only on the dirty spot, trying to disappear into it like it's a black hole. My lids grow heavy. I don't fight them. I let sleep come.

ELLA

(NOW)

WE ARE FINALLY HOME. I breathe a sigh of relief that there's no reporters outside our house. I can't help but wonder how long it will last. Mom opens the door for our entourage and we step through the door. It's surreal, like stepping back in time.

The living room is filled with people who shout out, "Welcome home," instead of Happy Birthday. It stops me in my tracks. There's balloons and flowers everywhere just like in the hospital. A large banner hangs over the staircase and reads, "Welcome Home Ella and Sarah."

This isn't her home. It's mine.

Everyone cheers and claps, patting each other on the back and hugging like we're soldiers coming home from war. I scan their faces quickly. Half of my church is here. There's my Sunday School teacher and the youth pastor from the camp I volunteered with last summer. Some of my teachers from school are huddled by the fireplace. My teammates from cross country are sprinkled throughout the room. Jaycee's face breaks through the crowd and she runs toward me with her arms out wide. I step back before she can grab me. I don't know why. I just do it.

She stops. Her face falls in disappointment, but she quickly erases it and replaces it with a smile. "Hi," she says nervously. "I'm so glad you're home and safe." Her eyes fill with big tears as she stares at me.

"Thanks," I say stiffly like she's somebody I'm meeting for the first time instead of my best friend since second grade.

Mom moves into the crowd, engulfed by their outpouring of emotion. She's all smiles, hugs, and tears as she's passed from person to person. The bodies move together as they celebrate, breaking into groups to let Mom through.

I can't move from my spot. I look toward Sarah whose taking it all in with me. She looks tired and pale. Her lips are pressed tightly together and she's wringing her hands in front of her.

Jaycee glances back and forth between us. My eyes slide to the big clock above the fireplace to avoid meeting hers. Naomi and Parker emerge and come stand next to her, linking arms with her. I feel trapped and claustrophobic even though they're my friends. Jaycee and I were the closest and spent the most time together, but we all ran cross country and took the same honors classes so we hung out a lot. Their faces are perfect, bright, and clean. I never noticed how clear their skin was before and I don't remember them being so shiny, but they shine now, radiating their innocence. I don't want them to get too close because if they do, they might catch the disease rotting away my insides.

I have no idea what to say. My mind draws a blank. They don't know what to say to me either. Naomi coughs, Jaycee focuses intently on picking lint off her shirt, and Parker nervously chews on her fingernails. The silence stretches out between us. It's so awkward you can feel it.

Sarah finally speaks, easing the tension. "Hi, I'm Sarah."

"Hi," they respond in almost perfect unison, eager to have broken the silence.

"How was the flight?" Jaycee asks with too much enthusiasm.

Sarah and I exchange a look.

I shrug. "It was okay."

Randy said I had a panic attack on the flight. I don't know what happened. All I know is I felt like I was going to die as soon as the doors closed. There wasn't enough oxygen and I had the most primal urge to run, but I couldn't which only increased my fear. Everything spun around me and I almost passed out. They had to give me drugs to make it stop.

"Everyone is so glad you're back," Jaycee says, tentatively. "Everyone keeps texting me and asking if you're here yet."

I force a smile. It doesn't feel right on my face.

Mom comes up to us, her face flushed and cheeks wet with spent tears. She tries to scoop all of us up in an overgrown group hug. "Girls, why don't you go into the kitchen and get something to eat?"

The thought of eating turns my stomach, but I follow everyone into the kitchen. It's hard to walk with my boot, but at least it's easier than the crutches. Our small kitchen is covered with food crammed in every possible space. The counters are lined with casseroles and salads. The table is littered with more desserts than you'd find at a buffet. Jaycee, Parker, and Naomi grab a paper plate and start working their way through the food, piling their plates high. They look grateful to have something to do.

Sarah's eyeing the food. Mom told me she threw up on the plane and I can't imagine she feels like eating any more than I do. I pick up a plate and hand her one. Her face pales. We follow the three girls, but only fill our plates enough to be polite.

There's no room to sit at the kitchen table so we head back into the living room. Jaycee moves us through the crowd and I keep my head down. Everyone reaches out to touch me as I walk through and I cringe with each soft pat on the back or rub on my arm. It's a sea of arms reaching out to me like zombies and I have to bite my cheek to keep from yelling at them not to touch me. Whoever was sitting on the couch, jumps up and makes room for us.

Sarah and I sit next to each other on the lumpy brown couch we've had since I was in fourth grade. We balance our plates on our laps. The others surround the old trunk we use as a coffee table and sit on the floor cross-legged. Jaycee, Parker, and Naomi dig into their food immediately. They giggle and laugh, talking about school and the upcoming student council elections. Everyone is staring at us but trying not to and they're constantly moving like they've forgotten how to stand still. They extend smiles toward me with tearful faces. The room is filled with excited chatter, but it makes my head buzz.

All of it hurts. Their kindness. The voices. The laughter. The sounds of people chewing. I can hear them swallowing their food. The lights hurt my eyes. They're too bright. My body is uncomfortable. It doesn't fit on the couch. People are behind me and I can't stand them behind me, breathing down my neck. My heart races and my palms sweat against the plate I'm trying to keep from falling off my lap. The air starts to leave like it did on the plane and I'm gripped with fear. I don't want to lose it in front of them. I'm spinning again. I can't take it. I set my plate on the coffee table.

"I'm sorry, I'm sorry," I hear myself saying, not connected to my voice. I push my way through the crowd. I hit the stairs and grip the rail to keep from falling as I stumble up the stairs to get to my room and away from it all.

ELLA

(THEN)

SARAH PEEKS HER HEAD in my door.

"Do you want to come watch TV with me?" she asks.

I look at her in disbelief. She's never asked me to do anything with her. She only lets me out of the room to go to the bathroom. Why is she being nice to me?

"Um, sure?" It comes out sounding like a question.

I get up slowly. It still hurts to stand. I shuffle into the bathroom to change my pad first. I don't want to bleed on any of his things. I don't think the bleeding is ever going to stop. I wash my hands when I'm finished, avoiding looking at myself in the mirror like I always do.

I walk over to join her in the living room. I've never been in the living room before. We only walk through it on the way to the bedroom. Like every other room in the house, it's designed to perfection, like a staged home, and there's nothing personal about it. Nothing sentimental. No pictures. Nothing on the walls. The only thing hinting at comfort is the white sheepskin rug on the floor, but it's so clean it's hard to imagine anyone has ever walked on it. I'm nervous to sit on any of the furniture in case my blood seeps through. I dismiss the two stiff-back upholstered chairs next to the fireplace and settle on the long L-shaped couch. It's big enough to hold ten people. I sit at one end and Sarah sits at the other. It's not a couch you can sink into. It's stiff and doesn't give in to my weight.

A large flat screen TV hangs above the fireplace and it feels surreal as she flips through the channels. I eye her cautiously. Why is she doing this? I stare at the blinking light directly above the TV. It's like he's staring right at us. What's he going to say when he finds out she let me out of the room to watch TV with her? Maybe he told her to do it. I scan the room to make sure we're alone.

"What do you like to watch?" she asks.

It takes me by surprise. I haven't thought of TV in months. I can't think of a single show. I used to watch TV, but all my memories have vaporized.

"Um, we can just watch whatever you want to watch," I say.

She flicks through some more channels before settling on *Gilmore Girls*.

"I know it's old, but I just love this show," she says.

"That's cool," I respond like what's happening is perfectly normal.

What's Paige doing downstairs? Is there somebody else down there with her now? Does she know I'm still up here? Is she okay? Does she think I'm dead?

"How's Paige?" I ask.

She shrugs. "I brought her down her food this morning. She's pretty bored."

I take a chance. I might not have another one.

"Can I talk to her?" I ask.

She crinkles her face. "Why?"

"I just want to let her know I'm okay."

"I don't think that's a good idea."

I don't push. I settle back on the couch, but I can't get comfortable. I can't ever get comfortable anymore. The only time I feel good is when I'm asleep. I think about the wine in the cupboard and how good it would taste. I miss the way it made me feel.

"Do you think I could have something to drink?" I ask timidly.

"No," she snaps.

I fold my hands in my lap, trying to look casual but something is wrong. They have to be planning something. I scan the room, searching for John or other signs of what's to come.

"He's not here," she says as if she can read my mind. "If he was, we wouldn't be sitting here watching TV."

"Why are you doing this?"

"I don't know."

I study her face as she stares at the TV, trying to decide if she's telling the truth or not. She looks dazed like she's watching the screen without seeing anything happening. She looks unnerved. I've never seen her this way.

And then it hits me—he's not here. It's just us.

I don't think. There's no plan. No forethought. I just get up and start moving toward the glass door.

"What are you doing?" She sits up straight.

I don't say anything. Just keep stepping toward the door, gauging her response.

"Don't even think about it." She jumps up and runs to block the door. "There's an alarm, you idiot."

I stop in front of her. "So what? I'll be gone before he gets here."

She shakes her head. "No, you won't. He's five minutes away."

"I run fast." I don't know how I'll run when it hurts to walk, but I have to try. I might never get another chance.

Her eyes dare me to move. "Do you know how far the gate is?"

"I can make it," I say with more conviction than I feel. "Now move." I try to move around her. She plants herself and stretches her arms out even more.

"There's dogs out there. He's not lying. I've seen them." Her eyes are wild.

"You've been outside?" I can't hide my shock or disdain. I thought she was locked in here with us, but she goes out into the world? Any hope I had that she might be a nice person evaporates. She's just like him. She's as evil as he is. Rage seethes through me.

I shove her. She stumbles but stays rooted in front of the door.

"Don't. Don't do it." She shakes her head like a mad dog.

My insides are on fire, but I ignore them and push past the pain. We wrestle in front of the door, vying for control of the handle. I take my elbow and slam it into her gut as hard as I can. She falls back and in that second, I grip the doorknob and twist. The alarm wails. I sprint like a gun has just gone off.

SARAH

(NOW)

"ARE YOU COMFORTABLE? Can I get you anything else?" Jocelyn asks. They have an old-fashioned wooden futon that she opened up and made into a bed for me. She keeps fluffing my pillows, bringing the blankets up, and tucking them underneath me. "I'm sorry you don't have your own bedroom."

"It's okay," I assure her.

Their house is small and only has three rooms. One is Ella's and the other is hers. The third bedroom is a combination guest room, office, and storage space. There's stuff everywhere. An entire wall is covered in floor-to-ceiling bookshelves that are so full books are shoved on top of other books on the shelves. An old pine desk is wedged in one corner with stacks of paper on top and the other corner is filled with boxes marked *Christmas decorations* and *Goodwill*. Ella's diplomas, stretching from kindergarten through middle school, are framed and fill the center wall. With the futon unfolded, the space is so tight, you can barely walk through to get to the door.

"I didn't know I'd be bringing anyone home with us or I would've cleaned up in here. I'm sorry it's such a mess." She wipes her hair away from her face with the back of her hand.

"You don't have to keep apologizing. It's fine. Really."

She's so nervous and jittery around me. She second-guesses everything she does. There's been so many times today that she reached toward me like she wanted to touch me, but she didn't know where to touch me or if I wanted it so she just let her hand drop.

"Now, I'm in the room next to you and Ella is at the end of the hall if you need anything. Anything at all. Don't worry about waking me up." The crow's feet deepen around her eyes when she smiles. "I probably won't be sleeping anyway. I'll be a nervous wreck checking on you girls all night long." She points to the only window in the room, its blinds tightly drawn. "It doesn't matter that they're out there, I'm not going to feel safe until he's behind bars."

There's a squad car parked in front of the house. There's going to be someone there 24/7. Randy is staying in a hotel room close by and Blake is in the living room. Jocelyn made a bed up for him on the couch, but I'm not sure he plans on sleeping.

She pats the blankets again. "Oh, and I set a glass of water on the desk for you too. Just in case." She anxiously looks around the room.

"I'm fine. Really, I'm fine. Thank you for being so nice to me."

She's the kindest person I've ever met. Her eyes are so soft and warm she reminds me of an innocent puppy. Her friends were as nice as she is. After Ella went upstairs, they approached me one by one and introduced themselves. I let them hug me even though they're strangers because they seemed like they really wanted to. Some of them cried. All of them told me they wanted to help me in any way they could and said they'd be praying for me. It feels nice to have people care about me.

After telling me about the nightlights in the hallway and that she had a sleeping pill for me if I couldn't sleep for the third time, Jocelyn tiptoed out of the room and shut the door softly behind her. I listen to the sound of her footsteps down the hallway.

"Ella? Ella? Can I come in?" She's whispering but I can still hear her because our rooms are so close together.

Ella never came back downstairs. She stayed in her room for the rest of the night, refusing to see anyone. Not even her friends. I remember hearing about Jaycee. She used to talk to Paige about her all the time. I thought her friends would leave when she did, but they stayed close to me.

"Is it really weird for you to be here?" Parker, the one with the freckles sprinkled across her face, asked. She reminded me of a Strawberry Shortcake doll with her matching red hair and round face.

Jaycee slapped her arm playfully. "Of course it is."

She blushed. "Sorry, that was a stupid question."

I smiled. "No, it's okay. Don't worry about it. And yes, everything about this is weird."

They all giggled nervously.

Parker tried again. "Are you going to go to our school?"

"I think so."

"We'll help you at school if you need it. Some of the girls can be kind of mean," Jaycee said.

Everyone had been so kind and it didn't seem like they were faking it. I hated all the questions in the hospital, but I answered theirs all night long. It was much easier. They seemed genuinely interested in me and besides, their questions weren't about what happened at John's house. They wanted to know what I liked—food, music, movies, and books.

It was hard to know what to say because I don't know what I like. I'm not sure I even know who I am. Maybe I've never known. I like what John says I like. I do what John says is acceptable for me. And before that? I never had a choice either.

SARAH

(THEN)

S HE OPENS THE DOOR and runs, hurtling herself down the stairs and into the vast darkness. I slam the door, locking it tightly. I'm frozen to my spot. The alarms scream. They're so loud. I cover my ears.

"He'll be here soon. He'll be here soon," I chant out loud.

I imagine the dogs grabbing her, tearing apart her flesh with their sharp teeth. What will he do when he finds her running through the yard? She's never going to make it. Not in the condition she's in. It's too far and there's no way she's getting over that gate.

Sickening dread covers me. He's going to blame this on me because I let her out of the room and it's against the rules. In all of our years together, I've never broken the rules. I can't see outside. It's too dark. There's no lights. I strain to hear the sounds of the dogs, his voice, or hers, but all I hear is the alarms screeching.

How long do I wait? How long has it been? We've been through this scenario before, but only in practice. He's told me what to do. We rehearsed it. How much time?

I race into the kitchen. I stare at the clock on the microwave: 6:47.

He'll be here. He'll be here before I have to do it. I don't want to do it.

I love this house. It's the only home I've ever had.

And what about Paige?

I can't do it again. I still dream about Tiffany. Her screams jolt me awake. It doesn't matter where I sleep, she comes to find me there. I've relived that moment over and over again. I can't do it again.

John, where are you?

I stare at the digits: 6:47.

They're not moving. They're laughing in my face. Mocking me.

He'll be here soon. He's just outside taking care of Ella. Poor Ella. I feel sorry for her and the baby. Nobody should have to live through that. Nobody. I hope it's painless for her. Quick. It will have to be because he has to move fast. Unless he brings her back into the house.

He can't bring her back into the house. She'll tell him everything. She'll tell him I was the one who let her out. He can't know that. He can never know that. I'll tell him I let her out to go to the bathroom and that's when she did it, but he's going to see I let her watch TV when he reviews the video. What am I going to say then? Is there any way to erase the video? Where is he?

6:48

ELLA

(THEN)

I DON'T HAVE TIME TO THINK. I just run. I jump down the stairs, furtively looking around for the dogs. I don't see them. My feet hit the pavement and I sprint faster than any race I've ever been in. I hear them first, before I see them, but I don't waste time looking behind me. I just keep running.

There's a gate in front of me. My lungs are on fire. I ignore them. I look over my shoulder just as one of the dogs catches me and snags my sweatpants. I twist, leaving a piece of my sweatpants in his teeth. He whips it around like it's alive. The other one is behind him, snarling, baring its teeth at me.

I stop.

"It's okay. It's okay," I say in the calmest voice I can muster. I'm inching backward now. Slowly. Step by painful step. Everything hurts. I ignore the pain. The first one tosses my pant leg aside, bored with it. He's realized there's no flesh. They're both walking toward me now, eyes glowing yellow in the dark and teeth bared.

I will myself to stay calm and rational. Think. Breathe. They're only dogs. Just dogs. They're not monsters.

"Hi, I'm Ella." I keep my eyes focused on them. They're eyeing me cautiously. I smack into metal. I'm pinned against a wall. "Shh, shhh. It's okay. I'm not going to hurt you. It's okay."

It's just like other runs. I've had dogs chase me before. It's just like other runs.

The other one hears something and takes off barking and running in the opposite direction. I breathe a sigh of relief at my good fortune. I finger the material behind me. It's smooth. Flat. Cold and hard. I've made it to the gate. I frantically feel for anything I can grab or step on. I need something to help me scale the wall. There's nothing. It's slippery smooth.

I don't dare sneak a look behind me. I crouch down slightly, forcing myself to be still even though my muscles are straining to run. I stick out my hand only through the greatest exertion of will. "Shh... Shh... it's okay. It's okay."

He steps cautiously toward me and sniffs my hand. I hold my breath. He's got to smell the fear oozing out of me. He moves past my hand and begins circling me, sniffing all over. I start edging my way along the wall. I stay flat, only taking small shuffling sideways steps, holding back the urge to sprint. It's only a matter of time before the other one returns, or worse— John.

We move around the gate, the huge house always in front of us, the focal point of our circle. This place is huge. I keep moving. Step. Shuffle. Step. Shuffle.

"Easy boy, easy," I say with each movement.

He's following me cautiously, still not sure what he wants to do with me.

I spot a tree. It's not next to the gate, but it's close enough that some of the branches tower over the gate. I edge my way toward it. I don't take my eyes off the dog as I slowly wrap my arms around the base of the trunk. It's so wide, they can't encircle it. He growls. I start to hoist myself up.

I look away for a second and that's when he pounces. His teeth sink into my calf. Searing pain shoots through my body. I scream. I twist. He holds on. He's not letting go. I scream again. I scramble up the tree, kicking my leg. It does no good. My muscles rip and tear apart. I clench my teeth, forcing myself to stay conscious. The weight of him is so heavy.

I grab onto the branch above me and tear off a long stick. I strike him on the top of his head. It doesn't faze him. I scream and try to stab his eyes. I stab again and again. Finally, I connect. He yelps and lets go.

I scramble up the tree, ignoring the blinding pain in my leg. I climb higher and higher. He's at the base yelping and barking. The other dog joins him. I keep going, crawling out on one of the large branches extending toward the gate. I shimmy along carefully. It's high. I don't look down. I focus on getting closer to the gate. Nothing else. Soon, I'm above the gate. The edge is skinny. It's too narrow to jump on. I pull myself to crouching position, steadying myself. If I fall backward, I'm dead in the yard.

I take one last look behind me and then pitch myself forward. My wrist snaps as I hit the ground. I hear the bone break. Mind-numbing pain. White spots flash on and off in front of me. Hard concrete underneath me.

I'm over the wall. I'm the over the wall.

I force myself to stand, holding my wrist against my side limply. I clench my teeth together and move, hobbling down the street. There's headlights in the distance. I run to the side of the road and throw myself into the ditch. I tumble down. The road is too dangerous. He might be up there. I start to crawl. I have to keep moving. Just keep moving.

ELLA

(NOW)

THEY REFUSE TO LEAVE me alone. They've been coming up to my room all morning. Mom twice. Randy once. I don't want to, but I force myself to get out of bed. Last night, I got to sleep in my own clothes. My favorite pajamas hung on me, I've lost so much weight. I had to flip over the elastic waist to keep them from sliding down. I slip on my track hoodie and pull it up over my head, stuff my hands in the front pocket, and shuffle down the stairs.

Mom, Randy, and Sarah are already in the kitchen. It's disorienting to see them in my house. Randy and Mom look up at me. Sarah stares into her mug.

"Finally, sleepyhead," Mom exclaims. "Are you hungry?"

I shake my head.

"But you haven't eaten anything since yesterday. I can make oatmeal."

I turn up my nose.

"Or toast with peanut butter? Cereal?"

"I said I'm not hungry." It comes out sounding angry even though I didn't want it to.

I walk to the coffee maker and pour myself a cup. I join them at the table, staring at the refrigerator. My report card from last semester is still hanging there with my cross country schedule next to it. Both are hung with the magnets I made in elementary school with polymer clay. One says *Home Sweet Home*. The other is supposed to be a flower but looks more like a dilapidated windmill. Mom's had them for so long the colors are fading.

"How are you feeling?" Randy asks.

I shrug.

"Did you sleep okay?" she asks.

"I guess," I say.

I wouldn't call what I did sleeping. Half the time I couldn't tell if I was asleep or awake. Every sound sent me into a panic. I don't remember our house being so noisy but it creaked all night long. I heard every car driving down our road and the slightest rustle outside of my window sent me into a frenzied search for something out there. I must've looked out the window at least five times.

"Blake and Phil are on their way," Mom says.

As if on cue, there's a knock on the door.

I jump.

Mom lets them in. "Can I get you some coffee?"

They each hold up travel mugs from Starbucks. Mom ushers them into the kitchen. "Are you hungry? Can I get you anything to eat?"

They decline. Mom bustles around the kitchen, wiping off the counters and putting the dishes away from whatever food people ate last night. Sarah jumps up to help. She walks over to the sink and grabs the towel draped over the stove. She picks up a dish and starts drying it.

Mom grabs the towel from her hand. "Oh sweetie, thanks for your help, but that's fine. It's okay. I've got this. Why don't you take a seat? The detectives want to talk to you girls."

The kitchen is cramped with too many people, but its where we've always had our important conversations. Randy gets up, giving her seat at the table to Phil. Blake motions to Randy and they step into the living room and speak to each other in hushed whispers.

All I could think about in the basement was going back home and getting back to my life like the basement was a bad dream and I'd wake up from it like you wake up from all your bad dreams, especially the really bad ones—sweaty, heart pounding, breathing hard, and scanning the room to see if the bad guy is still there. You breathe a sigh of relief and slowly relax once you realize the nightmare is over. But this nightmare is never going to be over.

Phil wastes no time getting down to business. "We have some news on the case." He gives all of us a moment to prepare ourselves before continuing. Mom grips the countertop. "The remains found at the crime scene have been positively identified as Paige. Her family was notified last night. It won't be long until the media gets wind of it and we wanted you to hear it from us first."

"No!" Sarah cries.

I whip my head to face her. "Why do you even care?"

"Because..." she stammers. Her cheeks flush with embarrassment. "Because I do."

"Ella, that's not nice," Mom says to me in the same voice she used when I was a little girl and didn't want to share my toys with someone I was playing with.

"Nice? I'm not nice?" I point to Sarah. "Do you know how mean she was to us?"

Randy interjects, "When young girls are victimized, they often do whatever they need to in order to survive the situation. It doesn't always make sense, but whatever Sarah did, she did it to survive."

"Seriously? She helped him. For years. She never stopped him."

I want to slap the tears off her face. How dare she cry for Paige now?

Mom rushes to her side and puts her arms around her. Sarah buries her face in her shoulder. I jump up and slam my chair into the table. The coffee mugs shake. I turn to Phil. He hasn't moved. He's watching the events unfold around him, observing us like a scientist.

"Did she burn?" I ask.

"We're unsure how she died, but yes, her body was burned. We don't know if she was dead prior to the fire or if it was the fire that killed her." He struggles to keep the emotion out of his voice.

I'm sick to my stomach. This is all my fault. Blame washes over me. I did this. All of it.

SARAH

(THEN)

6:57

H E ' S   N O T   B A C K . He's supposed to be back and
he's not back. I have to do it. I don't want to do it, but
I promised him I would. I promised him if it ever came
down to this, I'd do it.

I walk slowly into his office. I open his laptop on his desk as
if I'm in a trance. I log in with the password he gave me years
ago. For a while, he quizzed me on it every night. I watch as
my fingers type it in. I go to the folder and open the program.
The display opens up. All I have to do is push the button now.

My heart is pounding. Images of Paige lying downstairs on
her cot flash through my mind uninvited. She's probably curled
up reading a book. Something she's already read three times.
She has no idea what's happening up here or what's about to
happen to her.

I couldn't save Tiffany. It had to be done. But I can save
Paige. I can.

I race back out of the office and down the hallway to the basement. I tug on the door. It's locked tight. Of course it's locked. He never leaves it open and I don't have the access code. It's the one thing he never gave me. He always refused. She can't even hear me if I called out to her and gave her some kind of warning. I could press the intercom, but what would I say? *Paige, you're about to die.* And then what? Maybe it's better that I can't warn her.

I slide down on the floor, bringing my knees up to my chest and wrapping my arms around them. Where is he? Why isn't he coming? None of this makes sense. The alarm wails. I stare at the front door, gaping open. I could just follow Ella. I could try to run too. But there's no place for me to run. I have nowhere to go. I shake off the thoughts, beating myself up for being weak. He chose me because I'm strong. I can do things other people can't. I have to be strong and if I don't follow through, he won't take me with him when he comes back. He'll never trust me again.

I walk slowly back to the office. The system is still blinking at me, asking me the question. All I have to do is click yes and it'll be done. Over the years, the girls have always argued over stories they've heard about the walls being wired with bombs. I would never give them a definite answer, but the truth is—yes, they're wired. They're programmed to explode.

I click yes.

Instantly, a loud boom like a firecracker goes off downstairs. I run for the door and race down the stairs to the driveway.

ELLA

(THEN)

PART OF ME WANTS TO STOP because the pain is so intense. I can't even tell where it's coming from anymore. Everything hurts. I pause to catch my breath and then force myself to keep crawling. It feels like I've been crawling for hours in this ditch, but I can't go on the road. It's too risky.

And then I see a gate. Another barricaded home. I can barely walk as I emerge from the side of the road, frantically searching and scanning for any headlights. There's an intercom on the side of the gate. I press it. My fingers are caked with dirt.

Nothing.

I press it again.

Nothing.

Then, I start frantically pressing it over and over again so close together nobody has a chance to respond.

"Help! Somebody help me! Help!" I scream so loudly it hurts my throat.

Finally, there's a voice. Not from the intercom but from behind the gate.

"What's going on?" a male voice demands.

"Please, please, you have to help me." I'm sobbing through my screams.

"Miss, are you okay? What's going on?" He still doesn't open the gate.

I pound on it with my fists. "Please! Hurry! He's going to come. He's going to find me! You have to let me in. Help me!"

The gate slowly opens inward. I race inside. A tall man stands staring at me. He's holding a flash light and stares at me in bewilderment.

"Shut the gate! Shut it!"

"Miss, what's going on?" He moves toward me.

I collapse in front of him.

When I open my eyes, there's a police officer shining a flash-light into my eyes. The man is off to the side talking to the man. I grab the police officer's arm, clutching on to him. "Please, please help me. He's coming. He's coming."

"Who's coming? What's your name?" he asks.

"Ella. I'm Ella Stevenson. He kidnapped me."

He stares at me for a moment. "Wait here."

He walks over to his partner. I curl myself into a ball. Sirens are in the distance. They're getting closer. He walks back over with his partner.

"Ella, the paramedics are on their way. You're safe now. We're going to help you," he says. "I'm just going to put you in the back of my car until they get here."

ELLA

(NOW)

I AM A MURDERER. I KILLED A BABY and I killed
Paige. It doesn't matter how many times Mom comes in my
room and tries to comfort me or Randy says none of this is
my fault. Their words don't reach me and even if they did, they
don't have any meaning. They don't know the truth.

Mom and everyone still thinks John butchered my insides to
get rid of the baby. They don't know it was me and for some
reason, Sarah hasn't told them. She's keeping the secret too.
And yes, I didn't pull the trigger to blow up the basement, but I
might as well. I knew that trying to escape put her in danger. It
put all of us in danger. I hoped we'd all get out, but there was
always the possibility they wouldn't, and I chose myself. I killed
Paige to save myself.

They're meeting downstairs again. Everyone split into different rooms. They're on a rampage to find John since he's moved
from a kidnapper to a murderer. Blake's got Sarah cornered in

the living room unleashing rapid-fire questions like he does. Phil's in the kitchen with Mom combing through my Facebook and Instagram accounts for what seems like the hundredth time. I can't stand to look at those pictures anymore. The smiles. The brightness. The happiness. I look so innocent and pure. Untainted.

People keep stopping by. I hear the knocks at the door continually and Mom's voice greeting and inviting them inside. They keep bringing us food like she forgot how to cook.

It's been like this for the last three days. I haven't gotten out of bed other than to use the bathroom since the news about Paige. I haven't showered or eaten. I just lay here in nothingness, staring at my bedroom wall. I've unplugged my brain, detached it completely. I lay for hours drifting into sleep. I wake up crying just so I can cry myself back to sleep again.

Mom keeps trying to get me up. Come downstairs. Eat. Do something. Anything.

But I just can't.

It's like when John first started raping me. I gave up. It wasn't a decision or anything I thought about. It just sucked all the life out of me. It's the same way now. There's no reason to get up.

Mom loves me and hates seeing me like this. I wish I could change it. At least for her sake, but I can't. She touches me like I'm made of glass and if she pushes too hard, I'll break. But I'm already broken. Irreparably broken. It's only a matter of time before she realizes that.

SARAH

(THEN)

I WATCH AS THE REST of the house goes up in flames. There's so much smoke. Flames leap out every window. Every now and then, the firecracker sound. Something else exploding. The heat scorches my face. It's so hot. The flames dance toward the sky. Billows of smoke.

Still no John. Where is he? He's supposed to be here by now. We're supposed to be gone. On our way to a faraway country with new names and identities. That's what he said. What he promised. I refuse to believe he's not coming back to get me. Something just went wrong. He wouldn't leave me. I'm too important to him. He needs me.

The sirens are getting closer and closer. It was only a matter of time before someone noticed the smoke no matter how faraway the neighbors might be. They're outside the gates yelling at each other. More sirens. More voices. There's a loud crash followed by others. I watch as the gate comes down. They bash it with huge clubs and axes. Once they have a small opening, they drive one of the fire trucks right through it, ripping the gate to shreds and scraping their truck as they plunge through.

I can't move. I stand watching them as they move into action. They're scrambling around like ants, winding and unwinding, jumping, running. Everywhere. They're everywhere.

A man runs up to me. He says nothing, just grabs my arms and throws me over his shoulders like I weigh nothing. He carries me down the driveway and sets me down.

"Is anyone else inside?" he asks.

I shake my head, too afraid to speak.

"Do you live here?" he asks.

I nod.

"Who lives here with you?"

"Just me and my dad," I respond exactly like he told me to.

"And your dad isn't in the house? Are you sure?" His walkie-talkie cackles.

"Yes, I'm sure. He's at work. He should be here soon."

He has to be here soon. He promised. The ambulance arrives and the paramedics rush to surround me. They strap an oxygen mask on my face, but I swat it off. I don't need oxygen. They start trying to put me on a stretcher.

"Wait, what are you doing? Where are we going?" My voice is frantic.

The EMT responds. "We're taking you to the hospital. It's standard procedure. We need to get you checked out."

"No. I don't want to go. Please, I have to wait here for my dad." I swing my legs over the stretcher about to jump down. He stops me and pushes me back on the stretcher.

"Your dad can meet us at the hospital. You need to come with us. We have to get you out of here. It's not safe."

"No!" I'm yelling now. I can't help myself. They can't take me with them. This isn't part of the plan. I'm supposed to wait. He's supposed to come get me. "No! John!" I scream louder each time I say his name.

They start putting straps around me. Just like the basement. I'm trapped. Everything is moving so fast. They can't take me away. They can't. They lift and slide me into the back of the ambulance. The doors slams shut behind us.

"Just try to calm down. Everything is going to be okay," he says.

"John!"

ELLA

(NOW)

MOM AND RANDY ARE OUTSIDE my door again. They think I can't hear them, but I can even though they're trying to whisper.

"If you rush her, it will only hurt her. It might make her withdraw even more into herself," Randy whispers. "We might not be able to pull her back. We don't want that to happen. Just go downstairs. Let me check on her."

I can't hear Mom's response. In a few seconds, I hear footsteps walking away. Then, a knock at the door. It's Randy's voice.

"Ella? Is it okay if I come in?"

I say nothing.

She comes in anyway. She walks over to the space between my bed and the wall. She plops down on the floor so she's eye level with me. Her breath in my face smells like hamburger and cheese. I want to gag.

"I just wanted to check on you and see how you're doing."

I stare at her without really seeing her and don't bother to respond. I wish they'd all quit asking me how I'm doing.

"I'm worried about you." Her face tenses, drawing wrinkles in her forehead. "I know you're going through a lot right now and it's probably difficult to share with your mom what it's like because I know how much you love her and want to protect her, but you can tell me. There's nothing you can say to me that would surprise or shock me. Believe me, I've heard it all."

My pain is too big for words. Silence stretches out between us. Mom can't handle it when I don't say anything and eventually, she just starts rambling. But not Randy. She sits patiently, waiting for me to talk, but I can't.

"I imagine you feel very alone right now and I just want to be here for you in whatever way I can." Her eyes glisten with unshed tears. "Why don't we try something small?" She puts her arm on the bed next to me and sticks out her pinkie. "How about you see if you can just hold my pinky?"

I don't move.

She wiggles it in front of me. "Come on. It's just a pinky. You can hold a pinky."

I stick out my hand and link my pinky with hers. The human contact makes me start to cry. She doesn't move to hug me or tell me it's going to be okay like Mom does. She's just there while I weep quietly.

"I know it's tough having Sarah here," Randy says softly, choosing her words carefully. "I don't want you to think I'm saying anything bad about your mom because she's a great person and has a huge heart. She loves you so much and when she looks at Sarah, all she can think about is how much she would want someone to help you if the situation was reversed. I understand why she feels that way. She comes from a sweet place and just wants to help, but remember how I advised against this in the hospital?"

I nod.

She continues. "This is why. I was afraid having Sarah in your home would affect you like this. It must feel like you're being violated all over again and in the space that was the most sacred to you."

"I hate it." I almost choke on the words. "I hate it so much. I can't stand that she's here. I can't get away from her. She's everywhere. Sitting on my stuff. Eating our food. Having coffee with my mom. Seeing the way she acts with my mom is the worst."

Randy's eyes fill with compassion. "Sarah is a victim too and needs help as much as you do, but it doesn't mean putting the two of you together is the best solution."

"Everyone looks at her like she's this sweet innocent victim, but she isn't. She chose to be there. Chose it." I don't know why it's so hard for everyone to see that.

"I don't expect Sarah's behavior to make sense to you, but it's very common for girls like her who are abducted so young to act the way she did. To help their captors. Even love them. However, I want you to know that it's okay to feel whatever you need to feel about her right now, even hate her if you need to. There's nothing wrong with your feelings." She lays her chin on the bed. "Are you hearing what I'm saying?"

"I am." I force a smile.

"Good." She looks pleased. "I'm sorry that she's here and that your mom didn't listen to you about it or respect your wishes."

"What does Mom think is going to happen? Is she just planning on letting her stay with us forever?"

I won't be able to handle it if she does. I see him every time I look at her.

"I hope not. I've tried to talk to your mom about it. Not just at the hospital, but since we've been back too. She's determined to give Sarah a home and thinks this is the best place for her even if I disagree. How about this—why don't we set aside some time and talk to her about it again together?"

"I don't think she'll change her mind. I told her how I felt about it when we were in the hospital. It wouldn't be anything new." It still hurts that she insisted on bringing her home with us even when I begged her not to.

"It might make a difference now that you're home and she's seeing how it's affecting you. It can't hurt to try another time. What do you think?"

I shrug. "I don't know. My mom doesn't really even know me anymore. She still thinks I'm a good person, but I'm not."

"What makes you say that?"

I take a deep breath. "She doesn't know about the things that happened there and she acts like Paige isn't my fault, but she is." Saying her name makes me start crying all over again.

"Why is Paige your fault?"

"I knew she might die if I tried to escape and I did it anyway."

"Did he threaten to kill her if you left?"

"No. Paige warned me not to try and escape, though. She told me the basement was wired with bombs but I didn't believe her because everything about the basement was passed down second hand from other girls so we never knew what was true or not. We were always trying to figure out which stories were real and which ones weren't. Like the dogs. Paige told me she heard he had dogs with rabies patrolling the yard in case one of us got out. Supposedly, he starved the dogs to keep them hungry and only fed them raw meat, but I never saw them when I looked out the windows so I always thought it was just something he said to scare one of the girls and the story had grown as it travelled down the line."

She doesn't interrupt with any questions. She patiently waits for me to go on. I swallow the emotions in my throat before continuing.

"I never believed her about the bombs either. On one of my first days locked in the basement, Paige told me there were bombs in the walls. I remember thinking, bombs? How would you even put bombs in the walls? I thought it was just another threat to keep us afraid." I pause, assaulted with memories of what it was like when he first took me. "She always said, if we tried to run or got out of hand, he'd blow up the basement and everyone would die. I didn't believe her. But she was right and I set them off when I left. I killed her. I killed Paige." I pull my pinky away, tucking my arm underneath me. I don't want to be touched anymore.

"You didn't kill Paige," she says.

"I did. Please, don't try to make me feel better."

"I'm not. You didn't kill her. Yes, she died in the fire, but you didn't trigger the bombs by opening the door."

I sit up so fast it makes me dizzy. It takes a second for my head to quit spinning. "I didn't? How do you know?"

"The explosives in the basement weren't linked to the house alarm system. They were linked to an external source for detonation. Someone had to activate the system and you were already gone so you couldn't have done it. It had to be Sarah or John."

It doesn't make me feel any better. "Still, if I didn't leave, they wouldn't have blown the place up."

It's true. She can't argue that. It's still my fault no matter what she says.

"I can understand how you could feel that way and nothing you're going through right now is unusual. It's extremely common for victims to blame themselves. But I want you to understand something—it's not your fault that Paige is dead. There's nothing you could've done to save her." She pauses, making sure I'm paying attention to what she's saying. "She would've died even if you stayed. The only difference is that you would've died with her."

"What do you mean?"

"It'll take a long time before we have any definitive answers, but John didn't let the girls go. None of them were returned to their families. He killed his victims after he was done with them. None of you would've survived even if you hadn't escaped." She lowers her voice. "Paige's remains weren't the only remains found on the property."

SARAH

(NOW)

I CAN'T STOP STARING AT JOCELYN. I'm fascinated with her. I've seen moms on TV before, but I've never had one myself. I don't even know what my mother looked like and the foster mothers I had weren't real mothers. They were only interested in collecting the check they got for allowing me to stay there. Most of them didn't even care about their own kids, especially not kids like me that were picked up from the streets.

Nobody cares about street kids. Maybe when we're young, little, and cute, but as soon as you reach a certain age, everyone looks at you with the same disgust they give your parent, like somehow you're choosing to be homeless too.

But Jocelyn is different. She treats me like I'm a real person. One with feelings and thoughts. Ideas and interests. She never forces me to talk which actually makes her easy to talk to.

She has to be exhausted but she hasn't stopped taking care of people since we got here. She's constantly on her feet. She bustles around the kitchen making sure the coffee never runs out and rotating the food from the fridge to the counter. The phone rings constantly. Mostly, it's people from the media asking for interviews, but she won't turn it off because sometimes it's their friends calling to see how they're doing. Everyone asks about me too. It's not just Ella they care about. It feels weird to be grouped with them like I'm part of the family.

She's always smiling and stopping to ask people how they're doing. She's gotten comfortable touching me. She rarely walks by without reaching out for me in some way, patting my head or touching me on the back softly. She reaches out and squeezes my hand whenever she thinks I might be uncomfortable. It's like she doesn't want me to forget she's there. A safe feeling comes over me every time she touches me. I fantasize about what it would be like if she was my real mother, how it would be to grow up with her touches, her reassuring looks, and her comforting words.

Their house is so different from John's. It's not just that it's so much smaller, but that it's lived in. You can feel the love and it's cluttered with pieces of them. There's framed pictures everywhere. I've seen Ella at every age. There's pictures of them together smiling in front of oceans and mountains and an entire wall devoted to Ella's artwork in the hallway leading to the bathroom.

The living room is comfortable and inviting. John's living room was beautiful but you could never relax, not like theirs where you just want to grab a book and curl up by the fire in one of the throw blankets they knitted themselves. The mantle is lined with personal touches—shells and rocks they collected at the beach and on walks, misshapen vases they made at a pottery studio, and stacks of travel magazines with the pages marked on places they want to visit. The couch swallows you up when you sit in it. The coffee table in front is a trunk carried over by their ancestors from Sweden.

The kitchen is no different. The fridge is covered with magnets and Ella's schedules. There's a Formica table John would hate and appliances that aren't sparkling, clean stainless steel. Spices fill small jars on a shelf above the stove and pots hang from hooks next to the refrigerator. Plants grow in one of the corners next to the window where they get the most sunlight and they add even more life to the room. Everything about this place is quietly comfortable.

Jocelyn's been trying to keep our spirits up since the news about Paige. It's cast a shadow over our homecoming. It doesn't help that Ella stays locked in her room. She doesn't even come downstairs to eat meals with us. It's worrying Jocelyn. She looks wistfully at the stairs every few minutes just waiting for her to make an appearance. I can tell she's been crying whenever she comes back downstairs after she's tried to get her to come down. I don't like how sad it's making her when she's already been through so much. Last night she told me all the things she did to try to find Ella and bring her home.

It was hard to hear because nobody ever looked for me. There were no searches. No candlelight vigils. My face wasn't plastered on flyers around the neighborhood. I wasn't on the news. I disappeared and nobody cared. It was like I didn't exist. There's nobody for me to call and tell I've been found because nobody's looking for me.

Not even my real father. I never let myself think about him. I buried him a long time ago, but Blake and Phil resurrected him. Everyone knows I'm the girl that nobody wanted and they can't hide their pity. They don't even try. I can see the "poor girl" in all their looks. It's why they're all so kind to me. They feel sorrier for me than they do for Ella.

My story is worse because my own father gave me to John. I keep telling them I don't remember the day, but I do. I remember how my dad took me into the bathroom at the homeless shelter we'd been staying at that month and washed my face. I sat on the toilet very still, soaking in his attention because he never touched me unless he was punishing me. I didn't tell him I was old enough to wash my face myself.

He'd told me the night before we had a special errand to do together. Most of the time, he forgot I was even there. He was always leaving me places and forgetting to come back for me even though he promised he would. One time he left me behind a dumpster for three days. I stayed because he'd told me to and I always did what he said, but I was terrified. I crawled underneath the dumpster at night when it got dark and stayed there until morning. I was only five.

He held my hand like a friend that morning and he'd never held my hand that way. Usually, he only grabbed it if he wanted me to hurry or to drag me somewhere I didn't want to go. He held it like he cared that day. I remember how I marveled at the way my hand fit in his and how our fingers were the same shape. I was hoping he was finally getting sober and we were on our way for him to check himself into a rehabilitation center that let people keep their kids with them while they were there. One of the other moms at the shelter had told me all about it. I skipped along next to him, excited for the possibility of starting our life over.

My heart leapt when I saw we were walking toward the park because I thought he was finally taking me there to play after all the times I'd asked him to. We frequently panhandled in the park with others in our crew and I would stare for hours at the other children as they scampered up and down the playground equipment, wishing I could be them. I'd beg to go, but he never let me. I'd long ago given up pining over the park, but I got excited that he was going to try to make up for it. It'd be weird to play on the equipment because I'd be the biggest kid there and nobody my age played at the park anymore, but I was willing to do it if it made him happy.

Instead of stopping at the equipment, he picked up the pace. My hope faded as we walked to the left edge of the park where all the crackheads hung out behind the bathrooms. I gripped his hand tighter. I hated crackheads, the way their eyes bugged out of their head and how they twitched around like someone was shocking them, always talking but none of it ever making sense. My excitement evaporated. It was going to be just like any other day.

The man who liked to give us money at the shopping mall appeared. He was dressed in jeans with holes in the knees and a baseball cap pulled low like he was trying to blend in, but he stood out because his clothes were clean and he had tennis shoes on his feet. Most of them didn't wear shoes or if they did, they were held together with tape. He stepped toward us. Him and my dad shook hands. My dad's eyes nervously darted around. He let go of my hand and I felt the absence immediately. I fingered the palm of my hand where his sweat had met mine.

"Do you have it?" my dad asked.

The man nodded. He pulled out an envelope from his back pocket and handed it to him. My dad quickly opened it and counted the bills. He slid it underneath his pants straight into his underwear where he hid all his important things. He put his hand on my back and pushed me toward the man. "Petra, you're going to go with him."

The man reached out and grabbed my hand. His grip was tight. I twisted around to look at my dad.

"Dad, I don't want to go with him. I want to stay with you," I pleaded.

He never let me go with his friends. He always had to be there too. This guy didn't look like one of his friends, but I didn't want to go with him either.

His voice was stern and punishment loomed in his eyes. "Do as you're told. No arguing. Go!" He motioned toward the man.

"Dad," I cried out again, but he was already walking away, moving his way quickly through the people.

The man peered down at me. His eyes were a crystalline blue. "There's nothing to be afraid of, sweetie," he said. "I'm going to take good care of you."

I don't like to think about that day, but it comes back every time they mention Enrique. I used to think it was what made me special and set me apart from the other girls. He'd stolen them, but he'd paid for me. Now, I'm not so sure.

ELLA

(NOW)

TOMORROW NIGHT THE COMMUNITY is
throwing a big welcome home party for Sarah and me
at the church. My grandparents are going to be there
along with my uncle Jack and his family. I don't want to go, but
Mom isn't giving me a choice. She says it will be good for me.

I've been waiting for the last two hours to make sure everyone is asleep. It's been over an hour since Mom left Sarah's
room and retired to her own. She goes into Sarah's room every
night after she leaves mine and stays for a long time. I don't
know what they talk about and I don't care. Randy and I still
haven't talked to Mom about her not being there. I think Randy
is nervous about it so she's avoiding it.

Mom never liked her opinions at the hospital and she's grown
even more resentful toward her now that we're home. She still
treats her nice and politely because Mom would never be mean to

her, but I know when she's just pretending and she's definitely faking it. I'm sure Randy can sense it too.

I get up and tiptoe to my door, opening it carefully. The hallway is lit. Mom put night lights in all the outlets so we wouldn't be afraid in the night and Sarah could find her way to the bathroom. Both their doors are shut. I creep down the hallway, thankful the carpet muffles any sound. The stairs are a different story. They're old and wooden.

I take them one step at a time. Each creak freezes my heart and I strain to hear Mom calling out for me. It's not like she'll be mad or anything. She'll just be worried that I'm up in the middle of the night and no matter what I say, she'll insist on staying up with me. She can't stay up with me. I need a drink. Ever since I had the idea, it's all I've been able to think about.

I make it safely down the stairs without waking anyone up. It doesn't take long for my eyes to adjust to the darkness. I peek out the window just to make sure the squad car is there. I breathe a sigh of relief to see them parked with their lights off in front of our house. I can't help but wonder what it will be like when they're not keeping watch over us at night. They can't guard us forever. What happens if they never find John? I push the thought away.

I plod into the kitchen and head straight for the liquor cabinet. Mom isn't a big drinker. She never has more than one and even with only one, she starts to get giddy. She always has alcohol, though, for special occasions. She likes to make a Kahlua and coffee drink on Thanksgiving and Christmas and there's always a bottle of wine for when her friend Greta comes over. They're old friends from college. I hop up onto the counter and open the cabinet.

I grab one of the bottles of wine. It's the one that's already opened since I'm not sure how to open a bottle of wine. Sarah or John always did it. I'm about to hop down when I decide to grab a bottle of vodka too. I've never even seen her serve it and don't know anyone who drinks it. The only thing I know about vodka is that you aren't supposed to be able to smell it on someone's breath, at least, that's what I've heard the kids at school say.

I hug them close to me and head back upstairs. I'm just as careful on my way back up. I shove the bottle of vodka underneath my bed and plop on my bed with the wine. I can't unscrew the top fast enough. I take a long drink. It's sweet, much sweeter than the wine I used to drink with John, but I don't care. It feels good just to hold the bottle in my hands and feel the liquid going down my throat, leaving a warm trail throughout my body.

I sit with my back against the headboard savoring each sip. It's the first time I've been able to breathe since I got home. It doesn't take long for it to begin to work its magic just like it used to. My head starts to get fuzzy, all of my thoughts blurring together. The tension in my body slowly unwinds. I force myself to stop drinking even though I want to keep going. I don't want to waste it because I've got to make it last. I tuck it underneath my bed along with the vodka, pulling a bag of old clothes in front of the bottles. I curl up underneath my covers, bringing them up to my chin. I close my eyes without fear. A bubble surrounds me. I can't be touched. Nothing can reach me. Sleep comes easily for the first time since I got home.

SARAH

(NOW)

PHIL AND BLAKE ARE GOING to be here soon to take us to the welcome home party. It's the first time we've left the house since we arrived and I wanted to do something special with my hair rather than pulling it into a messy ponytail. I've never liked my hair. It's mousy brown and dull, not like the vibrant rich brown I've always envied on other girls. It's halfway between curly and straight like it can't make up its mind, but I wet it tonight and scrunched it up with product, taming the bushiness and making it roll nicely over my shoulders.

"You look pretty," Jocelyn says when she sees me.

I look away, feeling self-conscious that she noticed.

"I know you don't have much to wear and I promise we're going to take care of that soon. My friend Greta is organizing a clothing drive for you and she dropped this off for you earlier today." She hands me a dress on a hanger. It's a cotton dress with a floral print. There's a soft white sweater to wear over it. "What size shoes do you wear?"

My cheeks flush with heat. "I don't know."

I haven't worn a pair of shoes in years.

"Well, why don't you put the dress on and I'll go dig around in my closet to see what I can find?"

I step out of my jeans and t-shirt after she leaves and slip the dress over my head. I slide the sweater on and breathe a sigh of relief that it reaches my wrists so it hides my scars but the dress only reaches mid-thigh and there's no way to hide the ones on my legs. I put my jeans on underneath the dress.

Jocelyn returns and looks at me oddly when she sees the jeans. "Honey, why don't you take the jeans off? I think it will look better that way."

Ella hates it when she calls her anything sweet. She yells at her every time she does, but I don't mind. I like it. It makes me feel special.

I hang my head. "I don't want people to see my scars."

The color drains from her face. "Oh, I'm sorry. I didn't know. What did he do to you?" She clamps her hand over her mouth. "Oh my gosh, I can't believe I asked you that. I'm sorry. It's none of my business."

"It's okay."

"No, it's not. I'm sorry. Really, it just popped out. I wasn't thinking."

I don't like seeing her so uncomfortable. I push the sleeves of the sweater up and hold my arms out to her. She fingers the scars as her face crinkles in sadness.

"He is such a monster." She sucks in her breath.

I shake my head. "It wasn't him."

She looks at me in bewilderment.

"My dad was the one. He... he..." I clear my throat. I've never told anyone what he did to me. "He liked to torture me when he was high. His favorite game was to hold cigarettes next to my skin and see how long I could last. I got really good at it."

Tears drip down her face. She pulls me close to her, hugging me tightly against her body. She kisses the top of my head and rubs my back. I let her safety envelop me and sink into it. Too soon, she pulls away and kisses me on the forehead.

"Let me see if I can find you something else," she says, wiping her nose with her sleeve.

She scurries out of the room and comes back with a yellow blouse. "Here. I think this will look pretty with your jeans and the sweater."

She turns around while I change and hands me a pair of black flats when I finish. I slide my feet into them. They're a little big, but they'll work.

"You look pretty," she says.

I don't feel pretty. I feel like I'm wearing a costume. The clothes are tight and they itch, but I try to hide my discomfort because I don't want Jocelyn to feel bad.

We head downstairs. Blake and Phil are waiting for us, but Ella still isn't ready. She doesn't want to come but Jocelyn insisted. She finally appears and Jocelyn rushes to the end of the stairs to meet her.

"You look beautiful," she gushes.

Unlike me, she can't hide her scars. Her bruises have gone from purple and red to greens and yellows. The greens and yellows look even more hideous. She hasn't shaved her head since the first time she did it and it looks like she has a buzz cut now. Short stubble all over her head. She's wearing a long skirt since jeans don't fit over her bandages. It will be another two weeks before her staples get taken out. She glares at Jocelyn and I want to shake her. She could at least try to be nice to her mom. She doesn't even try.

"Okay, let's go," Jocelyn says.

Phil and Blake surround us as we walk out the door just in case any media is around. They camp out during the day, but they clear out as soon as the sun sets. We pile into the same black SUV that we rode from the airport. We even have the same driver. This time he doesn't make the mistake of turning on the radio.

Jocelyn chatters away, filling up the silence but I'm not listening. I stare out the windows trying to catch a glimpse of where we're at. I felt so sick on the drive here, I wasn't able to pay much attention. The tree-lined streets are filled with a jumble of different style houses ranging from bungalows to modern mountain homes. The yards are neatly manicured and most of the homes have two cars in the driveway. The streets are nestled between mountains lining all sides, their tips covered in snow. All of it looks like it belongs on a postcard. It doesn't take long until we reach the main streets where the residential areas give way to mom-and-pop restaurants and specialty shops. We pass a large fountain as we round a corner before coming to a stop at a red light.

Jocelyn leans forward and squeezes my knee. "This is the only light in town. It was a big deal when they put it up."

I smile back at her as we pull into the parking lot of a large, brick church. The sign in front reads: Christ Community Church. The only time I've ever been to church was when we would go to the one on 42nd street for the free meals, but they never let anyone inside the church. They had tables and food set up in the parking lot and we filed through. There were always fights over who took too much and somebody getting seconds when others didn't. The parking lot is filled with cars. How do they know so many people?

Ella hesitates before getting out of the car and Jocelyn nudges her. She looks dazed. Her eyes are glassed over. She's not handling any of this very well. Phil and Blake don't join us. They're going to be outside standing guard, but they escort us to the front door like our own private security.

"You ready for this, girls?" Jocelyn asks as she pushes through the heavy wooden doors.

She leads the way. I hang back with Ella.

"How are you doing?" I whisper to her.

She turns her head to look at me. It takes a while for her eyes to catch up.

"I'm fine," she says.

She doesn't look fine. I know that look. I've seen it on her face before. She's drunk.

ELLA

(NOW)

VODKA IS A LOT STRONGER than wine. I didn't know that before I drank it. I only took a few drinks while I was getting ready, but it's hard to keep my feet moving in the same direction. The world tilts if I move my head too fast. My throat still burns and I can taste the vodka in the back of my throat. My tongue feels swollen and it's hard to speak around. So far, Mom hasn't noticed. She's too busy making sure we get inside without anyone taking our pictures. Sarah grabs my elbow and keeps me from falling when I trip on the step in the doorway. I don't want her touching me, but I'm grateful she doesn't let me fall and make a fool of myself.

Mom leads us to the social hall. It's where they have all the big receptions—funerals, weddings, baby showers, important meetings. I've decorated the place numerous times because Mom always volunteered to help with the major events. It was one of her favorite things to do, especially weddings.

"I just love how happy people are at weddings," she'd always say.

Everyone is already there when we enter. The room buzzes with excitement and chatter. Children are running through the tables chasing after each other just like I used to do when I was younger. Soft music plays in the background. Streamers loop from one side of the room to the next, meeting together in the center. Long fold-out tables fill the room and are covered with matching tablecloths and elaborate centerpieces. The women from the auxiliary club are already lined up behind the counter with their spoons, ready to serve us our food.

My grandparents are the first to greet us. My grandma smothers my face with kisses. I hope she can't smell the vodka. Grandpa stands off to the side, unsure what to do. He's wearing the same suit he wears to church every Sunday.

"Oh, our little Ella Bear, you're home." Tears glisten in her eyes. "And you must be Sarah." She doesn't wait for Sarah to respond. She scoops her up in one of her big bear hugs, smashing her against her large chest. Whereas Mom is wiry and thin, Grandma is just the opposite. She's round and short. Her chin rests almost on her chest, obscuring her neck with its rolls.

"Let's hope you didn't get the fat gene," she's joked since I was a little girl.

But her size never seems to really bother her. She's been that way since I can remember. Never even tried to lose weight. Her personality is as big as she is.

"Come. Come." She fits herself between the two of us, taking one of us in each hand. "The entire family is here."

She drags us into the crowd. We move from one person to the next. Everyone touching, hugging, and saying the same things:

"We missed you so much."

"We're so glad you're home."

"You look great."

"I never stopped praying for you."

"We love you so much."

I feel like a ping-pong ball, bouncing off people and smashing into the next in line. Their faces blur in front of me. All distorted. It makes me dizzy.

"Grandma, I need to sit down," I blurt out.

"Certainly, sweetie. Let's find you a chair."

I don't bother to tell her not to call me sweetie.

I take a seat on one of the aluminum chairs. Sarah plops down in the one next to me.

"Are they always this friendly?" she asks.

I can't help but smile. "Yep. Always."

My family has always been close since it's so small. Mom only has one sibling, Jack, and I spent just as much time at their house growing up as I did my own. I'm not sure how Mom would've managed raising me without them. Jack has two boys and we were as close as siblings. They are a few years older than me and off at college but they'd made it tonight.

Aurora is a tight-knit community where everyone knows everyone. Small communities rally together whenever there's any kind of a need so it's no surprise that half the town is crowded into the room. It doesn't take long for Jaycee and our friends to rush over to the table and join us.

Jaycee points to the ones who weren't at the house and introduces them to Sarah. "This is Jade, Rachel, and Morgan."

"Hi," they sing out.

"Hey," Sarah says.

The vodka is starting to wear off. My head is beginning to hurt. The room is so loud and bright.

"You look great," Morgan says.

I wish everyone would stop lying.

We've huddled together at tables like this so many times over the years. They're the kind of friends who know everything about me. What I was like in preschool. My phase of only wearing purple in second grade. How much I hate scary movies. The things that make me cry and the stuff that makes me laugh. We used to be able to finish each other's sentences and had all kinds of private jokes we shared.

They talk and laugh together like we've always done—interrupting, talking over, and finishing each other's sentences. There was a big football game on Friday and a school dance afterward. They launch into detailed descriptions of what everyone was wearing and who danced with who. Rachel's ecstatic because the guy she's been crushing on since last summer broke up with his girlfriend and he danced with her twice. Jade's bummed she had her period because she swears she looked awful in her dress.

"I was totally bloated and gross," she says.

Everyone laughs and assures her she looked great. They all slept over at Jaycee's house afterward since Jaycee's house is the perfect spot for sleepovers. In eighth grade, her parents let her move into the attic so she basically has her own little private suite. She even put a mini-fridge in there. It's been our favorite spot forever.

They're excited to see me and want to catch me up on everything I've missed, but all I can do is watch them and wonder how I was ever a part of their circle. It feels so weird to be here. I want to be the person they remember. I want to return their smiles and laugh at their jokes, but I can't even look at them. It hurts too much.

Their movements are so fast and quick. I can't keep up with their conversations like they're running and I'm one step behind. Have they always been this loud? They talk around me, but not with me. When they do pause to try and include me, their eyes look around and over me, but never directly at me like I'm too painful to look at. It's the only time their voices slow. They speak to me like they're talking to a toddler.

I listen to them talk about the things that used to ground me in the world—school, friends, and church—but it only magnifies the gap between who I am and who I used to be. They're trying to put me back into my life, but I don't fit. I've been disassembled and even though they think I've been put back together, I'm not. Parts are missing.

It's hard to sit still. My fingers twitch and my skin itches. I claw at my forearm, the one not in the cast. I can't help it. I have all this energy humming through my body making it feel like bugs are crawling underneath my skin.

Their cellphones keep buzzing and dinging. I jump every time. I have no control over it. My body remembers what alarms mean. It will never forget. They're constantly going off.

Ding.

Look down.

Buzz.

Look down.

I want to slap the phones out of their hands.

I feel like I've aged twenty years but they all look the same with their long hair combed perfectly straight. We used to sit for hours in front of the mirror making sure there weren't any kinks or stray hairs in the back. They flip their hair from side-to-side like the twitch of a horse's tail as they talk. Every other word is *like*. Is that how I used to talk? I'm sure it was but I don't remember.

I'm exhausted by the time the party is over. People never stop swarming us. Sarah did better than me at making conversation, but she still looked uncomfortable. I'm totally sober by the time we get home.

I race up to my room, tear off the clothes that had clung to me all night and change into my pajamas. I want a drink. I'm acutely aware of the wine underneath my bed but I can't have it until Mom comes in. Thankfully, it doesn't take her long.

She plops down on the bed next to me. "Tonight was fun, huh? It was so good to see everyone."

"Yeah, it was," I lie.

She launches into a discussion about everyone that was there and the conversations they had. She explains what different people and organizations had done for me while I was away and all the things they've planned now that I'm back. She wants to know what I think we should do about the reward money that was raised during my disappearance.

I interrupt her. "Mom, do you think we could talk about this tomorrow? I'm really tired." I feign a yawn.

She looks hurt. "Sure. Sure, of course."

She kisses me on my cheek. "I love you. I'm so glad you're home."

"I love you too, Mom."

She turns around at the door. "See? I told you we could get through this."

She's barely closed the door before I reach underneath the bed and grab the bottle.

SARAH

(NOW)

I'VE NEVER BEEN IN a police station before. It smells musty and dank. They separated us because they don't want us to feed off each other. Ella went in first. She looked petrified. She had another panic attack yesterday when we got the call that they'd found John.

I still can't believe it. He's here, in the same building as me right now, at least if they've got the right guy and they're pretty sure they do. They tracked him down in Florida. He screwed up somehow trying to get a passport. Something flagged their people and they ambushed him in a small hotel in Titusville, Florida.

I'm so nervous. I know he'll be behind the glass and can't see me, but I'll be able to see him and he'll sense my presence. Even though we can't talk, I'll know what he wants me to do just by looking at him. Our connection doesn't always require words.

He's claiming not to know us or have any idea what this is all about. He says he's never lived in California or heard of Simi Valley. They want me to say it's him. If I say no, does he go free? Do they leave him alone then? Let him go?

The door opens and Blake leads out Ella. She looks like she's seen a ghost. Her face is drained of all color. She always looks like she's one step away from losing it completely. I don't even like being in the same room with her. You can feel her crazy seeping through her pores. What did she think was going to happen if she ran away? Did she think this was going to be easy?

They open the door on the opposite side of the room and Jocelyn and Randy are there to embrace her. Jocelyn gives me a nod and smile for encouragement. Blake returns for me. He sticks his arm out for me like he's walking me down the aisle at my wedding. "You ready?"

I take his arm and follow him into the room. The room is split evenly with one-sided glass. Blake motions to the uniformed officer standing inside. A door opens and men walk into the room in a single-file line. I recognize him immediately. He's third. He walks with the same confident strut like this is just another day. They all turn to face me. He holds up his numbered sign just like the others.

My pulse pounds. It's so loud I can hear it. It's strange to see him in an orange jumpsuit. He only wears black and white. There's nothing with color even hanging in his closet. He stares intensely through the glass. The specks of silver in his crystal blue eyes shimmering.

He sees me. I know he sees me. He's looking right at me. He sees into my soul like he's always done. I can't look away. I'm mesmerized.

"Sarah, I want you to take a good look at all the men and let me know if any of these men is the one who kidnapped Paige and Ella."

My name isn't included on his list of victims. They are his real victims. I can't tear my eyes away from him. I don't look at the other men even though I know I should. It's what you're supposed to do in situations like these.

I shake my head. "I don't see him."

Blake whips around to stare at me, unable to hide his surprise. "Take your time. Don't rush. Look again. Did you live with one of these men?"

I lock my eyes on John, hoping he's proud of me. "I've never seen any of these men."

ELLA

(NOW)

CAN'T STOP SHAKING AND CRYING. Randy and Mom hold me. One on each side. Mom is crying too.

"What happens now?" she asks.

Randy lets out a deep sigh. "To be honest, I'm not sure. Everyone expected Sarah to make a positive ID so this isn't something we saw coming." Anger flits across Randy's face. It doesn't fit with her normal calm. It looks unnatural and out of place.

"How could she do that?" I cry. "It was him. I swear, it was him. I'm not lying."

"Shh. Shh," Mom soothes, wrapping her arms tighter around me. "We know. We believe you." She turns to look at Randy. "What would make her lie?"

"Sarah's bond with him is strong. In her mind, he took care of her. She's convinced he loved her and she was a girl who was never shown love. You have to remember that she lived with him for four years. That's a long time." She pauses before continuing, trying to reign in her emotions. "It can take a long time to break the hold these men have over girls. They're a lot like domestic violence victims. So many times, women call 911 while their spouses are beating them, but once the police get there, they deny it ever happened. We see it play out time and time again. It might help you explain her behavior if you can think of Sarah like a battered wife."

"Will the police still be able to charge him? They can't let him go, can they?" Mom's body is rigid next to me. I can feel her fear through her shirt.

Randy nods, reassuringly. "He's already been charged and I doubt he'll post bail. I'd be surprised if they even gave him the option. The trial is when it will get tricky because they don't have a lot on him that isn't circumstantial. They've got the connections on social media to the girls, but that doesn't necessarily prove he kidnapped them. Without Sarah's corroboration, there's not any evidence they were kidnapped besides Ella's testimony. We have Enrique's statement that he sold Sarah to John, but I have to be honest with you—they could charge him with sex trafficking for her, but it might be hard to stick especially because Enrique is a convicted felon." She notices Mom's horrified expression at the possibility that John could get away with what he's done to us. "But don't worry, they're still gathering more evidence on him. They're focusing all their efforts on getting him to confess and I promise you that our best guys are on the team."

It doesn't make me feel better. I'm so angry with Sarah I want to run into her room and shake her. How could she do something like this? How could she lie to protect him after everything he's done? I've always said she's as sick as he is, but nobody believes me. Everyone just feels sorry for her. Maybe this will make them see what she's really like.

She came out of the police headquarters with a smug look on her face like she was actually proud of herself. I wanted to slap the look off her face. I want her out of my house more than ever. I can't spend another night with her under the same roof.

"Mom, please can we get rid of her?" I beg.

Mom's face is contorted in conflict. Her shoulders sag with the weight of the day. "Don't say it like that. We're not getting rid of anyone."

"You know what I mean. She needs to live somewhere else. She can't live here. I can't handle it."

Mom rubs her forehead. "She can't help her behavior. She's been completely brainwashed by him. Didn't you hear what Randy said?"

"Randy agrees with me," I snap.

"What?" Her eyes flare with anger.

Randy never gets rattled. She's the Queen of Calm and her voice doesn't waver as she speaks. "I do. I–"

Mom's face is bright red. "How can you say everything you just said and then think we should kick her out onto the streets? How can you–"

Randy raises her hand to stop her. "First and foremost, nobody's getting kicked out onto the street. Like I told you before, there are really great therapeutic foster homes we could place her in. It's not the same thing as having a family, but Jocelyn, this isn't any more like a family to her than a foster home would be."

Mom shakes her head, refusing to give in. "But it could be. It's only been two weeks. You said yourself that it takes a lot of time."

"That's true," Randy concedes even though she doesn't want to. "However, having her here is making it extremely difficult for Ella. Her presence is a continual reminder of what happened. It makes this space unsafe for her and safety is the most important thing you can give her right now."

Mom jumps up and places her hands on her hips. "Are you saying I'm a bad mother? That I don't care about my own daughter?"

Randy shakes her head compulsively. "No, not at all. That's not what I'm saying. You're misinterpreting it. I'm only point-ing out how hard it is on Ella to have her here."

"Ella is strong. She's always been strong. She's going to be okay. She'll make it no matter what because she has so many people who care about her." She pauses to flash me a proud and encouraging smile. "But Sarah? She doesn't have anyone. Ella has a solid base to draw on. Sarah has never known any form of stability or care. She's got nothing." Her voice cracks.

Randy stands and goes toward her. She places her hand on Mom's back. "You have a heart of gold and I understand how difficult this must be for you too. I'm not saying you need to make any kind of a decision tonight, but do you think you could think about it? Maybe there's someone else in your family who could take her in?"

Mom puts her face in her hands. "What if I tried to talk to her? What if I could get through to her about how important it is that she's honest about Derek? That she needs to help the investigation?"

"You can try," Randy says, but she doesn't sound very confident. She turns to me. "What do you think, Ella?"

"I don't want her here."

Mom moves to kneel beside by bed. "Hon—I'm sorry—Ella, I know this is hard for you, but I think it'd be hard on you even if she wasn't here. I really do. Just think about how she must feel. Think about what it would feel like to be all alone in the world."

I don't have to think about what it would feel like to be all alone in the world. I am all alone. I've been alone since John grabbed me and threw me in the trunk of his car and I woke up in the basement.

SARAH

(NOW)

PEOPLE HAVE BARELY TALKED to me since we left the police station so I'm surprised when there's a knock on my door after I'd already shut my light off.

"It's Jocelyn. Can I come in?"

"Sure."

She walks in. Her eyes are puffy and red.

"Can I sit down?" she asks pointing to my bed.

I nod.

She sits and rubs her forehead like she has a headache. Her disappointment in me is so strong I can feel it. She turns to look at me. "Why did you do it?"

I don't have to ask what she's talking about. "I don't know."

I can't explain why I did what I did other than it was what he would've wanted me to do.

"I know I don't push you. I never make you talk about things you don't want to talk about, but if you're going to stay in this house, you have to be honest. We've all got to be on the same page and we can't do that if you're not telling the truth. Does that make sense?"

I nod. There's a lump in my throat.

"I'm going to ask you again. Why did you do that today? I really want to understand. Please help me to understand." She doesn't try to hide her desperation.

"He loves me." It sounds pathetic, but I don't expect her or anyone else to understand our relationship.

"Oh sweetie, I know you think he loves you, but that's not love. People that love each other don't hurt each other on purpose." She struggles to control her emotions. "What he did to you was wrong and what he made you do for him was wrong. You were desperate for love and that's not your fault. It's what kids do and he knew that so he took advantage of it. He was a grown man. A sick, controlling grown man."

Randy says the same things every time she meets with me. For so long, I've kept the bad things he did separate. I took all of it and tucked it away in a secret compartment in my brain and marked it "other."

"He took care of me. Nobody ever took care of me like he took care of me," I say, feeling flustered.

"Sarah, he tied you up and locked you in a basement. He starved you unless you did what he wanted you to do. He raped you." She chokes on the word *rape*.

"He didn't rape me. I let him do it."

He was kind and gentle with me. He went slow and talked me through the whole thing. He explained everything he was doing as he went. When it was over, he gave me another bath and helped clean me up. He held me for a long time afterward, whispering sweet things to me.

Jocelyn moves up the bed and sits in front of me. She crosses her legs and grabs both my hands in each of hers. "You were only a little girl. He was a grown man. You must've been terrified."

I wasn't. The men my dad used to give me to were rough. They never cared about how I felt or what they were doing to me.

They were the ones who terrified me. Dad used to stand guard while it happened, making sure they didn't have sex with me. He drew the line there, but everything else was fair game. They were the ones who hurt me. Not John.

"Can I tell you something I've never even told Ella?" she asks.

I snap my head up. She has a secret she's never told Ella?

"When I was in high school, I had a boyfriend named Steve. We grew up together so I'd known him my whole life. We were best friends before we became boyfriend and girlfriend. In tenth grade, my feelings started changing and I realized I was falling in love with him. I was beyond happy when he told me he felt the same way." Her eyes drift as she tells the story, caught up in the memories. "He was my first love. Your first love is always different and you think you'll be together forever. I was sure he was the man I was going to marry. We went to the same church and both had the same conviction about waiting to have sex until we were married so I was surprised when he started pressuring me to have sex during the summer of our junior year. One night after a football game, he had a few beers at a party we went to afterward." Her voice slows. The words fall further and further apart as she talks. "He forced himself on me that night. I kept trying to get him to stop, but he wouldn't. It was like he was a different person. Afterward, he sobbed in my arms and told me how sorry he was."

She stops. I wait for her to go on, but she doesn't.

"What'd you do?" I ask.

"I never told another soul and I told myself it was only because he was drunk. I blamed myself for being a tease because I'd worn a short skirt that night. I didn't break up with him. I stayed with him into our senior year and it happened every few months. Eventually, I didn't try to fight him. I just let him do it because it was easier that way." She blinks rapidly as if she's trying to pull herself from back there and into the present with me. "Do you know what the really sad part is?"

I shake my head, hanging on her every word.

"He was the one who eventually broke up with me. He moved on to another girl in our class and I was beyond devastated."

She squeezes my hands. "I know what it's like to love someone who is hurting you and what it's like to hate yourself for it, but feel powerless to stop it. I know the confusion, the pain, and the hurt."

The room fills with her secret.

"But you seem so normal." I don't know if it's the right thing to say, but it's what comes out.

She smiles. "We all have our pain and our secrets. None of us get through this life unscathed. It took me years of therapy to work through what happened to me, but I did. I needed someone to walk me through it. I needed someone to help me untangle all the lies he told me and the ways he manipulated me, but the hardest part was letting go of my shame. I had so much shame, not just over what happened, but because I stayed after it did."

We sit in silence for a while. She hasn't let go of my hands.

"I'm only telling you this because I think it will help you and I want to help you. What I went through doesn't compare to what you went through, but you're not alone. You can find your way back to the truth."

How do I do that when my entire life has been built on lies? I don't know how to separate the two. My brain is tangled in knots.

"How?" My voice is barely a whisper.

"You can start by admitting he's the one who hurt you."

ELLA

(NOW)

SHE'S STILL HERE. She and Mom had some kind of big breakthrough a few nights ago and Mom's convinced things are going to change. She says she got through to her and we just need to give it more time.

Randy's found a therapist for me. It's someone she says specializes in trauma and PTSD. I always thought PTSD was for people who'd been to war, but she thinks I have it too. She's going to find a therapist for Sarah, but I can tell she's not happy that Mom is as convinced as ever that it's best Sarah stays with us.

Everything is changing since they arrested Derek. I haven't seen Phil or Blake since the police station. They don't need us as much now that they have him. They're focusing on breaking him and getting him to confess. I hope it works. It feels weird without them around. I didn't realize how used to it I was until they were gone.

The police no longer hang around outside our house at night because there's no reason to. They say we're safe now, but I don't feel safe. At night, I dream he's escaped from jail. He sneaks through my bedroom window and grabs me. Sometimes he uses a knife. Other times it's a gun. Once, it was even just like when he took me. He showed up in my room and said he'd lost his dog.

Randy's preparing to leave too. She doesn't come right out and say it, but I know that's what she's getting at with all her talk about the acute phase and the long-term phase of adjustment. She says she's mainly involved in the acute phase and long-term recovery is something that takes years.

The phone still rings constantly. The media are the only ones who haven't left. They're even more obsessed with us since they found John. They've offered Mom all kinds of money for us to tell our stories or even just give them a picture. Everyone wants to be the first to hear what we have to say. Mom's thinking about it even though she doesn't want to. She's been out of work for almost five months and it's been a huge hit on our finances. She doesn't talk about it but we don't have the kind of money for her to be out of work for this long. I don't know how she's survived until this point.

She's talking about going back to work once we're more stabilized and back at school. For now, she's focused on how to become Sarah's legal guardian. Sarah's thrilled. The two of them exchange knowing glances all the time like they share some big secret.

I'm almost out of alcohol and that's the thing that scares me the most—going through my day without a drink. It's the only way I get by. The wine is gone. That's what I drink at night because I don't have to worry if anyone smells it on me. Once Mom says good night, I'm left to myself until the morning and I drink until I fall asleep. When the nightmares wake me up, I drink until I fall back to sleep.

I reserve the hard alcohol for the daytime. It must be true that you can't smell vodka because nobody has said anything to me about it yet. Nobody gets too close to me anyway. I've gotten good at emitting a "stay away from me" vibe and it seems to be working. Yesterday when Jaycee came over, she looked at me like she was afraid of me.

Mom popped popcorn and made brownies for us so we could sit down and watch a movie like we used to. Of course, she included Sarah. She's determined that we're all going to be friends. I made it through about the first hour of the movie before I couldn't take it anymore. The sound of Jaycee chewing her popcorn grated on my nerves and the way she laughed nervously at things that weren't even funny got so annoying I couldn't stand it. Finally, I just said I didn't feel good and had to go up to my room. She looked like she wanted to cry. I wish I could care, but I don't. She's too shiny and clean. Everything about her sparkles. It only magnifies the dirt on me.

I left her downstairs with Sarah. She's fascinated with Sarah like she's this exotic creature from the zoo and Sarah eats it up. She loves the attention. It's fine, though. She can have it. I don't want it. I'd rather they pay attention to her and leave me alone.

My room is dark, just the way I like it. I keep the blinds closed at all times. Mom's given up opening them in the morning because she knows as soon as she leaves, I just shut them again. I'm spending the day doing what I did yesterday, picking the scabs on my legs and peeling back some of the stitches. I've gotten lots of them out myself. I drink, pick, and then pull. Drink. Pick. Pull.

SARAH

(NOW)

"**Y**OU READY FOR THIS?" Jocelyn asks.
This time I'm not alone in the police station
waiting room. They let her stay with me until it's
time to see John again. She asked Phil and Blake to give me
another chance to identify him and they agreed.

I was feeling fine about it on the way here. It's easy when
Jocelyn is next to me. She's so strong and I feed off her strength.
But as soon as they open the door and usher me inside, my
stomach drops to my feet. This part I have to do alone. She can't
be with me. Just Blake. They don't want her to influence me.

"You can do it," she cheers, waving me through the door.

I nod, take a deep breath, and square my shoulders. I follow
Blake through the door and back into the divided room from a
few days ago. Nothing has changed. They file in the same way
as before. This time John is number five. He's wearing the same
orange jump suit. I wait until they are lined up facing me.

"Do you recognize the man who kidnapped Paige and Ella?" Blake asks in the exact same manner he did before.

I freeze. Once I step over this line, there's no going back. I know that and I don't know what happens next. I don't want to do it. I don't want to say it's him, but then I think about Jocelyn waiting outside for me and what she'll say if I tell her I couldn't do it. She might make me leave their house. I don't want to leave her.

"He's number five," I say.

"Do you see the man who kept you in his basement?" Blake asks.

"It's the same man," I hear myself say in a voice that isn't connected to me.

I'm so sorry, John. Please forgive me.

ELLA

(NOW)

I HAVE NO IDEA WHAT to expect when I walk into the therapy room. Everything is neat, organized, and in its place. There's a long leather couch in the center of the room as the focal point, but it's not set up like a couch in a living room. There's no throw pillows or blankets to make you more comfortable. Two fabric, winged-back chairs create a half circle around the couch. The book shelves hold nothing but self-help titles. The artwork on the wall frames pictures of nature lined with inspirational quotes. There's even some kind of fountain in the corner surrounded by plants.

The therapist looks nothing like I expected. I've gotten used to Randy's hippy attire and her laidback approach, but this woman is formal and stiff. She's dressed in a pantsuit like she has an important meeting to get to when she leaves. She's wearing heels that click on the wooden floor as she walks over to introduce herself and the sound makes me cringe.

"Hello, Ella. I'm Dr. Hale." She sticks out her hand formally like we're business acquaintances meeting for the first time. I take it. Her grip is tight. She turns to Mom. "I'd like to meet with her alone first. You can have a seat in the waiting room."

Mom looks taken aback. Randy always asks permission to meet with me alone but Dr. Hale has left no room for objection. Mom quickly heads out of the room, throwing me an anxious look over her shoulder as she shuts the door behind her.

Dr. Hale clicks back over to the center of the room and takes a seat in one of the wing-backed chairs. She crosses her legs and waits for me to join her. I have no choice but to sit on the leather couch because it'd look too weird if I sat on the chair to her right.

She reaches onto the end table beside her and picks up a yellow legal pad behind the box of Kleenex. She flips over a piece and grabs a pen from the table. She stares at me expectantly like I'm supposed to know what to say.

The couch is as uncomfortable as it looks. My body doesn't fit right. I don't know what to do with my legs. I feel like I have four arms and I don't know what to do with any of them.

"Let's talk about why you're here."

Is she serious? She knows why I'm here. Randy set this whole thing up. There's nothing to talk about. Her eyes bore holes in me as she waits for me to speak.

"Randy says I have to start seeing you now." It sounds lame but I don't know what else to say.

She nods, tucking her long, blond hair behind one of her ears. "Yes, that's right. I'm not sure how much Randy explained to you about me, but I'm a clinical psychologist with a specialization in traumatic stress. I work with children and families who have experienced traumatic events. I help people process what they've been through."

I'm glad I had a drink while I was getting ready because this is going to be intense.

"My goal is to help minimize the long-term effects of traumatic experiences. We work on important tools like learning how to deal with trauma reminders and reducing some of the internal effects. I emphasize restoring a sense of safety and protection through identifying the family's core strengths and using them as a way to develop resiliency."

She keeps explaining but she sounds like she's reading out of a textbook and I can't follow her. It's a while before she's finished and when she's done, I nod my head like I understand what she's just said but I don't have a clue.

"Let's start with something small. Why don't you begin by telling me what it's been like since you've returned home?"

"It's been hard."

She raises her eyebrows. "Of course it's been hard. We're trying to go a bit deeper than that and figure out specific areas where you're struggling."

She doesn't make any sense. At least Randy makes sense when she talks to me. I shrug.

"How about this? Why don't you tell me what a typical day looks like for you now that you're home?" She's holding her pen, ready to write when I start talking.

"Well, mostly I just stay in my room." The leather underneath me sticks to me whenever I move my legs. I feel like I'm sitting on tape.

She scribbles on her pad. "What do you do while you're in your room?"

"I sleep."

And drink, but she doesn't need to know that.

"What's your sleeping like?"

What kind of a question is that?

She recognizes the confusion on my face. "Let me be a little more specific. Are you able to fall asleep when you want to?"

"Usually," I say.

"Are you able to stay asleep?"

"I guess." I shrug.

She takes a moment and scribbles some more. What is she writing? I haven't even said much.

"Do you have nightmares?"

I nod.

"Can you tell me about some of your nightmares?"

I freeze. I don't want to talk about my nightmares.

"I can see this is making you uncomfortable."

It's making me want to throw up.

"Let's get back to your nightmares later. I have some other questions. Maybe those will be easier for you."

She spends the next thirty minutes asking me about all kinds of things. Am I eating? What kinds of things am I eating? Have I been outside? What's it like when I leave the house? Am I scared of loud noises? All of her questions make my head spin. I have no idea if I give her the right answers. They come so fast, I don't have any time to think about them and she writes everything down. Her writing makes me nervous.

I breathe a sigh of relief when it's finally over and it's Mom's turn. I hope I don't have to do this every week. I sit in the waiting room picking at my fingernails, counting the minutes until we can leave. I need a drink.

SARAH

(NOW)

"**NO! NO! No!**"

    She's been screaming like that for the last fifteen minutes like a spoiled toddler. I don't see what the big deal is. It's only a picture. They're not even going to ask us any questions. Jocelyn made them promise not to. I think it's exciting. I've never had my picture taken by a professional before. John's the only person who's ever taken my picture. They're even going to do our hair and make-up.

I can't decide what to wear. Jocelyn's friend Greta dropped off a bunch of clothes for me last week. I gave her back the things that didn't fit, but a lot of it did and there's some nice stuff. People were really generous. I'm deciding between the black jeans with a cute light blue top or the jeans with the holes in the knee that make me look more relaxed when Jocelyn knocks on my door before coming in.

"Did she finally calm down?" I ask. She's not screaming anymore so that's a good sign.

Jocelyn shakes her head. The lines in her face grow by the day. "She doesn't want to do it."

My heart sinks. I've been looking forward to it all day.

"Did you tell her she had to?"

"No, I can't make her." Her shoulders droop.

"But did you tell her why she needed to?" I press.

Jocelyn tells me things she doesn't tell Ella because she knows I can handle things she can't. When she first brought up allowing ABC News to take a picture of us to release to the press, she confessed she was only giving in to them because she needed the money.

"I didn't want to make her feel bad," she says with a frown.

"Well, you should tell her. She'll do it if you tell her why."

She better do it. Jocelyn needs her to.

"I'm just so tired." She sits down on my bed. "I feel like everything I do for her is wrong. I fail at every turn." Her eyes fill with tears.

I rush to her and put my arms around her. "You're not failing." I can't believe she even thinks that. "You're doing everything you can for her."

She pats me on the back. "Thanks, Sarah."

"I'm going to go talk to her."

I head for the door.

"No, don't do that," Jocelyn calls. "It will only upset her."

I ignore her and march into Ella's room without knocking. She's curled up on her bed, laying on her side, and staring at the wall. "Get up," I order just like I used to when I needed the girls to do something. "You're going to do this because our mom needs you to."

She jolts like I've shocked her. Her eyes are wide, manic.

"She's only doing this because she needs the money." I point to the clothes scattered on her floor. "Get moving and put something on."

She stands like she's in a trance and moves toward her clothes. She picks through them in a daze. I push her aside. I grab a long skirt and matching top and toss them to her. "Wear this. You'll be fine."

I head out her door and back into my room. Jocelyn is still sitting on my bed with her head in her hands.

"She's getting dressed now," I say. "She'll be ready soon."

Her face lights up. "Are you serious? How'd you get her to change her mind?"

I shrug and smile. "I have my ways."

ELLA

(NOW)

CAN'T STOP SHAKING WHILE I get dressed. I pull out my bottle and drain the last of it. I don't know what I'm going to do. I've drank everything in our liquor cabinet. Last night, I finished off the Kahlua. Mom is going to freak when she finds out. Somehow, I have to replace it, but I have no idea how I'm going to do that.

I throw on the clothes Sarah laid out even though I don't want to. I've never liked getting my picture taken, even before. I brace myself for what's to come and head downstairs. Mom and Sarah wait at the bottom for me. Mom's eyes are puffy underneath. She's been crying again. I can't seem to do anything but make her cry.

"You look pretty," Mom coos.

"Thanks," I say sheepishly even though I look awful. My hair looks like I belong in the military. I liked it better when I was bald.

The camera crew is set up in the living room. Mom only allowed one photographer, the producer, lighting crew, and make-up artists, but our small living room is still cramped. They're buzzing around trying to decide where they want us to sit. The make-up people grab us and shuffle us into the kitchen. They get to work quickly.

"You have such beautiful eyes," the guy says as he starts rubbing foundation all over my face. He's close enough to kiss me and it makes me so uncomfortable it's hard to sit still. I hold my breath so he doesn't smell the alcohol. It makes me dizzy because he stays in front of me a long time before grabbing his palette of colors.

He keeps trying to talk to me while he works on my face but I can't think of anything to say. I never can anymore. I've forgotten how to talk to people. I sit like a statue, mute, while Sarah rambles on and on with the guy doing her make-up. She giggles and laughs while he dabs on her lipstick commenting about her full lips and how pretty they are.

They move on to her hair, but since I don't have any hair to do, I'm finished and I can't get out of the kitchen fast enough. I'm still mad Sarah made me do this. The producer has Mom cornered. She's talking her ear off, trying to convince her to let her ask us a few questions. Mom keeps shaking her head and saying no, but it doesn't seem to be getting through to her. What did she expect would happen when she let them into our house? Mom spots me and uses it as her excuse to get away.

"How are you doing?" she whispers in my ear.

"Fine," I say with a clipped tone. I'm still mad at her too.

In our last session, Dr. Hale told us we need to work on re-establishing our relationship and getting to know each other again. She said it after Mom cried because I don't talk to her like I used to and still haven't opened up about what happened to me. She explained how we used to be able to talk about anything and how I always confided in her. She doesn't feel like she knows what's going on with me or how to help me. She looked really torn up about it. Normally, I can't stand it when she cries and there's nothing I hate worse than hurting her feelings, but I feel so dead inside.

It takes forever before they finish with Sarah's hair, but they finally do, and when she walks into the living room to join us, I'm shocked by her appearance. She looks amazing. They've done her hair in long spiral curls, flowing down her back. Whatever they've done to her eyes makes them pop. Her lips are plump and full, lined in red. I look like the ugly duckling next to her.

They start by putting us in front of the fireplace. The crew arranges the things on the mantle, making sure everything looks perfect. We sit on the stoop. Sarah crosses her legs and I cross my ankles. The lights start flashing and then the clicks start. I force a smile. It's awkward and forced, out of place.

"Can you put your arms around each other?" the photographer asks.

Sarah throws her arm around my shoulders, pulling me closer. Someone else rushes up to us and flips her hair around. They adjust my hands, setting them on my lap. They move our bodies this way and that. Then, the flashing starts again.

They move us from the fireplace to the couch, scurrying around to rearrange everything again. They work fast. Mom gives us the thumbs-up sign from behind the camera and Sarah beams at her. We go through the entire process again—the primping and adjustments of our bodies, lighting moved.

"We're done. Thank you, girls," the producer gushes once it's finished.

I jump up from my seat and head back upstairs. All of it makes me feel sick. Nothing feels real. I look over my shoulder when I get to the top of the stairs. Mom and Sarah are laughing together. Mom has her arm thrown around her lovingly like they've known each other for years.

I can't get to my bedroom fast enough. My skin is crawling. I'm sweating. My face feels hot. My heart races. I need to calm down. There's nothing for me to drink and being without it fills me with a horrible sense of impending doom. I can't shake it.

I creep into the bathroom and throw open the cabinet. Tylenol. Benadryl. Cough syrup. Moisturizer. Our sleeping pills.

I grab the bottle of sleeping pills and pour a handful into my palm. I shut the cupboard door and move to the drawers underneath the sink. There's an unopen bottle of Scope. I read the label. 15% alcohol. I ignore the shame of knowing I'm about to drink mouthwash. I grab the cough syrup too, remembering that kids used to drink it in junior high and get really messed up. They called it a robo-trip.

I peek out the door, listening to see if anyone is coming upstairs. They're still talking and laughing downstairs. I rush back into my bedroom. It calms my heart just knowing I have something to help me feel better.

I open the mouthwash and take a huge drink. It burns all the way into my gut, settling like a firecracker. I take another drink. My stomach threatens to reject it. I toss the pills into my mouth. I use the water on my nightstand to wash them down.

I sit, taking small sips of the mouthwash, and wait for the bubble to come. I don't have to wait long. As they start to work their magic, everything relaxes and I settle into it. Everything becomes dull and faraway. Nothing matters as I sink into oblivion.

SARAH

(NOW)

JOCELYN GOES UPSTAIRS TO SEE if she can get Ella to come down for lunch. I doubt she will. She usually takes her food up in her room and even then, she barely eats anything. She's skinnier than she was before.

"Ella! Ella!" her blood-curdling screams pierce the air.

I drop my coffee mug and run for the stairs, taking them two at a time. I run to Ella's room and throw open the door. Ella is crumpled on her bedroom floor. Yellow vomit spills out of the corner of her mouth. Her head is limp, eyes closed. Jocelyn hovers over her.

"Call 911," she screams.

I run back downstairs, grab the kitchen phone, and punch in the numbers.

"911. What is your emergency?"

"I'm not sure. Ella's passed out on the floor. She might have choked on her puke."

"Is she breathing?"

"I don't know."

I keep the phone to my ear and race back up the stairs. Jocelyn leans over Ella's body, rubbing her back. Her shoulders shake with sobs.

"Is she breathing?" I ask.

"Yes. I checked," she says.

"She's breathing," I tell the operator.

"Tell them to hurry. Hurry!" Jocelyn screams. "I can't wake her up. She won't wake up."

The operator hears her. "How is she laying?"

"On her side."

"Good. Keep her there. Can you see anything in her airway?"

"Check her airway," I order Jocelyn. "See if there's anything in there."

She lifts her head, opens her mouth, and peers inside. "I don't see anything." Her voice grows more frantic with each word. When she lets go, Ella's head flops to the side.

"Keep monitoring her breathing. The ambulance is on its way."

ELLA

(NOW)

WAKE TO BLINDING FLUORESCENT lights. My throat is on fire. I turn my head to the left. Mom is sitting next to my bed. I'm in the hospital. How did I get in the hospital again? My movements startle my mom. She scoots her chair closer to the bed. She rubs my cheek with the back of her hand.

"Hi... you're awake." Emotion thickens her voice.

"What happened?" I croak. It hurts to talk.

"You tried to kill yourself." Pain etches her face.

It all comes flooding back. The sleeping pills and mouth wash, but I didn't try to kill myself. I just wanted to numb out. I shake my head, "No, I didn't."

She cocks her head to the side. "Well, it certainly looked like you did. You took a bunch of sleeping pills and drank mouthwash."

"I didn't try to kill myself."

"Then, what were you doing?" Randy's voice breaks into our conversation and she moves into view.

I should've known she'd be here. It's just like before.

"We found the empty liquor bottles under your bed." She glances over at Mom.

I start to cry.

"That's a lot of alcohol," Randy says.

"Have you been drinking every day?" Mom asks like she's not sure she wants to know the answer.

I nod. I'm crying too hard to talk.

Mom grabs my hand, careful not to jerk out the IV, and squeezes it tightly. "We can get through this. We can. We're going to be okay," she says with conviction.

I pull my hand out of hers. "Stop saying that! Please, stop saying that. Stop acting like it happened to us. It didn't happen to us! It happened to me! I'm the one he took! He tortured me—not you. He raped me, Mom. He didn't do anything to you!"

My entire body shakes with sobs. Mom looks like I slapped her. She reaches up to touch her cheek as if she's searching for a mark.

"Good. Good," Randy coaxes. "Tell her how you feel, Ella. Let it out."

"I hate being at home. Hate it! I drink every single day because it's the only way I can stand it." I sit upright in the bed and point my finger at Mom. "You won't make her leave. All I want is for her to leave. Do you know how awful she was? Your second daughter?"

Mom is weeping now, but I can't stop.

"She helped him! And she liked it. She never tried to help us. Not once. Not any of us. Do you know how many of us there are?"

Randy is beside me now. She places her hand on my back for support.

"He was a monster and she is too. I don't care what you say. I don't care how sorry you feel for her and her sad little life. Every time I look at her—I see him. His face. And you cuddle and laugh with her like you're best friends."

Mom hides her face in her hands. Her shoulders shake.

I slide up against the wall behind me. Spent. Exhausted. Depleted.

"I'm so proud of you, Ella," Randy says.

She waits for a few minutes before walking over to Mom. She kneels beside her chair, puts her hand on her back, and speaks in a soft voice. "I know this is hard to hear, but you have to take it in. You have to listen to what she's saying. Really listen."

"I'm so sorry. I'm so sorry." She leaves her head buried in her hands. "I almost lost you again. It would've been my fault." When her sobs subside and she looks up, it's like she's seeing me for the first time. Not the Ella she knew before, but the Ella I am now. "I don't know what to do. How do I make it better?"

I fold my arms across my chest. "She has to leave."

SARAH

(NOW)

'VE BEEN WAITING ALL NIGHT for Jocelyn to get home and it's taking forever. She sent her friend Greta to stay with me like I needed a babysitter. It feels weird to be in the house without her. We've been watching TV for the last two hours, but I'm not even paying attention to what's on. I can't. It's another hour before she comes home and when she does, I've never seen her look so wrecked.

She and Greta chat quickly in the kitchen before Greta leaves. She walks into the living room and sits down next to me on the couch. She turns the TV off.

"We need to talk," she says.

"I'm here for you. Whatever you need."

I'd do anything for Jocelyn. She's done so much for me.

Her eyes fill with tears. "This is really hard for me. Did you know Ella has been drinking since she's been home?"

What do I say? If I say I knew then she'll wonder why I didn't tell her. She'll think she can't trust me. She has to trust me.

"She was drinking?" I ask, doing my best to feign surprise.

"Yes. Every day since she's been back." Her eyes are so sad. She's never looked so sad. "She's having a very difficult time adjusting to being back. Much harder than I even knew." She stops looking at me. She shifts her gaze to the fireplace, staring at the pictures on top of the mantle. "I'm so sorry..."

What's she sorry for? She doesn't need to apologize. She hasn't done anything to me. She's the only person who's ever been good to me.

"I really thought I was doing a good thing. I just wanted to make things right. It's all I wanted." Her eyes are wet.

She's not making any sense. She needs to get some rest. This is all really taking a toll on her. Why does Ella have to be so weak? I was wrong about her being a fighter.

"Maybe you should just go to bed. You look tired," I interrupt.

She lets out a deep sigh. "I thought this would be the easy part—the getting better part. I never thought it would be so difficult."

I reach out and place my hand on top of hers. I want to comfort her the way she always comforts me. She places her hand on top of mine and turns to look at me.

"When I found out about your childhood while we were in the hospital and that you were going to have to go into the foster care system, it broke my heart. It literally broke my heart." Her voice cracks. "I couldn't stomach the idea of you being shuffled around and not knowing if you had someone to really love and take care of you. I hope I've been able to show you that since you've been here."

"Jocelyn, you have. You've been so good to me." I look deep into her eyes, hoping she can see that I'm telling the truth. Why is she beating herself up so much?

She wipes her eyes. "Thank you." She turns to look at me. "Having you here has been very difficult for Ella. Randy told me it might be, but I didn't believe her. I thought it'd be good for her. Good for both of you to be together. I thought you'd be able to help each other. Unfortunately, it hasn't worked out that way."

Hasn't she seen the way I've tried to help Ella? I was the one who was able to get her dressed for the photo shoot. She never would've done it if it hadn't been for me. It's not my fault Ella is so stubborn.

She clears her throat. Clears it again. "Ella can't move forward with you here. I'm so sorry. She doesn't feel safe with you because it reminds her of everything that happened and she needs to feel safe. She can't get better if she doesn't feel safe. I'm so sorry."

All the air gets sucked out of the room.

"Wh–what are you saying?" I can't wrap my brain around what's happening.

"Randy is looking into finding a foster home for you. She says there's some really good homes that work with teenage girls who've been through similar experiences–"

"I have to leave? You're making me leave?" Everything is spinning. I can't believe it. I didn't even do anything wrong.

"I'm so sorry, honey," she cries. "We can still stay in touch. I want you to know I'm always going to be here for you."

"I have to leave?" I ask again, still shocked.

She struggles to say the words, but she does. "Yes, you're going to have to leave."

ELLA

(NOW)

FOR THE FIRST TIME since I escaped, I can breathe without feeling like I'm going to choke on the air. Mom told Sarah she had to leave last night. She cried about it this morning, but Randy assured her she was doing the right thing even if it's painful. It didn't seem to make Mom feel better, but she understands that Sarah needs to leave and says she'd never forgive herself if something happened to me because she didn't make her go.

It's going to be awkward at the house for the next two days. Randy thinks she's found a foster home for Sarah, but all the paperwork won't be done until Thursday. I'd rather stay in the hospital until she's gone for good, but the doctors are going to discharge me this afternoon.

They say I overdosed on the mouthwash and sleeping pills. I didn't do it on purpose, but I'm still not sure Mom believes me. Part of her thinks I was really trying to kill myself no matter how many times I tell her I wasn't. I didn't want to die, at least I don't think so. I just didn't want to feel anything. Everything was just too heavy.

I'm glad I was unconscious when I got here because they had to pump my stomach and it sounds terrible. The last thing I remember is the taste of Scope in my mouth and the next thing I was waking up here. For a split second, I thought it was all a dream and I'd never gone home. But it was real.

I can handle two more days with Sarah if it means once she's gone, I never have to see her again. It's not like I want bad things to happen to her. I hope wherever they send her, it's a place where people can help her. I just don't want any part of it.

We get to ride in the car by ourselves on the way home from the hospital. It feels strange, but normal. I can't help but think of all our morning rides to school. Even though I could've rode the bus, Mom always insisted on driving me. I have to get to school earlier than I would if she didn't, but I've never minded. Mom's silent as we drive. She's lost in her own thoughts. I don't mind the quiet. It feels good not to have to fill up the space. It isn't long before we turn onto our street.

"What's she been doing all day?" I ask.

"She was really upset last night after I told her. She got really angry and said I was just like everyone else. That I never really cared about her because if I did, there's no way I could do this to her." Her face is lined with pain. "She stormed up to her room and didn't come out for the rest of the night. She didn't even let me in when I knocked to tell her good night. But it's been a little strange today."

"How so?"

"She was in the kitchen making coffee this morning like nothing happened. She didn't even bring it up. She hasn't said anything about it all day. I think she might be in denial about the whole thing. I asked Randy about it and she said that's probably what was going on. I've never been so grateful for Randy than I was today. She was a huge help for me. I should've listened to her all along and I wouldn't have added to her pain. Or yours."

We pull into the driveway. We don't get out even after she's shut off the car.

Mom turns to look at me. "I'm sorry, Ella. I should've listened to what you needed. I promise from now on, I'm going to listen to what you need."

"It's okay, Mom. I still love you."

"I love you, too. So much."

She gives me a huge hug before we head into the house.

SARAH

(NOW)

JOCELYN AND ELLA LOOK shocked when they come in the door and see the table filled with food. I spent all afternoon cooking for them. We've been eating leftovers and frozen casseroles from things people brought for us, but I figured it was time we had a real home-cooked meal. It felt good to be in the kitchen cooking again. It'd been a long time. Their kitchen is so much smaller than what I'm used to, but I was able to make it work.

"Hi, Sarah. You cooked?" Jocelyn raises her eyebrows.

I smile. "I did. I figured you guys would be hungry and hospital food is terrible."

"I'm not really hungry," Ella says.

Jocelyn shoots her a pointed look. "You should try to eat something."

Ella glares at her, but sits down.

We haven't ever sat around the table with just the three of us before. I fill their water while they pass the food around. Ella barely takes anything but Jocelyn fills her plate. I appreciate the gesture.

Randy is coming over in the morning to discuss what happens to me next. She wants to show me pictures of the family I'll be living with. They live somewhere in Iowa. It's probably in the middle of a cornfield. She called me today expecting me to be sad and was surprised when I wasn't. I had my moment of being sad last night, but I refuse to stay in that place. What none of them realize is that I'm not one of the weak ones. I'm a fighter and I know what I have to do.

ELLA

(NOW)

HE'S HERE. HE'S coming for me. I can't see him, but I'm next. I know I'm next. I scream, but the sound gets caught in my throat. My eyes snap open. There's no air. My pulse pounds. I'm dripping with sweat. My night gown sticks to me. I try to calm myself, "It's only a dream. It's only a dream. You're awake now."

But I can't shake the sleep off me. I can't wake up. My lids are so heavy. I force myself to focus, trying to adjust to the darkness. My room slowly comes into view. Everything in slow motion. There's pressure on my bed. Slowly, the silhouette of someone sitting on the end of my bed comes into view. I try to clear the cotton from my brain, force myself to wake up.

I'm still dreaming. I'm awake. What's happening?

I blink, close my eyes, and blink again. There's still a figure on my bed. I focus on my breathing, using the techniques Randy taught me. I try to move, but I can't. Something's holding me.

I struggle against it, trying to fight my way out of the darkness and back to wake.

I'm awake.

My arms are tied to my headboard.

This is real.

Sheer terror shoots through me. I try to scream but I can't. My mouth is taped shut. Just like before.

Sarah's face comes into view above me.

"Oh, Ella. I had a feeling you'd wake up. You should've eaten all of your dinner." She brushes her hand on my cheek.

I try to pull away from her, but my reactions are dull. It's like moving through quicksand. My head just rolls.

Sarah throws her head back and laughs. "You can make this easy on yourself or you can make it hard. Your choice."

What is she talking about? Is John here? How did he get in the house? How did this happen? Where's Mom? Did he hurt her? Liquid fear pools my insides.

"Did you really think I'd just let you get rid of me? Your mom loves me and she'd never make me leave if it wasn't for you. All of this is your fault. All of it." She tightens the straps holding my wrists back. "These are just to be sure. I bet you can't even feel your body right now, can you?"

What did she do to me? I try to scream for Mom. It comes out muffled.

"She can't hear you. She's fast asleep. I made sure of that." She laughs again. It's a different kind of laugh, one I've never heard her make.

I move my head back and forth, scanning for a way out.

"Here's what's going to happen. I'm going to take your gag off and you're going to take more of these pills." She points to my nightstand. A glass of water surrounded by pink pills—the same ones I overdosed on. "I already gave you your first dose at dinner, but sometimes it's not enough and the girls wake up."

It hits me with a sickening realization that she's done this before.

"You made this way too easy for me. Everyone already thinks you tried to kill yourself and now, they'll just think you finished the job." She pulls the tape off my mouth. Duct tape.

"Mom! Mom! M—"

Her fist slams into my face. The taste of blood fills my mouth.

"If you scream again, I'll kill her. I mean it. I gave her pills in her water too so she'll never even know I'm coming."

"Why? Why are you doing this to me?" My words slur like I have a mouthful of marbles I have to speak around.

"I'm not going to let you take her away from me. That's not going to happen." Her lips are set in a straight line.

"Okay, okay. I get it. You can stay. I promise. I'll tell her I changed my mind. That I can make things work with you here." My words tumble over each other.

She shakes her head. "Do you really think I'm that stupid? You probably do. Just like the rest of them." She picks up the pills, cupping them in her hand. "No, this is going to happen. Trust me, it's totally painless. And if you struggle, some of them struggle, I've seen it happen before." She points to the pillow beside me. "Well, then I just help you along."

"You can't do this to my mom. Think about how much it will destroy her if I'm gone."

She doesn't care about me, but she does care about Mom.

"See, that's where you're wrong. She'll be devastated. That much is for sure, but it's only going to make her want me more. She won't be able to go on without a daughter to love. That's where I come in." She places her hand on my forehead again. I jerk back. "You don't need to worry about her. I'm going to take good care of her. I'll be there for her in her grief. Nothing bonds people together more than shared grief."

I have to keep her talking. The longer she talks, the clearer my head gets.

"How do you know it'll work?"

"You think this is my first time? Like I've never done this before?" She smiles. Her eyes light up. "I've been doing this for years. I give all the girls their last supper. Then, John takes care of the rest."

I want to cry, but have to keep my emotions in check so I can think. I bite my cheek hard to keep from crying.

"Are you done talking now? I'm really ready for this just to be over." She brings her hand to my mouth. "Now open your mouth and take these."

I clamp my jaw shut, gluing my lips together, jutting my chin out in defiance.

Her eyes flash with anger. "Open up."

I shake my head. I won't let her get away with this. I want her to smack me again. Beat me up so she'll leave marks for people to find. Blake isn't stupid. He'll figure it out. She reaches over with her left hand and pushes on my jaw bone. An excruciating pain radiates to the back of my head. She does it again. The pain is so great, it makes me feel like I'm going to pass out, but I hold on. She tosses the pills back on the nightstand. She's so furious she's shaking. Her hands are clenched in fists at her side.

She picks up the pillow next to me. I twist back and forth.

"Mom! Mom!" I scream. This time my voice is louder. My strength is coming back.

She smashes the pillow on my face. My arms and legs thrash against the ties binding them. My body screams for oxygen. My chest is going to explode and spray pieces of me all over the pillow. Black fills the edges of my visions. Darkness is coming. I stop fighting and let it cover me. I'm not scared any more.

Just like that I can breathe again. I gasp for air as Mom screams, "Get away from her!"

Mom grabs Sarah and flings her off the bed. She crashes to the floor and springs back up like a cat.

My lungs are burning.

"How dare you? How dare you?" Mom inches closer to her, her face contorted in rage.

Sarah's face twists in pain. "You love me! I know you love me. She ruined everything and you just let her. She doesn't even appreciate you." She starts grabbing things off my dresser and throwing them at Mom. She rips the posters off the wall, screaming incoherently.

Mom doesn't take her eyes off her. She fingers the ties around my wrist; her other hand against Sarah's chest. "Ella, I'm going to untie you and when I do, you run downstairs and call 911."

But it's not going to work. The ties are too tight. She can't untie them with one hand. Sarah shoves Mom aside and bolts for the door. Mom leaps up and grabs her by the hair, snapping her back. She pulls her into the room and slams her onto the floor. She gets on top of her, pinning her arms back and sitting on her stomach. Sarah screams like she's possessed. Spit flings out of her mouth. Mom holds on. She bucks her around, but Mom doesn't let go. Finally, she goes limp. The room stills. Sarah starts to sob.

"But you love me. You know you do. How can you do this to me? Please, Jocelyn, please. I'm a good daughter. I am." She sounds like a little girl.

Mom's voice is calm and steady, "Sarah, I'm going to untie Ella now. You aren't going to move. Do you hear me?"

She doesn't respond. She lays there like she's dead. Mom inches her way to me. I watch Sarah while she unties me. She curls herself up into the fetal position.

"Ella, go call 911," she says.

Sarah whimpers on the floor. "I'm sorry, Jocelyn. I'm so sorry. Please, give me another chance. Please. I just didn't want to leave you. Please. I'm your daughter."

I hear Mom's voice behind me as I hurry downstairs, "You are not my daughter."

ELLA

(ONE MONTH LATER)

THEY ARRAIGNED JOHN TODAY. There's not going to be a trial because he worked out a deal with the lawyers. They took the death penalty off the table if he agreed to life in prison with no chance of parole in exchange for identifying the girls and leading investigators to the bodies. So far, they've uncovered six. He swears that's all there is but I don't believe him.

Blake asked if I wanted to make a statement at his sentencing but I refused. I never want to see his face again. Mom, Paige's parents, and some of the other parents of the dead girls are going to read letters to him, though. Mom tries to connect with the other parents but they don't return her efforts. They resent her because I'm alive and their daughters are dead. It's too hard for them.

Paige's parents had a nice service for her. It was closed casket. There were so many people, they couldn't all fit inside the church. Her real dad showed up and she would've liked that. I couldn't help but wonder if he was wracked with guilt for missing out on her life and not having a chance to make it up to her. They asked me to read the poem, "I'll Lend You a Child," and I cried through every line. We didn't go to the reception. There were too many people and I hate crowds now. Instead, we went home and watched reruns of *Modern Family*. I have to be careful about TV because I never know what will trigger a panic attack.

Mom is back at work and last week I went back to school. She drove me there just like the old days except things still don't feel real. Everything feels plastic like I'm living in the movie set that used to be my life. I still haven't made it through a full day. The bell signaling the end of classes makes me jump out of my skin and I hate the way everyone pushes and shoves each other in the hallways. There's too many people. Too many hands. Sometimes I freeze. Other times, I throw up. My new therapist, Dr. Hale, is meeting with the administration on Tuesday to talk about making special accommodations for me. She wants to work out a way for me to leave my classes a few minutes early so I can avoid the mob. She's also going to let them know I need to sit in the back of the classroom so I can see all the doors and nobody's behind me. I have to be against the wall so nobody can take me by surprise again.

I meet with her twice a week and I'm slowly starting to like her. We've started doing a type of therapy called Trauma-Focused Cognitive Behavior Therapy. She says it will help with feeling like I float. I'm covered in bruises again because I constantly bump into things. Mom laughs and jokes about me being clumsy but Dr. Hale says it's because I'm not in my body. Randy agrees with her. She calls it dissociation and says it's what people do who've experienced horrific abuse. She calls once a week and emails me too. She's proud of me and encourages me to keep doing the things Dr. Hale suggests.

My friends try really hard to be there for me, but they don't know how. I don't blame them because it's not their fault. I wouldn't know how to talk to me either. I've turned into a loner, preferring to be by myself or with Mom. I'm not sure it will always be that way, but right now, that's how it is. They keep begging me to run track this spring and tryouts are coming up in a few weeks, but I'm not going. My running days are over.

Mom hasn't pressured me to do it. She's started respecting my choices and boundaries about things. She's doing her own therapy and it's really helped her work through her own pain and give me the space I need to heal. She's finally accepted that we can't go back to how things were and our job is to figure out what our world looks like now. She took me to the salon to get my hair done in a cute pixie-cut. She said I could shave it again if I wanted, but I'm not going to. I'm definitely keeping it short, though. I might even dye it red for something different.

I don't know what I'd do without Mom. My moods are like a roller coaster and she rides them with me without complaining. She lets me rage if I need to or holds me tight while I sob. Sometimes when it gets really bad and I go to the dark place where I can't move or speak, she just sits with me until it passes without saying a word. At night, she hovers outside my door. Even though I can't see her, I know she's there. I promised her I'm done drinking, but it's going to be awhile before she trusts me again.

I still can't talk about what happened to me. I just can't. It's too big and doesn't have words. Instead, I will myself to forget—his voice, his face, the way his cold hands felt on my body. Some days it works. Other days it doesn't.

Sarah's locked up in a psychiatric facility until she's twenty-one. She worked out a plea bargain with the lawyers too. They didn't charge her for helping John kill the girls or what she did to me. They didn't want to punish her because they say she's a victim too since she was a kid when he took her and brainwashed her. They blame everything on her Stockholm syndrome. Randy petitioned for her to be rehabilitated in a locked mental health unit rather than go to prison and the judge agreed. I still don't feel sorry for her. I never will.

Mom still does, though, even if she won't admit it. Sarah writes her letters almost every day. Mom hasn't written her back. She says she won't, but I know she still cares about her. It eats her up inside, the way the whole thing went down. She says she's past it, but she's not. She hasn't let it go because even though she doesn't write her back, she still reads her letters and doesn't throw them away. She keeps them in a locked box and sometimes I catch her reading them when she doesn't think I'm looking.

SARAH

ONE MONTH LATER

HIS PLACE IS SUPPOSED to be a punishment, but it isn't so bad. I've definitely lived in worse. I have my own room and I can decorate it however I want. I've filled the walls with my drawings to keep my spirits up. Most of them are of me and Jocelyn.

My room is locked and so are all the other rooms on the unit. You have to knock to get let in and out. Most of the kids freak out when they first get here, but not me. I'm used to waiting to get let out. They have an intercom they make announcements on and every time it plays, I keep expecting it to be John's voice.

The food isn't as bad as I thought it'd be. We all have a job on the unit and I asked to help out in the kitchen. Staff didn't let me at first. I had to start out with cleaning the bathrooms, but I did such a good job that it didn't take them long to allow me to work in the cafeteria. They don't let me make any of my own dishes yet. I have to follow their menus but my therapist is open to letting me have one night a month where I get to make a dish. I'm looking forward to it. I think I'll make my pesto chicken.

Everyone under eighteen has to attend school and I go to the learning center every day. I'm studying to take my GED. Once I do, I can start taking college classes if I want to. I could be halfway through my bachelor's degree by the time I get released. Most of the kids complain about having to go, but not me. I like it. Yesterday, I passed the reading portion and it won't be long before I pass the science. Math is the one I'm most worried about, but one of the education aides has been spending extra hours tutoring me.

Everything operates on a points system and you have to earn enough points to be allowed certain privileges. I'm already on Level Three. Some kids never get off Level One. Level Three means I get to go outside for an hour every day and it's beautiful. There's trees everywhere and a huge garden with multi-colored flowers. I've started reading up on all the different kinds. Once I earn enough points, I can help out in the garden. It's going to be a great way to pass the time.

I still miss John even though I tell my therapist I don't. He's in prison and never getting out. He confessed about the girls and led the police to the graveyard. I still can't believe he's the one who broke. He was always so worried about me, but he didn't even have enough strength to follow his own rules. There's a chance he might end up in the same correctional facility as my dad and I laugh every time I think about it.

It turns out Ella was a fighter. She surprised me. It's not the first time, though, and probably won't be the last. You never know which side of the spectrum they'll fall on.

As much as I miss John, it doesn't compare to how much I miss Jocelyn. I write her every day. At first, all I did was apologize again and again for my behavior, but after a while, I ran out of apologies. Now, I just tell her about my day and the things I'm learning. I talk to her about how much I've changed. So far, she hasn't written back, but she will. She just needs time.

I have to be here for another three years, but three years really isn't that long. It will be over before I know it and I'll be free—totally free. The first thing I'm going to do is find Jocelyn.

ABOUT THE AUTHOR

Dr. Lucinda Berry is a clinical psychologist and leading researcher in childhood trauma. She uses her clinical experience to create disturbing psychological thrillers that blur the lines between fiction and nonfiction. She enjoys taking her readers on a journey through the dark recesses of the human psyche. Her other thrillers include *PHANTOM LIMB* and *MISSING PARTS*. If she's not chasing her eight-year-old son around, you can find her running through the streets of Los Angeles prepping for her next marathon. To be notified of her upcoming releases, visit her on FACEBOOK or ABOUT.ME/LUCINDABERRY.